The Cobra p[illegible]g and shaking, its engine [illegible] of the ladder was snagging at the trees as the chopper staggered through the air on its drunken dying run, shredding leaves from top-growth, tearing branches off wholesale.

The thought that raced through Hardin's mind at that instant was that nothing was going to save the Cobra. Not Marco's renowned skill as a pilot – which might now be precisely nil anyway, depending on how badly he'd been shot up – nor anything else save an act of God. And Hardin didn't believe in God.

Any second now the Cobra was going to belly-flop into the jungle and a few hundred tons of dead metal were going to be smashing straight down on top of him. There wasn't going to be enough of him left after that to fill a soup-plate.

Also by Jack Hamilton Teed

GUNSHIPS: THE KILLING ZONE
GUNSHIPS: FIREFORCE

GUNSHIPS:
Needlepoint

Jack Hamilton Teed

A STAR BOOK
published by
the Paperback Division of
W. H. ALLEN & Co. PLC

A Star Book
Published in 1984
by the Paperback Division of
W. H. Allen & Co. PLC
44 Hill Street, London W1X 8LB

Printed in Great Britain by
Hunt Barnard Printing Ltd, Aylesbury, Bucks.

ISBN 0 352 314842

To

MICHAEL LAKE

A friend indeed

PROLOGUE

McMahon knew he was a dead man when the second gunship hove into sight. It came hurtling low over the tree-tops at an ugly angle, seven o'clock, a dark and terrible shape silhouetted against the thickening band of light on the far horizon, nose and side-mount guns stabbing long glittering lines of tracer that curved spectacularly towards him.

One was bad enough. Two was an outright disaster.

McMahon pulled on the collective lever at the side of his bucket seat and the chopper shot high. His eyes flicked round, right to left and back again, as he tried to locate the first chopper. But it wasn't where it had been, lancing in from the left. That meant it had switched to the rear, was probably even now swooping down towards him from behind. He swung the cyclic, booted the left pedal, sending the bird into a tight turn so that his belly was only exposed for mere micro-seconds. Fear was like bile in his stomach, rising in an acid flood into the back of his throat to choke him.

Beside him Carney, white-faced, was babbling into the intercom, his voice high-pitched with panic.

'What gives? Who are they? What the hell is going on?'

McMahon felt like swinging a fist at him. Normally Carney was reliable, steady. A solid guy to have with you as back-up. Now it looked like he was on the hinge; about to topple right over, in fact. McMahon cursed savagely. It was a bad enough situation already, without that happening. Without your goddamn co-pilot falling apart.

'What the hell d'you think is going on? They're trying to kill us is what's going on!' He screamed suddenly, *'They're trying to fucking kill us!'*

He poured on power and the Huey streaked away to the west at top-foliage level. Any lower and the bird would snag and tumble, pancake into the trees in a tearing eruption of fire and smoke. As he gripped the cyclic and stared at the uneven carpet of green that unrolled in front of him at high speed McMahon realised that that was probably how it was going to end anyhow. A bucketing, careering plunge into the forest and at the end of that the best you could hope for was a broken back and a broken neck and maybe as much as a third of your bones intact. Maybe. As a future prospect, it was bleak.

There were just a couple of things in their favour. As low as this they were a lousy target, unless the bad guys had truly sharp door-gunners who could train down. Not easy. In any case, the bad guys had to catch up with them first.

The other thing was that McMahon was a shit-hot pilot. There were no two ways about that. He knew it, everybody back at Base knew it. With a bit of luck – and even the greatest, most shit-hot flyboys needed that sometimes – the bad guys would be getting the message ricky-tick. Most ricky-fucking-tick, goddamnit.

He felt hammer-blows at his rear and struggled with the cyclic, keeping the bird on even keel, his eyes glued to the plexiglas windscreen in front and the sea of dark green beyond. All it needed was one branch curling upwards above the canopy, one tree-tip a foot or so taller than the rest. Just one. Jesus, at this height, all it actually needed was one startled bird rising upwards in front of him and it'd be enough to kick him all over the fucking forest.

He kept low, low and fast, heading west but easing on the cyclic left and right, left and right, so that he was shimmying like a flying eel. The bad guys' gunners would have to be really Number One to nail him like that.

Now he could see their shadows extending past him across the trees on each side, thrown by the growing light from the east, behind.

That wasn't so good. They were bracketing him. They could stitch him up with their MGs and Mini-Guns from both sides at once. It was about time the door-gunners he'd inherited this trip earned their keep.

Why in hell weren't they firing?

The answer came through the intercom even as he was preparing to curse them.

'They're too tight.' That was Colehammer, the port gunner. 'I can't get a fucking sighting like this. They're maintaining our speed.'

Smart, thought McMahon. Kind of, anyhow. Because it also meant that if his own gunners were unable to fire at them, they couldn't fire back – with any hope of properly nailing the chopper, anyhow. It was a stand-off. They could race round the fucking world like this.

McMahon didn't like the smell of it. They were shepherding him, and that was surely bad news.

'I'm gonna bounce,' he snapped to Carney. 'First chance you guys back there get, cream the mothers! Blow 'em outta the sky!'

It was getting less dark by the second, and that was bad news too. He wanted to get shot of these two long before day was fully up. Now in the half-light of dawn, he was a bad target and they knew it. They, too, were waiting, and it looked like they could afford the time.

Another voice in his ear. It was one of the civilians this time, the one who called himself Martins. McMahon didn't believe his name was Martins for a moment. These guys probably lied to themselves in their sleep.

'Who are they?'

'I didn't ask,' said McMahon – then, furiously, 'How the hell should I know who they are? You tell me! You guys are more likely to know the answer than I am!'

Martins said, 'I don't want for us to be compromised.'

McMahon turned to Carney, utterly outraged now.

'Take over! Keep us low! Kissin' the trees!'

He tore off his cans, unpopped his straps, disengaged himself from the harness, clambered back past his seat and into the main section of the Huey. Colehammer and Spidelski, the two gunners, were peering out of their respective doors, bleak-faced, both clearly as pessimistic about the outcome of all this as McMahon was himself.

The two civilians, Martins and the other one – he called himself Burns, but McMahon didn't think he looked like a Burns at all; more like a Rocco or a Russo or a Grazziano – were crowded up into the back, both sitting on upturned ammunition boxes, Burns with an M-14 rifle across his knees.

As McMahon tramped past the open doors, through which air roared in a gale, Spidelski fired off a short professional burst upwards then shook his head sourly.

McMahon squatted down in front of Martins and screamed at him, 'Fuck you and your compromised!'

He was extravagantly pissed off with the whole business. He had his orders; he carried them out. He knew with a stone-cold certainty that brooked no denial that what he was doing was illegal in some damn way or other – apart from anything else, his flights were never logged – but on the other hand he never questioned his orders for the simple reason that those orders were given to him by someone so high in the military hierarchy that it would probably mean a firing-squad at dawn if he even so much as intimated that he'd like to think about them first before he committed himself. That had to be admitted. But in any case, all he was doing was ferry-work, and where was the harm in that?

On the other hand, he had more than a vague notion about exactly what he was carrying, and this, together with the presence of the CIA goons (never admitted by anyone, but you'd have to be a dimbo not to recognise the symptoms) who invariably acted as couriers on every flight, was bound to lead to disaster sometime or other. He'd figured that out months before. That he'd been dead right – judging by what was going on outside this very minute – gave him no satisfaction whatsoever. It merely fuelled up his rage.

'I oughta toss you fuckers outta the chopper!' McMahon

yelled. He pointed at the attaché-case chained to Martins' left wrist. 'You and your goddamn merchandise! Maybe then those guys up there'd take the heat off! What d'you say to that, hah?' He repeated the last word in a hoarse scream. '*Hah?*'

Martins glared at him. 'Cool it, Lieutenant.'

'Screw you!' snarled McMahon – then, suddenly aware that both his gunners were now gazing back at him with open mouths, 'Watch the skies!' He swung back on Martins, jabbing a finger at him so that the man instinctively jerked his head to one side. 'It's gone beyond you fuckers being compromised, whatever the hell that means. As of five minutes ago, we're the closest things to dead men you'll ever see ouside of a fucking body-bag. You read me, mister? You patched in on my net? Jesus-*shit*!'

He turned to go back to the pilot's area but Martins was on his feet now, dragging the black bag with him, clutching at his arm.

'Find their wavelength. Tell them to back off. Tell them they don't know what they're playing with.' Martins' voice was hoarse, urgent. 'Tell them!'

McMahon bared his teeth in an ugly, death's-head grin. He thrust his face close to Martins', spoke with a barely controlled ferocity.

'Wise up, mister. I've got their wavelength. They're not bothering to answer. They don't give a shit. I don't know who they are, or why this deal has fucked up so badly – all I know is they're intent on nailing our ass. *To the wall!*'

He leaned back, watching Martins' face, waiting for him to give the logical command.

This was an American army chopper, ostensibly flying on a normal run from Laos to the northernmost tip of South Vietnam. The fact that the flight had not been logged should have no relevance at all to what was happening in the air around them. No one outside of a handful of people knew this flight was black. And yet here were two other US army choppers intent on knocking them out of the sky. There was no argument about that. These guys hadn't made some crazy error, hadn't mistaken their markings for those of North Vietnam. These guys were deadly serious. And seriously deadly. They were on a killing mission.

McMahon didn't know why. It looked to him like there was some kind of internecine dispute going on, and he was in the middle of it. And if he was right about the merchandise they were carrying this was not so goddamn surprising. In any case the why of it was unimportant, irrelevant. The truly relevant detail – what concerned him most – was that these fuckers were keen to blast him and his machine all over the jungle. That was *relevant*!

So the logical thing to do was yell for help – call in a bunch of F-4s from the nearest field and within minutes the bad guys would be bits of smoking debris fluttering down out of the sky. That was the obvious move. Except for one small thing.

On no account, ran McMahon's orders, are you to make official contact on your flights to and from Laos.

There was no argument about that, no court of appeal. That was it. Straight down the line.

No official contact.

Not even under the most provocative or vicious or perilous circumstances. Not even if you sprung a fuel-leak and had to land in the jungle. Not even if your instruments went on the fritz and you flew into a mountain in the dark. Not even if you got bounced by a whole goddamn squadron of EnVee MIGs.

No official contact.

Which actually meant no contact whatsoever with anyone at all. Even God.

So, pondered McMahon, what was the spook gonna do about *that*?

Martins stared at him. McMahon could tell that most of what he'd just been thinking, or something very close, was passing through Martins' mind at that very moment. It was decision-time. Martins held the aces in that, as it had been explained to McMahon – in typically convoluted sentences, sure, and in words of five syllables, but McMahon knew by now how to translate from the military – it was Martins who gave the orders on a trip like this one and McMahon who said 'yes sir' every time. That was why he was banking rather more each month than just about every other L-T who flew choppers in the whole of Nam.

All Martins had to say was 'call in our position'. That was all. That would save them.

Martins was biting his lower lip; his eyes had glazed over. He didn't look such a hard case now. He opened his mouth, shot a look at his impassive-faced companion, started to raise his right hand. Then the mouth shut again, the hand dropped. His face had turned the colour of old parchment and sweat was trickling down his cheeks. He turned away.

'That better be the right decision!' hissed McMahon.

He swung round, began once more to march towards the front.

Martins grabbed him again. 'Get us off the hook, McMahon!'

He was pleading. His face was chalk-white now, strained; there was real terror in his eyes. He clutched the black bag to his chest, as though it was some kind of body-armour.

'There's one thing you can do,' snapped McMahon above the roar of the rotors.

'Yeah, sure!' Martins pounced on this. 'What? Just tell me what to do!'

'*Pray.*'

McMahon enjoyed that. He enjoyed the look on Martins' face, the gaping mouth, the doomed expression in the spook's eyes.

This time he made it back to his seat and jammed himself down, connected himself up. There were still trees in front of him and more trees and trees that stretched for ever, and it really didn't look as though there was any way out of this one at all, but even so he felt more in control of events than before, more in control of himself. If they didn't make it, it would not be his fault.

He winked at Carney then snapped into his intercom, 'Colehammer!'

Colehammer's voice came back at him. 'Yeah?'

'Get ready.'

'Check.'

'And don't fuck up.'

'Rodge.'

McMahon hoped Colehammer didn't fuck up. On every mission like this he had different gunners, a different bird. Far better to have his regular crew, but that was out. This was the way they wanted it, and this was the way it had to be. So you could never depend on anything.

McMahon *prayed* Colehammer didn't fuck up.

He checked his dials, his mirrors; adrenalin was boosting into his system. Ahead the sea of green dipped down as the jungle fell away into a shallow valley. The dip was not much, more of a depression, but it was all that McMahon needed, or wanted.

As they sailed over the edge of the valley McMahon stabbed at the left pedal, jammed down on the collective and shoved the cyclic forward then tilted it to the left. The engine howled, the rotors tore air. The Huey dipped nose then yawed, swinging to port half on its side. Suddenly above the sound of the rotors came the thunderous racketing of an M-134 Mini-Gun – Colehammer's Mini-Gun, pouring out a devastating stream of rounds.

In the space of just two seconds, very slightly over the time it takes for the heart to beat once, the deadlock had been broken, the situation altered – and drastically, for the chopper on McMahon's port-side.

McMahon was now in a tight, fast turn, and Colehammer was in the perfect position to rake the bad guys' bird from tail to nose, his fire chewing into its body, stitching holes across it fore and aft and, as its pilot tried to escape upwards and over, along its belly too.

Electrically operated, the Mini-Gun's rate of fire was an appalling 6000 rounds per minute, optimum. Glancing to his left, McMahon saw with satisfaction that under this tremendous, concentrated onslaught the chopper was already starting to break up.

It was as though his Huey and the other were inextricably linked by that withering stream of blazing shells. As McMahon deftly turned so did the other chopper, and as it turned, hooked by Colehammer's fire-lines, so it began visibly to disintegrate. Struts, spars, skids flew off, its mangled rotors whirled away, the tail drive-unit exploded, the power-plant cowling tore apart, flapping bits into the air. A man fell from the open side-door, screaming, almost ripped apart at the waist; ammo boxes shot out after him, as though hurled from a grenade-launcher. Still the Mini-Gun spewed destruction.

Even now, even as McMahon watched, the whole of its port side buckled inwards under that hammering blast and at last smoke – thick and black and oily, with a tinge of orange – erupted from the dying bird.

The incredible, shocking sound of the Mini-Gun ceased abruptly. As though released from bondage, the wrecked Huey fell away from them – spiralling brokenly down towards the jungle, crashing into the top-foliage and almost instantly bursting apart in a fireball.

McMahon showed his teeth in a feral grin. For a few moments – and that was all the time that had elapsed since he'd bounced left and the engagement had begun – he'd lost the other chopper, but now he could see it again. It had sheered off to the right, to the east where the sun had now risen above the horizon, spilling a harsh radiance across the world.

Now it was diving at him again, and he swung once more towards the west. A low hill appeared, a mushroom-cap above the sea of green. To McMahon it was a beautiful sight, because it meant cover for just so long as he needed it, to manoeuvre once again – to fling his chopper up and round and nail the remaining Huey the way it had to be nailed. So that it, too, ended up a twisted mess of smoking junk below the forest roof.

He turned to Carney and laughed in sheer exhilaration. He was truly high. He'd been wrong all along. He wasn't a dead man. He was going to make it.

He was laughing when the third gunship sprang into sight over the brow of the hill ahead, forward cannon stabbing fire, quad-mounted MGs spitting tracer.

He was still laughing when his windscreen exploded inwards in a gust of plexiglas and steel, and rounds smashed everything in the pilot's area into a whirling, agonising chaos.

He died laughing.

I

One moment the car was there – parked a little way along from the National Assembly building on Le Loi Boulevard – the next it wasn't. Or at least, most of it wasn't.

It was only a small explosion – relatively speaking, for Saigon, a throwaway, a mere bagatelle – and it was at once clear to any spectator who had lived in Vietnam for more than a fortnight what had happened. Some smart operator, probably a kid – shoeshine boy, paper-seller – had deposited a grenade in the gas-tank. The grenade would have had its pin extracted and the spoon held down by a rubber band. It could have been in there for a day, a couple of days – maybe even as long as a week, but no longer. It all depended on the grade of gasoline.

Whatever, after a while the corrosive action of the gas would eat away the rubber, up would pop the spoon and – Bingo! Ragoût of automobile.

To the military, who delighted in acronyms, the device was known as a CACK, which made the uninitiated think instantly of messy diapers. What it actually meant was Corrosive-Action-Car-Killer, which summed things up pretty neatly.

To the Englishman it was just a bloody nuisance. He said as much to the Frenchman, who was sipping Pernod and whose hand did not even quiver at the bang.

Only minutes before they had been discussing the Bad News, which was the reason they were sitting at one of the front tables of the Continental Café in the first place. Also at the table was the American, who hid behind mirror-fronted dark glasses and didn't contribute an awful lot to the conversation, and the Corsican, who contributed even less.

The Corsican's nickname was La Bête, and this had little to do with the fact that he looked like a crazed gorilla, guzzled his food, was surly and boorish for most of the time, and had a voracious appetite for extremely young girls, although all these factors contributed. The real reason lay in his career as master-torturer for the French SDECE and the rather more notorious SAC in the cellars at the pretty, orange-blossom-choked Villa Dar Es Saada on Rue Fabre in Algiers. This particular job – one of many, although something of a highspot in the Corsican's life and one to which he often looked back with great nostalgia – had come to an abrupt end at 5 o'clock on the afternoon of the 29th of January, 1962, when the OAS turned the villa into a shambles with 150 kilos of high explosive. The Corsican had been one of only twelve men to survive, out of thirty-one, and had gone on to arguably greater things. But his reputation, certainly his name, was made at the Villa Dar Es Saada (which, being translated, meant 'house of bliss', although this would have been a debatable point to the majority of its inhabitants), and had clung to him ever since.

The Englishman did not greatly care for the Corsican. Although a fastidious man and a Member of Parliament, the Englishman himself was no angel. In this day and age you could not afford to be, was his attitude. What the Corsican had done in the past was of no interest to him; what he did in the present was of even less interest, as long as he got results. Even the Corsican's gross appetite for little girls didn't bother him, his own tastes being directed entirely in the opposite direction. What the Englishman mostly disliked about the Corsican was that the Corsican looked like an oaf, acted like an oaf and indeed had such vast reservoirs of oafishness within him that most people thought he was an oaf. But there were times when he wasn't. *That* was the point. He could, on occasion, be a cunning and intelligent man. The Englishman didn't like that at all. You never knew where you were with a man like the Corsican, and that was dangerous.

Take the time in Marseilles when one of the Fraternity had become aggrieved and taken his problems to the flics. The Corsican had gone berserk – had actually gunned the man down on the steps of the Hall of Justice *and been caught red-handed*! God alone knew how much money had been expended in springing him. Or the time when he'd tripped out on something or other, and gone stark staring mad in Joe Attia's plush Parisian restaurant *Gavroche*, shooting out whole racks of priceless claret and wounding the *maître d'hôtel* and two waiters. Joe had not been best pleased. It had taken a good deal of financial soothing to calm him down. And yet it was the Corsican who had masterminded the break-in at the Société Internationale Bank in Lyons, where the take had been upwards of two million dollars. And it was the Corsican who had overseen the setting-up of a dummy insurance company in Hong Kong's banking quarter, where over forty per cent of the Fraternity's profits were now being immaculately laundered.

And now, on learning the Bad News, all the Corsican had done was collapse into a broody silence. The Englishman didn't like that at all. There were signs that the Corsican was on the verge of wigging out too. Ever since the Englishman had arrived in Saigon, just two days before, the Corsican had been popping pills – all shapes, all sizes, all colours – as though tomorrow was by no means another day. Already the Englishman was beginning to wish fervently that he was back in Weybridge.

There were, after all, better things to do during a parliamentary recess than sit about on Saigon streets drinking not very good wine with a psychopath, right in the middle of a full-scale war.

He had had it all planned out. A month with Georges on the Greek Islands, a couple of weeks on his estate up in Scotland, a longish trip to California. There were one or two business deals to discuss, a particularly tempting take-over to firm up, other matters – not quite so important, but still interesting enough to warrant a certain amount of attention spent on them – to see to. The Englishman led a busy and active life. He liked getting things done. In his constituency he was considered good value, even by those who had not voted for him.

He sometimes wondered what those who did vote for him would say about his many and various extra-curricular activities, but in the long run that kind of speculation was pointless – there was no percentage in it, as his American friends would say.

Sipping his not very good wine, the Englishman returned to the attack.

'They obviously mean business.'

'Perhaps.'

'But good God, our source was talking about three hundred million dollars! Even in sterling that's by no means a small sum. Merely to bribe politicians, the police, the military, both top and bottom. *Three hundred million dollars!*'

'Lotta jack,' said the American, lighting a small cigar.

'Well, it scares the pants off me,' said the Englishman. 'If they're willing to pour that kind of money into just part of the operation, what in God's name are they throwing into the whole? Has no one considered that?' He gulped at the wine, made a face, and crossed one leg over the other, fastidiously lifting the crease of his linen trousers. 'They can be vicious swine.'

The Frenchman leaned across the table, a slow smile creasing his teak-brown face. He tapped the Englishman's right arm gently with his knuckle.

'So can we, my friend.' He turned to the Corsican. 'Eh? Eh?'

'They know nothing,' grunted the Corsican. 'They are pigs.'

'That's all very well,' said the Englishman testily, 'but it sounds to me as though this is war. They are quite deliberately striking into our territory. For God's sake, up until now *we've* been supplying *them*!'

The Frenchman shrugged.

'It is business. You know that. You are a businessman. They are merely cutting out the middleman.' He made an open-armed and very Gallic gesture which to the Englishman was particularly infuriating. 'It makes more sense. Their profits will be far greater.'

'And what about our profits?'

'Do not excite yourself, my friend.'

'The way you're talking, we might just as well allow them to march in without a murmur. Walk all over us.'

The Corsican's head rocked up and back, as though someone had just delivered a jolting uppercut to the point of his jaw. His eyes, to the Englishman, seemed quite literally to blaze.

'We'll destroy them!' he hissed. 'They won't stand a chance! We'll cut them down, Englishman – *un, deux, trois, quatre, cinq, six, sept, huit, neuf, DIX!*' He spat out the last number with such stark and unbridled ferocity that the Englishman flinched.

The Frenchman smiled at the Corsican, almost fondly.

'He is right, my friend. They won't know what hit them. I am confident that they will fail utterly. They have no conception of the depths to which certain of our number will descend – often simply for the pleasure of it – in defence of our territory. Our position. One might almost say . . . our *heritage*.'

The Englishman leaned across to the American. 'D'you know what he's talking about?'

'They got it in hand. Don't worry.'

'In that case,' grumbled the Englishman, 'I can't see why I was summoned to this godforsaken country in the first place.'

'Decisions must be made,' said the Frenchman sternly. 'In any case, as I'm sure you will agree, one's own best interests are always far better served if one is on the spot oneself.' His voice became silky. 'And after all, each of us here – as well as our brothers upstairs – has a stake in the outcome of this affair, to a greater or lesser degree.'

Something cold trickled down the Englishman's spine.

'My stake's as big as anyone's round this table,' he

blustered. 'And no one's mentioned the risks, either. I can tell you, I have far more to lose than just about anyone here. Or upstairs for that matter.'

The Frenchman patted him gently on the arm. 'Of course, of course. You are an honoured member of the Fraternity. It goes without saying. Your contacts have been, without doubt, extremely useful. You have opened up for us so many doors, my friend. Truly.'

Traffic careered by on Tu Do. Citroens, bicycles, ancient lorries, cyclo-taxis, mopeds. Exquisitely beautiful girls in *ao dais* and pantaloons and conical hats hurried past, chattering and laughing. A road-sweeper shuffled along the pavement, impassive-faced, his broom in front of him. To one side a newsboy was selling papers at the tables, under the watchful eye of one of the hotel barmen, lounging in the sun. The air was full of petrol fumes.

'And nor were you summoned, my friend. That would be much too strong a word. Men of your calibre and importance are never summoned. Only minions are summoned.'

The Englishman smiled thinly, aware that he was far too deep into this business to argue the toss as to whether the phone call that had reached him at 3.30 in the morning at his London flat only four days before constituted a summons or not. When you got right down to it, it was a matter of semantics, and there was really no percentage, again, in making waves.

The newsboy hurried across to their table, his wares jammed under one arm.

'You buy paper, mister? All the news!'

The American laughed shortly. The paper that was being waved under his nose was the *Saigon Post*.

'All the news that's fit to print,' he muttered, and snorted in derision. The Englishman couldn't see the joke.

He dug around in a pocket for the 15 piastres and was just about to proffer it when someone bawled out behind him.

'Hey! Y'little shit! Come here!'

Instantly the newsboy reacted. He grabbed the Englishman's money and bolted, without leaving a paper.

'Wait!'

The Englishman half-rose, waving an arm, then subsided. There was no point in making a fuss about this, either.

A tall American sprinted round the table then stopped, cursing. He wore steel-rimmed glasses, longish hair, and an off-white suit that was creased and slightly grubby. He was holding a copy of the *Post*.

'Goddamnit!' He appealed to those sitting at the table. 'How long have I been in this shithole of a country, reporting on this shithole of a war? Three fucking years – and I *still* fall for it!' He suddenly stared at the American intently for a couple of seconds then leaned across the table and gently pushed his mirror-fronted dark glasses down over his nose with the tip of a forefinger. He smiled. 'Hi, Luke. Thought I recognised you.'

The American pushed his glasses back up his nose again. Apart from a slight tightening of the lips, his expression did not give a lot away.

'Will.'

The man called Will smiled brightly, gazing round at the table's occupants. He homed in on the Englishman. 'Will Steeger. Journalist. Freelance.'

The Englishman felt a finger of panic insinuate itself up into his stomach. He should never have come here. The whole thing had been a mistake. His entire career could end in ruins simply because some stupid little Vietnamese boy had pulled some minor confidence trick, the exact nature of which wasn't clear to him even now. He summoned up all the vast reserves of diplomacy he had acquired over the years in dealing with the Press and managed a smile that, while there was not one ounce of humour or goodwill in it, at least did not reveal the sheer rage and hatred that he actually felt.

'How do you do.'

'You're English,' said Steeger, still smiling. 'But you don't look, if you don't mind me saying this, like you've been over here very long . . .'

There was obviously a question to be answered here. Indeed, a whole sackful of questions, to all of which, it was perfectly clear, the journalist was hoping for answers.

The Englishman's smile was just starting to slide into oblivion when the car-bomb went off.

The blast was minor, the shock-wave slight. Pieces of twisted metal clanged down on to the road amongst cyclists and Honda-riders who were already picking themselves up from where they'd been blown; a front wheel went bowling along Tu Do before cannoning off a parked jeep and sailing spectacularly into the window of a modish dress shop. As usual there were shouts and yells, the tooting of horns, a few screams – but these came from off-scene; no one near at hand seemed to be panicking. Certainly no one was running, either towards the scene of the explosion or away from it.

Most of the post-blast commotion was coming from the ARVIN guards, who were now dashing out of the Parliament building, waving their M16s threateningly and shrieking excitedly – a good enough reason, to anyone with even the slightest experience of life in Saigon, not to move at more than a snail's pace, ARVINs being notoriously trigger-happy and utterly careless as to whether they blew away friend or foe.

'Bloody nuisance,' said the Englishman irritably.

Sirens could now be heard, coming from the direction of the river. Any moment now and the entire area was going to be crawling with the military, both Vietnamese and American.

'I apologise,' said Steeger. He was still smiling. The smile seemed to be glued to his face.

'I beg your pardon?' The Englishman was icily polite.

'For thinking you haven't been here very long. You're obviously an old hand. Used to bangs. They don't bother you.'

'I was here during Tet,' said the Englishman as though that explained everything – which, in a way, it did. There had been a lot of bangs in Saigon during the 1968 Tet Offensive, when the Viet Cong had not only stormed the city but actually mortared the US Embassy in Thong Nhut Street.

The Englishman was about to follow this up with 'on a fact-finding mission', then decided, just in time, to keep his mouth shut on the subject. It would have been perfectly true, but also untrue. True, because he had indeed, together with a dozen or so other British MPs of all political persuasions, been rooting around in Saigon and the Delta in an endeavour, albeit mostly vain, to discover 'the feeling' of the Vietnamese on various aspects of the war and their 'attitude' to both the Americans and the Viet Cong guerillas, but untrue because this relatively high-minded investigation had masked, for him, the setting-up of a number of tasty and extremely lucrative deals, the exact nature of which, had the merest hint reached the ears of any of his colleagues, would have meant a thirty-year jail sentence at least and probably hanging, drawing and quartering, if that were possible in the last half of the twentieth century.

'It's just that you didn't jump much, or dive under the table, or run screaming down the street,' said Steeger.

'No.'

'Uh-huh?' Steeger's smile seemed now even more friendly than before. He positively radiated good-humoured joviality.

'Hey, Will.' The American shifted his chair back slightly, waved his cigar at the fast-gathering crowd on Tu Do. 'Looks like some real hot copy right there.'

'Oh I don't think so, Luke. Car-bombs. Dime a dozen.'

'Could be some top-echelon politico. You never know.'

'No, you're right there, Luke. You never know.'

Steeger took some time in extracting a pack of cigarettes from a pocket, tapping one out, lighting it, putting the pack back first in one pocket then in another until he felt, it seemed, he'd got it exactly right. The Englishman, normally cool, felt like heaving the table at him.

'Well, nice meeting you guys,' grinned Steeger, puffing at his cigarette. 'Gotta catch a deadline, as we old newshawks say.'

He waved, moved off, then – just as the Englishman was leaning forward angrily towards the American – swung round and marched back.

'One other thing,' he said to the Englishman. 'There's something I've gotta give you.'

The Englishman glanced round wildly, as though all

kinds of menacing forces were suddenly crowding in on him and there was no possibility of escape.

Steeger pitched his copy of the *Post* on to the table.

'Here. You better have this.' He became confidential, placing both hands on the table, leaning towards the Englishman and lowering his voice. 'It's crazy, but I still get taken in by it. I mean, like I said, I've been here for three years off and on, and mostly on, and the little fuckers can still take me for a sucker. Look!' He jabbed a finger at the paper as though he meant to nail it to the table.

'I really don't know what you're talking about,' said the Englishman in a voice that was almost shrill.

'The crossword!' chuckled Steeger, his whole frame relaxing. 'Goddamn! If I had all the piastres I've spent on papers that have been bought and read two or three times over by other guys, then begged back by the newsboys and neatly refolded and sold again, I'd be so rich I'd be able to one-finger all those fuckhead editors back in the World and tell 'em exactly what they can do with their assignments!' He put his head back and laughed, a rich, fat belly-sound. 'It's the only reason I buy this rag, to do the crossword. Although,' he winked melodramatically at the American, 'I have been known to appear in its columns myself, I have to admit. I gotta eat too! But it's a real kick in the ass to open your paper and find some other guy's already finished the crossword. Jesus! It's a racket! I've been thinking of taking it up myself. You know, 15 piastres is a lotta piastres for a paper – the newsboys, they make maybe eight, nine cents a copy. That's about . . .' he screwed up his face, narrowed his eyes, began playing with his fingers '. . . Uh, I dunno, two pennies, three pennies of your money, current rate of exchange. And *then* – they beg 'em back, iron 'em out, sell 'em again, this time getting 15 piastres a whack, all for themselves. Sharp's not the word, man. These guys, they got all the angles.'

The Englishman's face was a blanched mask. 'Fascinating,' he whispered.

'So as long as you have no strong yearning for the crossword, you better have the paper. You paid out good bread for it. I don't like to see an Englishman buncoed in the 53rd State. It's not right. Me, I wouldn't read the rag if you paid me. I know what goes in it. Hey, Luke?'

The American gave him a steely smile.

'Only kidding,' grinned Steeger.

He turned away again and the Englishman's upper body and head shot forward, not unlike a striking cobra.

'*Who . . .?*'

'Oh yeah,' said Steeger, somehow having appeared beside him again. 'Just one more thing. Your friend doesn't look too good.'

All eyes centred on the Corsican, who was sitting hunched in his chair looking towards his right but quite clearly staring at nothing. He seemed to be in a cataplectic trance.

'Gotta go,' said Steeger. 'See ya, Luke. Be in touch.'

This time he moved off the pavement and on to the road, walking quickly towards the scene of the blast, where barriers were now being erected and two old men in black pajama suits were sweeping glass and other assorted debris into the kerb. The ARVINs were still shouting; no one seemed to be in charge.

'Who the bloody hell was that?' hissed the Englishman.

'Will Steeger. Journalist. Freelance,' mimicked the American. 'Forget him. He's harmless.'

'Harmless?' The Englishman looked genuinely outraged. 'He was taunting me! Deliberately! D'you think he recognised me?'

'Does it matter?' The American thumped his cigar out in the ashtray. 'You're not over here incog, for Christ's sake. Any case, why should Steeger worry himself over some goddamn limey?'

'I am a Member of Parliament,' the Englishman reminded him in a voice that was as brittle as broken glass.

'Jesus wept! Look, forget Steeger. He's got a weird sense of humour is all. That apart, he's safe. He toes the line. He writes what he's told to write. He's perfectly happy to do us a snow-job on anyone or anything we care to name, as long as he gets paid for it. And the Company's got plenty of loot in its coffers.' He looked at the Englishman pointedly. 'As you have very good reason to know.'

The Englishman's stomach turned over a couple of times.

'Yes. Of course. Naturally.' He tried a light, offhand chuckle, but it sounded tinny even to him. 'I've always been grateful for your . . . aid in the past. And I don't believe it can be said that my own . . . services have been without a certain . . . value . . .'

This was half a question but the American said nothing, simply stared straight ahead, and all the Englishman could see was his own face, twice, in the mirrors of the man's glasses. The Englishman looked away quickly; it was not an attractive sight.

Out of the corner of his eye he could see one of the Fraternity heading towards them, steering a complicated course around the intervening tables. He took another sip at the wine and wondered why he bothered. It was dreadful. His gaze shifted down to the copy of the *Saigon Post* on the table in front of him.

'What was all that about the paper?' he said, a note of petulance in his voice. 'I don't understand what he was aiming at.'

This time the American laughed out loud.

'Oh that! No, I guess you wouldn't get that, you not being over here all that often. See,' he leaned forward, smiling, and the Englishman could sense, without seeing his eyes, that he was genuinely amused, 'the *Post* has a very tight editorial policy. Very tight. Takes a firm line on certain matters. We like to think you get the real facts in the *Post*.'

'The real facts?'

'No shit,' said the American, pronouncing the words very distinctly.

'Ah. I begin to see. I take you to mean that you are somehow involved.'

'The Company has a certain interest in it,' agreed the American. 'Not to put too fine a point on it.'

He was about to add more when there was an explosive sound from the Frenchman – a guttural eructation which expressed outrage, disgust and fury tinged with horror all within the space of perhaps half a second. The Englishman stared at him, then at the white-faced man who had been bending down to whisper into his ear but who was even now jerking back his head as though he feared the Frenchman was about to knock it off. A bearer of bad tidings, thought the Englishman. And then thought: Can anything be worse than that which we know already?

'One of our ferries,' snapped the Frenchman. 'Destroyed. Up near the Laos border. Two couriers, pilot, co-pilot, crew, and only the good God himself knows the exact value of the merchandise.'

The American gazed at him. 'Destroyed? How?'

'That is what we must discover. But they think it was shot down.'

'Shot down?!' The Englishman flapped one of his hands in consternation. 'The Communists? But I thought we ran the lines well away from their air-space. In any case, I understood they were generally . . . friendly?'

'I do not know the details,' snapped the Frenchman. 'How could I know them? I have only just been told!'

'You don't think . . .' whispered the Englishman. 'I mean – it couldn't have been . . . the opposition? Could it?'

The Frenchman didn't bother to reply. He glared at the Englishman as though what he was looking at was something that had to be stamped on instantly, then slammed back his chair and made off towards the hotel followed by the white-faced man. The American shrugged resignedly and did likewise. The Englishman thought about phoning an airline company and booking himself right out of this madness, then wearily got to his feet and plodded after them.

The Corsican watched them go.

At that moment he felt as though his brain was coming apart. The plates that held it down had corroded away and the pulpy stuff inside was leaking out. There was no pain there inside his head, just an increasing emptiness; everything was oozing away down his tubes. Leaving only acid nightmares behind.

Tall buildings began to sway like storm-tossed trees. Tables, chairs, trash-bins, shrubs in cask-like wooden tubs all began to slide away from him imperceptibly until his own table was at the centre of a vast concrete desert. There was a population shift going on too; beings with animal masks were moving menacingly around him, closing in for the kill. Cold winds howled like tortured demons across the plain. He blinked, shivered, shut his eyes. He was at the centre of the universe; there was no one else left alive.

'You want?'

The Corsican stared up at the impassive Vietnamese boy, neat in hotel garb, holding a tray of empty glasses.

'Yes. Now. I want it now.'

The boy nodded.

In the hotel room the Corsican kicked off his laceless shoes and stared at the wide bed then, turning slightly, at the long mirror beside it. A short stubble of black hair, prominent forehead, thick bristling eyebrows, dark eyes that lifted slightly at each corner, high cheekbones, broad nose, dense band of moustache, thick lips and wide chin, blueish where the beard was already starting to push through after only five hours' grace.

He threw his coat on the bed, stripped off his checkered shirt. A thick mat of dense black hair over a burned-brown chest. Old scars were deep white furrows in the leathery skin. In the old days, La Bête himself had been in bad situations; had taken almost as much as he'd given out.

A fat coackroach waddled out from under the bed. The Corsican watched it for a long time as, antennae quivering, it hustled this way and that across the carpet. Then he smiled with his mouth. It was heading for a crack in the boards. He stepped forward and stamped on it, twisting his bare foot sideways and back, sideways and back, hearing the sharp squidge of bursting carapace as he crushed it underfoot, feeling the wetness of its vital juices on his skin.

'No!'

He turned slowly, keeping his foot down. The boy looked

aghast. He was now muttering to himself in Vietnamese, staring down at the floor.

'What's your problem?' growled the Corsican.

'Not good thing,' the boy said in English. Then he reverted to French. 'You have made an unwise decision.'

Still keeping his foot where it was the Corsican reached out and grabbed the boy by the neck. The massive hand almost enclosed his throat, making the boy look as though he was wearing a surgical collar. Experimentally, the Corsican flexed the muscle of his arm, began to lift the boy into the air. The boy made frantic gargling noises. The Corsican's arm went higher and the boy's feet kicked in the air, his hands clutched round the man's knotted arm. The boy's face was scarlet, his wide eyes filled with tears. Almost lazily, the Corsican swung his arm around in a quarter-circle and unclasped his fingers. The boy, croaking, staggered against the bed, lost his balance, fell to the floor on his knees.

'I said, what's your problem?'

The boy clambered to his feet, a fixed smile on his flat face. He rubbed at his neck.

'Bad luck,' he muttered.

The Corsican laughed harshly. 'No such thing, *mon fils*. You make your own luck.'

'Is bad luck,' insisted the boy, although warily, ready to jump back in case the gorilla took another lunge at him.

'Tell me.'

'There is a story,' began the boy, 'about a poor student . . .'

The Corsican shook his head. He was beginning to see things again that no one else could see. Stories did not interest him. 'This business. This better be Number One.'

The boy cheered up instantly. Stomping on a cockroach was one thing, business was another, and this was sure enough Number One business. The best. A lot of money would very soon change hands, to his advantage.

'Real Number One. Yes, sir. You got it.'

'Fetch,' said the Corsican.

He blinked his eyes a couple of times, rubbed a hand over his face, sniffing hard and deep as though he was snorting a whole belt of the white stuff. He walked back to the carpet, rubbed the sole of his foot on its worn surface.

Pigshit bunch. That's what they were. They'd find out what it meant to play games with the Fraternity. They were amateurs. They might have got the US sewn up all ways and every way, but in the end they were amateurs. That was all. They'd find out what the professionals did to amateurs soon enough. Sooner. *Tout suite*. Pigshit bunch.

The door opened, closed again, softly. A girl stood by the bed. She was small – *très petite, très jeune*. A full-moon flat face, almond-shaped eyes, very black hair. She wore a thin Western-style frock that came to just below her knees.

For a second the Corsican lost control and her face underwent a hideous transformation. The thin lips curled, the eyes leered; suddenly she was a monstrous looming figure about fifty miles away down the room. But he blinked and everything shot back to normal again. He shivered.

'*Ma petite . . .*' he said thickly.

She came slowly round the bed, stopping in front of him, a foot or so from him. She was holding a thin nylon carrier-bag with a Marlboro advertisement printed on both sides. He gestured impatiently and she obediently dropped it to the floor; some clothes – linen frock, panties, tights, a cheap plastic belt – spilled out on to the carpet. He nodded, reached out for the round neck of her frock and with one swift, savage jerk ripped the dress downwards, tearing it off her.

Underneath she was naked. The Corsican gazed at her, his mouth dry. A pulse throbbed at the side of his throat. She had no breasts to speak of, not much pubic hair. A rounded, yellowish belly, small thighs.

Très petite, très jeune.

With an animal-like grunt of fury he hit the side of her face with the back of his hand, still clutching what remained of her dress. She gave a startled yelp, was spun round by the force of the blow and staggered towards the bed, tripping over the carrier-bag with the Marlboro advertisement on it. She sprawled on the floor in a rag-doll heap, one knee bent sideways and back, exposing the tiny, perfectly-formed sex. She looked utterly defenceless.

He threw the tattered dress from him and bent down, wrenching at her shoulder, yelling at her in several languages as he heaved her up bodily and threw her on to the edge of the bed so that she half-straddled it, one foot on the floor, the other leg bent on the bed, her buttocks high in the air. She did not move, except to half-turn her head, glancing back at him so that he could see her frightened eyes. Her body quivered slightly, like a tiny animal's.

The Corsican threw back his head, breathed in deeply through his nose again. The pigshit bunch would be destroyed and he would be the destroyer. The angel of death. He began to unbuckle his belt . . .

The boy was smoking a Ruby Queen in a cramped cubby-hole down near the hotel's boiler-room. He had a sheaf of ragged and grubby dollar bills in front of him and was dealing them out into separate piles of different denominations and very carefully, almost fastidiously, straightening out the creases.

There was a thick pile for one dollar bills, a not-so-thick pile of five dollar bills, and a thin pile of anything that was over ten dollars. Every time he reached ten dollars in the one dollar pile he folded the ten bills three times and slipped a rubber band round them, pushing the wad into his left-hand flapped shirt pocket.

The boy enjoyed this pastime. He was only thirteen and it was better than playing pitch-and-toss out in the streets. The old ones could do that. Better, too, than serving drinks to the idiot Yankees upstairs. So far he had three packets of one dollar bills, a lot of five dollar bills, and one or two ten dollar bills. This represented a good deal of extremely hard work, although the hard work had not all been done by him.

He glanced up as the girl came along the passageway towards his cubby-hole. She was staggering a little and looked tired. She certainly looked older than her age, which the boy happened to know was eleven years and eight months. And a few days. She sat down carefully on a broken-backed cane chair beside the upturned packing-case that served as the boy's desk. Closer up, she now seemed utterly exhausted. Her head drooped forward and her legs were splayed out.

The boy touched her on the shoulder and then gently squeezed the flesh through the thin material of her frock. She gazed at him blankly.

She said in Vietnamese, 'That one, he's a buffalo and a hog all rolled into one. I hate him.' She shivered, wrapping both her thin arms around herself. 'He's a madman, too. Crazy.' She used the phrase '*dien cai dau*', which meant literally 'off the wall'.

The boy squeezed her arm again, almost affectionately. 'Don't worry. His star is a bad one to follow.'

He told her about the cockroach and she giggled appreciatively, shifting about on the chair, her eyes lighting up with glee. The boy suddenly noted with irritation that there was some blood on her tights and a hole, just above the right knee. He shifted his gaze to the piles of bills, frowning. Now he would have to buy her some more.

The girl noticed this and stopped laughing. She pulled a face as she stared at the dollar bills on the upended packing-case.

'You gimme money,' she said, reverting back to American. 'You gimme money now.'

'You wait.'

'No. You gimme. I want shot.' Her face became a venomous mask. 'You gimme bucks. You no gimme money, you a bastard duck.'

This outraged the boy who banged his small fist down on the packing-case. They were still arguing over the spoils when one of the assistant head-waiters from upstairs arrived, looking for his missing bar-boy, and commandeered what was left.

II

Steeger said, 'You know those guys?'

Colonel John Hardin, of the US Special Forces, took a sip from the glass of Barracuda gin in front of him then reached across the formica-topped table to butt his cigarette, at the same time letting his eyes drift towards the long mirror on the wall behind Steeger.

The decoration around the outside of the mirror-glass consisted of a frieze of badly-executed pictures of naked women. For some time Hardin had been trying to make up his mind about the country of origin of the anonymous artist. It was hardly to be supposed that he was an American as, although the ladies themselves were voluptuously proportioned, quite unlike the general run of Vietnamese women – whose bodies in the main tended towards the delicate and the fragile in the matter of breasts, buttocks, thighs and so forth – their faces were definitely cast in an Oriental mould. Yet these faces were more akin to Japanese or Korean, the eyes in particular had a definite noseward slant to them, far more so than the eyes of most Vietnamese girls which leaned more to roundness, or at least a shape that was not so acutely inclined. The evidence, such as it was, all pointed to a Vietnamese who was intent on feeding the basic American idea of what a woman out East ought to look like, but seldom did. Or, to put it another way, what the average American wanted out of life in strange ports and foreign climes. It all came down to the same thing in the end: big tits and slant eyes. The fact that big tits and slant eyes were in short supply in Vietnam was beside the point.

In the mirror the room stretched away in front of him, a typically tacky Saigon bar in the Tu Do district, down near the river. The tables were round and small, and there were a lot of them. Each had two chairs to it, an American male and a Vietnamese female filling them. The Americans for the most part were civilian workers: oilmen, engineers, construction workers, maintenance men, clerks. There were some GIs. A few were quite clearly splashed out of their minds, heads down on the tables, eyes glassy, mouths wide open; dead to the world while their partners calmly played solitaire, or chatted quietly to the other bar-girls serving drinks. The girls at the tables and the girls with trays all wore extravagantly padded bras under their Western-style dresses, although it was impossible to see even a hint of cleavage as this would have given the game away, destroyed the fantasy. Most of those seated demurely sipped cold tea, munched crab meat sandwiches, and listened politely to tales of erring wives and utterly incomprehensible grouches from their not-so-drunk Occidental partners.

A long bar ran down one side of the room and some attempt had been made by the owner to introduce a jungle effect, with hanging shrubs, clumps of fern, trailing creepers. But this was sabotaged utterly by his own stupidity and bad taste (most Americans, especially the GIs, wanted to get *away* from the jungle; they certainly did not want a reminder of one of the more hellish aspects of warfare in Vietnam when they were having a quiet, or even rowdy, drink and trying to make it with the bar-girls), and by the fact that all the greenery was plastic, and had not been dusted for some months. The lights in the room were low, although this was not so much to create an intimate and exotic atmosphere as to hide the depressingly tawdry and gimcrack workmanship, the cheap fitments. Here, only the drinks were expensive – especially, for what you got in return, the cold tea.

Hardin's gaze took in the long room, the maudlin

customers, the busy bar-girls, the impassive barmen – and two sallow-faced civilians in sombre suits towards the far end of the room who were shooting glances at his back (although not at the mirror, and thus not directly eye-to-eye) and whispering animatedly to each other.

A frizz of mild warning prickled at the back of his neck. His brain-relays began clicking over at some speed, but nothing came out that was to any degree definite. He caught and locked on to the eyes of Captain Frank Marco next to him. Marco's expression was one a martyr might have worn just before being thrown to the lions.

'Shee-it, man,' he muttered, 'we in trouble?'

'I don't know,' said Hardin.

'Well?' asked Steeger.

'If I do know 'em, it goes back a long way. Too long.'

'The longer it is, the worse it gonna be,' said Marco darkly. 'These dudes, they be gunnin' for you for years maybe. Now, way out east, in the Or-eent, they spot your ass an' decide to mince it. This gonna be a bar-fight, I can tell. Knives, cudgels, fowlin'-pieces. It gonna be: Up against the wall, muth'fuck, you gonna be dead.' He pronounced it 'day-yud' and grinned a big fat coon grin with plenty teeth.

Frank Marco was black, tall, skinny; a street-wise kid from Harlem who'd made it. He held a degree in social anthropology and could fly as sweet as though he'd been born to it. The US army had no use for social anthropologists, but had always been a little tight on ace flyboys. Which was how come Marco was driving gunships in Vietnam.

'You're a real bundle of laughs,' said Hardin.

'I seen your face, babe. Warnin' bells ringin' in your mind. I got that ole doom-cloud hangin' over my head, sudden.'

'Fuck 'em,' said Hardin. 'They wanna start something, let 'em. I'm in a mood for murder.'

Steeger said sympathetically, 'They're still feeding you horse-pucky?'

'Sure. I got the plague again. It always happens when I do someone a favour. There's guys tramping up and down

Nam ringing bells and warning people off. They've nailed a big sign outside of MAC-Vee HQ. It says: Watch out for this man; don't touch the fucker; this guy can seriously damage the war-effort.'

Steeger picked up the bottle of bourbon he was using for re-fills and thrust it at Hardin, transforming himself into Steeger the ace radio newshound.

'Tell me, Colonel Hardin – what are your views on the High Command in South Vietnam?'

'Bout as big a bunch of crap as you are, Steeger,' grated Hardin.

Marco grinned. In the short time he'd known Hardin he had discovered very quickly that Hardin was an oddball among Special Forces vets. He didn't act much like his peer group, and he sure as hell didn't think much like them either. He was a maverick. He smoked dope, spoke his mind, and had weird – and at Command level the word 'weird' could be translated as 'treasonable' – views on South Vietnam, the management of the war, Command, politics and politicos, all the things he was supposed to be fighting for. Mostly he didn't like any of them. Well, sure – he cared for South Vietnam as a country, but he hated the head honchos, the fat cats who were skimming the thick cream of American power and money and influence off for themselves, and not even leaving much thin milk for the Vietnamese people. To Marco all of this was refreshing.

Yet he still fought – and, more to the point, fought hard; if needs be, dirty. Marco had seen Hardin in action at first hand. He didn't need to be roused in order to turn himself into a mean mother, a killer, a man who let nothing and no one stop him until he'd reached his goal, whatever goal it was he'd set himself. The guy was no powder-puff and he had the scars to prove it.

The latest scars had been awarded at the end of the fighting in a Laotian valley occupied by US army renegades with rogue CIA backing, when he'd narrowly missed being blown all over the landscape by a grenade.* That was less

* See *Fire-Force* by Jack Hamilton Teed.

than a month ago, and now Hardin was all patched up, back in business – only to find himself made redundant by the jerk-offs on high.

It didn't make sense to Marco. Hardin was a pro. The best. He knew the jungle – could *use* the jungle better than most men who'd grown up in it. He was a natural. Why the fuck keep putting him back on the shelf? Just another part of the general craziness, he decided.

'Well,' shrugged Steeger, 'if those guys back there don't bother you, they don't bother me.' He leaned forward, spoke confidentially. 'It's just that I suddenly remember I have a heavy date with a girl from Reuters, so I'll take a raincheck on the rest of the evening's activities, if you don't mind.'

Hardin laughed. 'Christ, Steeger, you're a fucking coward!'

'I wear yellow pajamas in bed,' admitted the stocky journalist. He began using the bottle of bourbon in the manner for which it had originally been intended. 'Physical danger always alarms me. There's a chance one can get hurt. Intellectual danger now, that's quite a different matter. I'd be happy to trade verbal punches with, say, Descartes or Immanuel Kunt – sorry, Kant.' He gave Marco a ludicrously exaggerated wink and took another injection of bourbon. 'I've been like this since he first knew me. Ya can't keep a good man down.'

Hardin and Steeger went back to San Francisco in the mid-fifties when Steeger had been 'Our Man In Frisco' for a UCLA student newspaper and Hardin had been peddling hot copies of Allen Ginsberg's *Howl!* at the City Lights bookstore – when, that is, he wasn't off on mysterious jaunts to remote corners of the world, the exact nature of which Steeger himself had never been able to nail down with any accuracy.

'You're also a fucking liar,' said Hardin, taking another shot of the Barracuda. 'I heard about that trip to Phnom Penh.'

Steeger looked suddenly depressed. 'Yeah, that was a bummer. Boy, was I glad to get outta that in one piece.'

'I heard about the cab-ride.'

‘Oh, that. Yeah. That was hairy.’

Marco raised an enquiring eyebrow. ‘I only a poor flyboy. I don’t never get to get the dirt on these impo’tant matters.’

Hardin said, ‘Buncha journalists in Cambodia, during the, ah . . .’ he grinned ‘. . . incursion. The Khymers were trying to beat up on everybody in sight, but particularly Vietnamese civilians. Lon Nol was putting it about that all Vietnamese were Viet Cong fifth columnists, even those who’d been there for centuries.’

‘Massacres, massacres, fucking massacres,’ muttered Steeger. He looked up at Marco. ‘See, there were a whole raft of us, we heard there was some action. Real VC troops in a shoot-out in a ville about twenty klicks from Phnom Penh. So we hired all the cars we could, raced out there in a fleet. All we found was kids and old women. The Khymers had had a duck-shoot. Teenage girls just lying in their own blood about a hundred yards from a goddamn hospital. The Khymer soldiers wouldn’t let the medics out, wouldn’t let the wounded in. The provincial chief was really pissed, he said the cross-fire was truly shocking. Actually, what he was pissed about was that there were so many of these poor fuckers still alive, that we’d arrived before they could start the old bullet in the back of the head routine. So we got mad at him and bundled all the WIA we could into the hire-cars, raced back to Phnom Penh. It was funny, actually. I had a photog with me and we had five wounded. They were all shot up bad. The guy was driving us refused to take us back, he said he wasn’t having blood on *his* seats. He said, Fuck you Jack, you ain’t staining *my* seats. He said, Up your ass pal, I ain’t having all this dirty Commie blood in *my* car. He said, Shit on you, fuckface, I want some *money*!’ Steeger was getting madder and madder.

‘So, uh . . . what happen?’ asked Marco.

‘So I bust him on the snoot, said add *that* to the bill.’

Marco let out a wild guffaw of laughter. ‘An’ you got back to Phnom Penh *alive*?!’

Steeger shrugged, embarrassed. ‘Yeah, well it wasn’t that bad. The photog was covering the fucker with a .45 while I was damaging him. Hey, did I tell you?’ He turned to

Hardin. 'Car-bomb outside the National Assembly building this p.m.'

Hardin smiled as Steeger wriggled clumsily off the hook. Actually, the stocky journalist had a lot of guts, as Hardin well knew. He also had a lot of nerve, which was not quite the same thing. Only Will Steeger, highly-regarded free-lance, would write to order for the CIA-run *Saigon Post* and also feed hot and deadly accurate scandal to the Undergrounds back in the World. Not to mention run a contact on the diplomatic staff at the American Embassy who brought in all kinds of unlawful pills and potions through the diplomatic bag. Steeger was a head, a freak of the first water.

'They kill anyone useful?' he enquired. 'Martinez, Wallgrave, Ted Shackley? They get value for money?'

Steeger shook his head in frank admiration. 'Man, you sure got it in for the spooks.'

'Sure I've got it in for the spooks. I hate their guts, mostly. They're the guys who bear the ultimate responsibility for fucking this country up.'

Steeger shook his head again but made no further comment on that. He had long since given up trying to work out Hardin's thought-processes in this particular area. When you got down to it, Hardin himself was a spook – or at least was someone who engaged in covert activities for a secret government agency, albeit not the CIA itself. Actually, when you got *right* down to it, Colonel John Hardin was a killer, an assassin, a man of blood. Luckily, that wasn't all he was. He was courageous and intelligent, and he was also a man of stupendous integrity; a man who, weirdly, because of his sometimes highly controversial views on the American presence generally, didn't seem like he ought to be over in Nam at all.

'No.' He returned to the car-bomb. 'This was just a minor incident, not worth a paragraph. Although . . .' he grinned, suddenly sharklike '. . . there were some strange people sitting at a table outside the Continental, watching the show.'

'Oh?' Hardin was not particularly interested. He was

pondering the two guys at the far end of the room, was still trying to work out who they were, why he should be under the impression he ought to know them, or had known them long ago. And how far back was long ago, anyway?

'Yeah. Luke Dowling. Three other guys.'

'Dowling?' A spark of interest now flickered in Hardin's mind. He said, 'Luke Dowling? He's one of Shackley's hatchetmen. Used to be attached to the CIA station in Vientiane. Before that, South America. I got a feeling he was in on the Bay of Pigs thing back in '62.'

Steeger filed this away for possible future use. Somehow. Somewhere or other. Hardin was usually at his most reliable when he used the expression 'got a feeling'.

'Are you saying Dowling had something to do with this car-bomb?'

'Jesus, no. That was just, you know, nothing. Pin-prick. Penny-ante stuff. Dowling just happened to be there.'

'Who else?'

'Dunno. There was an Englishman, middle-aged, fancy manners. Might've been a fruit. I tried to tickle his temper, but he didn't quite lose his cool. Another guy, he looked European, looked like he'd been over here for decades. Probably French. I didn't hear him speak. Then there was a guy put Frankenstein's monster in the shade. Man, he was big, I'm tellin' ya!'

'You're not giving me a hell of a lot,' said Hardin.

'There's not a hell of a lot to give. It was just – I dunno, something about them. The Brit was on edge, about ready to scream and jump about.'

'Not surprising. They don't get that many car-bombs in London.'

'Uh-uh. He didn't give a fuck about the car-bomb. Listen, he said it was *a bloody nuisance*.' Steeger chuckled. 'Can you beat it! No, he was an old hand. He was jumpy about something else, man. They didn't want me there.'

'It's your sunny personality and winning ways. I've told you before, Will, no one likes a smartass.'

'Okay. But it still doesn't explain – Jesus, I just don't know. There was a smell there I caught. Something outta line. It was spotting Luke Dowling there that started it. Why I ambled over in the first place. He's a funny guy, and I don't mean ha-ha. He deals in strange commodities.'

'He deal in dope?' said Marco, snapping his fingers. 'My connections ain't what they used to be. There a real drought goin' on round here.'

'As he was stationed up in Vientiane,' said Steeger sourly, 'the odds would not be against it. The spooks are running more junk outta that town than sand in the Sahara, and even though he's down here now stuff like that sticks. There's mucho payola there. But with Dowling, what I know about the guy, there's more than just dope. He has his fingers in some weird pies.'

'What about the big guy?'

Hardin threw that question in with no real enthusiasm, or desire for any detailed answer. He'd gone back to the problem of the two hoods – because that was more and more the impression they gave – down the bar. Ethnically, they were Mediterranean; possibly Italian, but more likely French. They had a touch of the kind of pimp you might bump into in the meaner streets of Marseilles. Dock-rats.

'Wow!' breathed Steeger. 'That guy! He was something else! Built like a bulldozer, and mean with it. Monster-man walks again! He looked to me the kind of guy has his own personal jungle, all over his body. You know? The last Neanderthal left on earth.'

'Shit, Will, you go way over the top!' Hardin chuckled reminiscently. 'Actually, I know the type. There was a guy I bumped into like that, but that was a long . . .'

He stopped dead.

A long time ago.

He stared at Steeger as though Steeger had just pulled a gun on him.

Except he wasn't focusing on Steeger at all; wasn't now even aware of his presence, as the camera that was inside his head sent flickering pictures across the screen of his mind.

A gross brute of a man, leaning over him, chuckling with genuine amusement as he casually inflicted pain.

'John? Hey, man – where ya gone?'

Quite suddenly he had stepped back in time and there was the stench of urine in his nostrils, the damp smell of mould on old brickwork. A reek of terror.

He saw once again the room, the man, the instruments. Saw the dancing highlights on highly polished, pristine steel caught by the powerful arc-lamps. Saw how they flickered and danced, dazzling his eyes.

Another smell came to him, the acrid stink of French cigarettes. Then another, overlaying it: the stench of garlic at close quarters. He heard heavy, wheezing breathing, a mumble of laughter in the background, the clink of steel on steel. Then, cutting raggedly through, an animal bellow of agony.

Had that been *him*? Had *he* screamed like that? It was more than likely. A man could only take so much; after a certain point, you either yelled or fainted. Or died.

Suddenly his mouth ached intolerably.

'John? For Chrissakes!'

Sure, that was all a long time ago. And the men down the other end of this crummy bar were maybe a long time ago. And a lot of things had happened a long time ago, and they were mostly utterly unconnected, one with another.

And, sure, the man he remembered so vividly did indeed look like he was the last Neanderthal left on earth – but then a hell of a lot of other guys in the world could, in all conscience, be so described.

It was just that, now he'd been reminded of this particular long time ago, now he thought about it seriously, these two guys looked to be precisely the kind of guys he remembered as being among those present and under the command of his own particular last Neanderthal left on earth.

He shook his head irritably, came back to the present – to other kinds of cigarette smoke, other sounds; to, crummy bar or not, an altogether different atmosphere. He was making all of this up, inventing mysteries where absolutely none existed; in fact, re-creating past terrors out of the mildest of coincidences.

So Steeger saw a guy who might possibly look like

someone who'd tried to break him eight years before. So two guys in a bar looked like they might possibly be discussing him. So these same two guys, maybe, looked like the kind of guys who'd been cohorts of the guy who'd tried to break him damn near a decade back.

So what?

Steeger said, 'Listen, when you finally come down to earth . . .'

Hardin laughed, off the grim roller-coaster of memory now, back in control of his own immediate present. 'Yeah, you threw me back for a moment . . .'

And he thought: Throwback. Beast-man. Brute. Neanderthal.

Then he thought: This is fucking ridiculous! I didn't even connect that bastard Guerini with the word 'Neanderthal' even when I knew him! Why in Christ's name should I do it now? Apart from the fact that he looked like one. But so what?

'Like I said, I knew a guy looked like he came straight outta the caves, too. Years ago.'

'You must have some sweet memory of him,' commented Steeger sourly. 'You been in a fucking trance for the past three hours.'

Hardin, in the middle of sinking some more of the Barracuda, choked on the liquid, spluttering with laughter.

'Jesus, Will, you go over the crapping top! How about thirty seconds?'

'So, uh . . . what this guy do to you?' said Marco carefully, as though he really didn't want to know at all.

Hardin shrugged. 'Some dentistry on my back teeth. But he was careless, forgot about the anaesthetic.'

Steeger sank back in his seat, raised plaintive eyes to the ceiling. 'Holy shit, that's a conversation-stopper if ever I heard one. What do we do for an encore?'

Steeger had always been slightly uneasy about the darker side of his friend's life, the destructive elements that must lurk somewhere in the background of any guy such as Hardin who lived always on the edge of, at best, physical torture and disfigurement, at worst death. He knew that vicious, appalling events occurred in the strange and stark world Hardin inhabited, and when it was someone other than Hardin who was involved with them, he could bring a measure of objectivity – the best kind of journalist's supreme gift – to bear on the subject. But it was different when you knew the guy, had known him for years, was as close to him as one could reasonably get. Way different.

Hardin leaned across the table, thumped him in the chest with his fist. 'I'll tell you what we do for an encore. We hightail it over to the Royal, have ourselves a couple of pipes a-piece.'

The atmosphere lightened considerably.

'Man,' said Marco, 'now you talkin'.'

Steeger said, 'You seeing Eileen this trip?'

'Uh-uh. She's out on assignment, down in the Delta. Snapping pix of kids with big eyes being given band-aids. Hearts-and-minds stuff for *Time Magazine*, or *National Geographic*, or I dunno. Any case, Marco and I, we gotta head back up north later tonight . . .'

All at once Steeger wasn't looking at him. Steeger was gazing beyond him. Behind him. Hardin's eyes flicked to the mirror.

There weren't just two of them now. There were five. No, six. Shit! There were *seven* of the fuckers!

The two civilians had been joined by five GIs, but Hardin could not see any empty tables. So where in God's sweet fucking name had these others come from? Somewhere at the back. A door, maybe, behind one of the plastic palms. Who knew. Who cared! This was going to be a bad scene.

To look at them, one might think that here were five well-juiced GIs and a couple of their civilian buddies. They were heading for the door. They'd had their fun. The evening had been fine. The jokes had rolled. The booze had flowed. They were *mellow*.

Hardin knew better. They were staggering, laughing loudly, bumping into tables, apologising profusely to bar-girls and scowling civilians. It was the apologies that were out of line. That was overdoing it.

'You got a piece?' he muttered to Marco.

'Ain't got a piece.'

'Fuck. Anything at all?'

'Ma wits.'

'Get ready to use 'em.'

'What I fuckin' doin'!' snarled Marco.

He was busy shovelling coins out of his pocket and on to the table-top. Steeger watched with alarm.

'Smile!' hissed Hardin.

The roisterers had reached the room's half-way point and were beginning to move faster. Hardin gave it another twenty seconds, maybe less.

'This fuckin' foreign crap,' mumbled Marco. 'Funny money. Loony-Toon tin. Wish I had me a few silver eagles.'

'Why don't we just beat it out the door?' said Steeger. His right hand was clutching at the bottle of bourbon.

'Because there'll be a goddamn reception committee out the door, dimbo,' snarled Hardin. 'And don't hold that bottle like it was a goddamn weapon.'

'It *is* a goddamn weapon!'

'Not yet it ain't. And when things start happening don't use it like a fucking club. Smash the bottom off against the wall and jab it at guys' faces. We're going out the back, right?'

Marco scooped all the coins he had into his right hand, fisted it. He dropped his hand under the table.

'Hey, buddy!'

Point-man had reached them, one of the GIs. He was a big guy, carrying a lot of beef. He looked to be in not bad condition despite this, although it was clear from the veins on his nose and cheeks that he had a more than merely nodding acquaintance with the juice of the grape or the corn or the juniper berry. He stood beside the table, swaying slightly. He belched a couple of times.

'Wow, Jesus, what a fucker. Hey, man. Ya gotta light?'

He slumped down into the seat next to Steeger, facing Marco. Marco was aware that someone else was standing just behind him. There was continuous movement there, shuffling and scuffling, a few belches, loud laughter.

'Hey, c'mon man, I said you gotta light, for fuck's sake.'

The beefy GI's expression was shifting from good-humoured oafishness into mild truculence. Steeger smiled wanly. Hardin fished into a pocket, pulled out his Zippo.

'Sure, man. Where's the smoke?'

The big man's expression now became belligerent.

'Shit, man, I don't want no fuckin' lighter. Doncha know how ta fuckin' act civilised, man? Ya get all lighter gas stinkin' up the smokes, man. Jesus, doncha know that? Ya must come from the fuckin' boondocks, man. I wanna match.' He appealed to those standing. 'He wantsa stink up my smokes. Jesus. I hadda good evenin' till this fucker came along.'

'Thinks he's king of the shit-pile,' said someone.

The beefy GI grabbed at this enthusiastically.

'Thass right! King of the fuckin' shit-pile!' He swung round towards Hardin again, thrust his face across the table. 'Listen, dickface, ya gotta match!' It wasn't a question.

'Sure,' said Hardin mildly. He slipped the lighter back into his pocket. 'Your face, my butt.'

He didn't give the guy even half a second to register outrage. His left hand came up, open-handed, fingers curled. He rammed the palm into the man's face and clutched, fingers jabbing into eyes. Even as the man gave an agonised yell Hardin shoved his head backwards. The crown smashed back into the mirror behind, shattering it, blood haloing round the broken glass in a fine spray as Hardin, still holding tight, dragged it sideways.

Even as the man shrieked Marco had moved with the speed of a striking snake. His hand, too, came up as he swivelled round in his seat and sank his loaded fist into the groin of the man standing behind him. With a wheezing grunt of agony the guy buckled, doubled-up, and Marco, still on the move, heaved. The guy careered back into his companions, toppling them like pins into chairs and tables. There was a bull-like roar from one of the oilmen which did not wholly cover the sound of Steeger trying to smash the short-necked bourbon bottle against the wall. Then, as one of the GIs lunged for Hardin's back, Steeger snarled '*Fuckit!*' and brained him instead. This time the bottle shattered. As the man sank to the floor Steeger could see that the juice of Indian corn mixed with rye did something very weird to the colour of blood.

Marco was methodically, systematically, heaving over more tables and chairs. Hardin suddenly found himself face to face with one of the sallow-skinned civilians who was spitting at him in hoarse French and pulling an automatic from under his coat. Hardin's fist shot out, gripped the gun-hand, wrenched it up. Bones cracked, the gun banged. The bullet went up through the man's jaw-bone and it must have been soft-nosed and carved because all at once the guy did not have a face, just a scarlet mess of pulped bone and homogenised tissue.

Hardin thrust the man away, keeping hold of the gun. He rammed the barrel into another man's face and snarled '*Out!*' He didn't wait to see if Marco and Steeger followed but hurdled the barricade of overturned tables, barrelled through a mass of screaming bar-girls and yelling customers and raced down past the bar, head down.

There was a door, and it was hidden behind the plastic shrubbery. He didn't stop to use the handle, just hit it with his shoulder and the door, cheap and flimsy in construction, burst inwards. There was a passage ahead. He sprinted down towards another door at the far end, aware that people were running after him. He didn't bother to check out who. If they weren't shooting at him they were on his side.

The second door presented even less of a problem than the first. It was so thin Hardin almost ploughed through it, leaving a man-sized shape, like in the funnies. Most of the woodwork ended up outside. Hardin breathed Saigon air. He was in a small yard enclosed by a high brick wall. Marco propelled Steeger through what remained of the door after him.

Steeger said, 'My God! The guy's head was harder than the fucking wall!'

He was white, shaking. Hardin understood perfectly that such explosive violence in a bar, when you were relaxed and off-guard, was way different from facing up to murderous guards who'd just massacred civilians in a battle-situation.

Still, he didn't for a moment imagine that Steeger was about to flake out on them.

He snapped 'The wall!' and at the same time dropped down on one knee, hands cupped in front of him. Marco left-booted into the hand and Hardin heaved. Marco shot upwards. Behind, there were sounds of angry pursuit.

Marco yelled, 'C'mon, c'mon! I can take him!'

Steeger too put his foot in Hardin's hands and was thrust upwards to where Marco, now straddling the top of the wall, grabbed at his arms and hauled him over. Marco then screamed '*Down!*' and disappeared from sight.

Hardin dived for the nearest corner, his right hand fumbling for the pistol in his pocket. Automatic fire chattered harshly. Where he'd been crouching, rounds chewed at stonework, ricocheting around the confined space of the little yard. Hardin, finally disentangling the gun from his pocket, recognised the sound. Someone had found himself an M16.

The firing ceased as suddenly as it had commenced. Hardin sprang to his feet, jumped to his right, the gun gripped two-handed. He was already squeezing the trigger as he leapt into the sight-line of the doorway. He pumped two rounds fast into the stooping figure of a man outlined against the passageway light and thought: Stupid sonuvabitch deserves to die, should've dowsed the goddamn illuminations.

The man spun round, staggered backwards, the M16 clattering to the floor as Hardin emptied his mag into a melee of guys behind the fallen figure. Then he swivelled, dropped, launched himself upwards.

His hands caught hold of the flat wall-top, fingers gripping the stonework. He heaved himself the rest of the way, legs kicking wildly as more shots rang out. But no one was thinking straight. No one grabbed for the M16 to rake his body. He swung himself up and over the top of the wall, let go, dropped, automatically bringing up his knees for the touchdown.

As he hit the ground Marco caught hold of him, steadied him.

'Ain't gonna be too long before the guys out front decide to come round the back, cut us off. If there were guys out front.'

'You betcha,' grinned Hardin. He was high on adrenalin; even his finger-tips felt like they were on fire.

Steeger was leaning against the wall, breathing harshly. 'Fuck this,' he said. 'This is a hell of a night out for the boys.'

'Get back to Tu Do,' said Hardin. 'Infiltrate the crowds.' He began shoving Steeger along the narrow alleyway. 'C'mon, Will, hurry the fuck up.'

'Where to?' complained the stocky journalist. 'The fuzz? The military? Where?'

'Like I said, we gotta date with some opium.' Hardin was laughing. 'I need to simmer down.'

III

There were king-size rats in the Royal Hotel, but long-time aficionados said that that was because it was clear the Royal was no sinking ship. Its captain, Jean Ottavj, on the other hand, these days often looked as though he himself was sinking fast.

No one seemed to know just how old M. Ottavj was. Certainly Hardin didn't; it was doubtful if M. Ottavj himself had more than a vague idea. Some said maybe in his seventies, others said around eighty. Actually, he looked about ninety. His face was lined, corrugated, contoured, wrinkled, and although he walked as straight-backed as he could, because he was essentially a proud and dignified man, it was necessary for him to use a stick at all times. He was frequently bed-ridden, plagued by rheumatism and other aching ills. Yet there was a lively intelligence in his dark eyes, and when he spoke, although it was often in a hoarse whisper, what he said was worth listening to. Even gossip that might not be entirely accurate. Perhaps *especially* gossip that might not be entirely accurate.

M. Ottavj was a French Corsican, born near Ajaccio some years – and who could number them exactly? – before the turn of the century. He had lived in South East Asia, mostly in Saigon, for the best part of forty years. It seemed likely he would die there. He had no reason to return to his birthplace, or even to France, and rarely spoke of either, even in moments of stress. In fact, when the melancholic fit took him, and a need to recall some memory or experience other than those associated with his years in Vietnam, he would be more likely to speak with sad nostalgia of the great glowing disc of a moon that hung over Aleppo, where he had once served in the French army. Steeger, who had never been to Syria in his life, used to say that the only thing he knew about Aleppo was that he'd once read they were keen on circumcising dogs there. This, M. Ottavj used to deny vehemently, or as vehemently as his nature allowed. Which on the Richter scale was about 0.5.

M. Ottavj was, like a lot of long-term expatriates, a character and much liked, even in a land where his countrymen were generally detested for what they had done in the bad old days of colonial rule. Even hardened journalists admitted the general truth of the Vietnamese complaints about the French: their brutality, stupidity, colossal arrogance; their economic and political blindness; their essentially short-term paternalism. 'The goddamn French!' sneered Steeger, whose grasp of the socio-political history of any country he reported on was usually fairly acute. 'In a hundred fucking years, the only thing they gave to Nam was a machine for filtering coffee!'

But M. Ottavj was respected. Perhaps because he loved the country, and had stuck to it through the most appalling debacles and personal hardships: the Japanese occupation of the forties (he'd been tossed in the slammer), the Viet Minh terror of the fifties (his only son had been killed in a mortar attack), and now the Viet Cong and the threat of a total North Vietnamese invasion. Throughout it all M. Ottavj had exhibited a measure of tranquillity and retained his sense of humour and balance – in short, kept his cool. The Vietnamese liked that. His staff was loyal to a boy, and *boyesse*. Some had been with him for a quarter of a century.

That was what Hardin liked about the Royal Hotel, its sense of permanence in a crumbling world. Sure, rats brushed against your legs in the bar, there were lizards in the bedrooms, gigantic spiders in the baths, and the wiring was lethal. But that was nit-pickey stuff, not worth bothering about. He always stayed at the Royal when he was in Saigon. Apart from anything else, M. Ottavj could usually be relied to come up with opium for his friends, although he invariably spoke of it dismissively, comparing it contemptuously with the opium of forty or fifty years before. 'Ah, *mon Colonel*, this trash!' he would say with a melodramatic groan. *'C'est frelaté!'*

Steeger was talking about adulterated opium now. He seemed to be obsessed with it. He was still looking shaken, even after three pipes, but this did not seem to affect the way he was kneading the opium, rolling it on the side of the bowl.

'All the guys I know say you got two pipes to the gramme in the old days,' he said. 'With all the crap they throw in now you need about six before things start popping.'

'Ain' it the truth,' muttered Marco.

He was sitting on the floor with his back to Hardin's bed flipping through a copy of *Mad Magazine*. Thus far, none of the jokes had started him popping, but he wasn't really concentrating.

'Everything's got shit in it,' grumbled Steeger. 'Every goddamn thing. Booze, food, junk. You name it. We're living in an adulterated world.'

Marco pondered whether or not to throw in a snappy one-liner linking adulteration with adultery, but the more he pondered the less snappy the one-liner became, until he forgot about it. He'd already had a couple of joints on the way up, prime Laotian red that Steeger had dug up from somewhere. He hadn't had a hit like that for some months and was already feeling fuzzy round the edges.

'Take a raincheck on the o-peem,' he suddenly said. 'Any moment now, an' I goin' . . .' His voice drifted off into a long yawn.

'Jesus,' said Steeger disgustedly, popping the pill into the wooden bowl and upending the pipe over the lamp-glass, at the same time tamping the pill in with a spill. 'This is a fuck of a wild party.'

Hardin was lying on the bed smoking. He'd had a couple

of pipes; it was enough. He had other things to think about. A couple of hours later, on the transport up north, the hits would start to take effect. They would make a tedious plane journey tolerable.

Hardin took relaxants, uppers, brain-poppers, and mind-expanders because he liked them and because he was intellectually interested in their effects. It was, in any case, a more civilised, indeed convivial, way of loosening up after a heavy situation full of blood and death than chugging beer or spirits, or both, with a bunch of rednecks. That often made things worse, had an utterly depressing effect even while you were actually indulging, although he didn't at all mind taking a drink as part of the social round. His personal drugs philosophy – no hard and fast rules – went back to his youth when marijuana had been freely available, and hallucinogens had been, as some wiseass had once put it, an expanding market.

He thought about the goons in the bar and wished that he'd had time to grab one of them. Not the GIs; they were just cannon-fodder, doing somebody a favour. 'Ya wanna bounce some guy around a little? Sure, sure.' They'd know nothing. One of the dock-rats now, that was different. They looked tough mothers but even tough mothers can be made to talk if you start cutting them up, a piece at a time. His mind flipped back. One of the dock-rats was dead anyway. With a snapped wrist and no face.

Why? Why had they jumped him? Who were they? Were they out of the past?

It had to be that. But which past? He had more than a few to choose from, a rich assortment of missions in various parts of the world where the end-result had been chaos and confusion, death and destruction. Hate lasted. With some guys, it lasted a lifetime.

'Hey,' said Steeger. He had just finished pulling at the pipe and was flat on his back talking to the ceiling. 'I heard a good one from Larry Wales of UPI. He was at the last Bob Hope thing at, uh . . . I dunno, Long Binh, I guess. Somewhere like that. But li'l ole Bob, he wasn't going down too well. There was a certain amount of, uh . . .' Steeger chuckled throatily '. . . like he wasn't, you know, connecting. There was a three-generation gap, dig? Anyhow, he's like, telling these bum jokes, and the cameras are on him, and there's dudes out in the audience, they're all getting restive and fingering at the cameras, and there's the director, he's going crazy trying to keep the cameras off placards in the crowd saying stuff like "Fuck Off, Nixon" and "The Vietnam War Is A Bob Hope Joke", things like that, and some really gross stuff, I mean Jesus, truly embarrassing, and then suddenly *bam!* – this groupa guys suddenly jump up on the stage and wave this banner around . . .' Steeger started laughing so convulsively that his head banged up and down on the floor. 'Jesus, it was rich, truly rich. The guys are MPs, right? Military Police. Really mean. Real motherfuckers, right? And they had this banner, really big letters, dayglo lettering – "Pigs for Peace"! Oh shit! *Pigs for peace!*' He went on snorting with laughter for some time.

Hardin went over in his mind the scuttlebutt of the past few months; the whispers, the rumours, the grapevine mutterings; intelligence reports that had come his way in the normal line of business. He could think of nothing significant, nothing that might connect up with his past. He thought: Maybe it's the spooks, the CIA? Maybe they're out for revenge? They've got no cause to love me. For one reason or another, some of those guys have every reason to want me dead. And then he rejected the thought. Even the CIA – who had once seriously considered a plan for making Castro's hair fall out and his toe-nails drop off – were not that dumb. Even the CIA would not contemplate something as crass as icing him in a Saigon nightspot under cover of a bar-brawl. Even though there were guys who'd just love to knock him off, they wouldn't come up with a scheme as inept as that. It was just too fucking stupid for words.

In any case, he and Steeger and Frank Marco had chosen that bar at random; there was nothing planned, nothing anyone could have caught hold of and said, Okay that's the place, we hit him *there!*

Nor had they been followed by anyone through the

streets of Saigon after they had been dropped by the taxi from Steeger's place on Pasteur. Hardin had an instinct when it came to being tailed, a gut feeling that triggered off all kinds of alarms inside his head. It had never failed him yet. He was, he knew, a lousy subject for any prospective tailer, however much of a professional the guy was.

Which meant it was pure chance. It was the only explanation that fitted the facts. Those two guys had spotted him, remembered him. Jesus, it's that sonuvabitch Hardin. Let's take him out. They'd summoned assistance (a nod to the bar-keep, a note to one of the girls – it didn't matter how), struck – and blown it.

The irony was, if these two guys hated him before, one of them was gonna be hating him double now!

Hardin thought: I can do without this crap. I have problems enough right now, trying to get myself off the hook with Command, and trying to push Lew Halderling into keeping his goddamn promises. I just don't need this extra aggravation piling up.

Steeger was saying, 'It's true, I'm telling you. I had it from a reliable source. The big H is on the upswing.'

Marco said, 'Bad stuff, baby. Don' do me no good. You see the dudes where I come from, man, they shakin' in the gutter, beggin' for it. They got a forest fire burnin' in their guts. They don' know if it bearshit or Christmas. They jus' gotta have it, man, whatever. That ain' for me, man. I mean, I got too much respect for my body.'

'Sure. All those needles. Shit, I hate that. Ya gotta stick it in ya for the burn. Holy Christ, I have troubles enough with the goddamn dentist.' Steeger stared at the ceiling. 'I gotta feeling in my bones. There's some big old shit-level wind blowing somewhere. Those guys at the Continental. Maybe I oughta look into that.'

'Yeah,' said Marco, not much interested. He was watching a fat cockroach, part of the Royal's private menagerie, scuttling across the carpet near him. Marco didn't like cockroaches, he'd seen too many of them; in Harlem they were taking over the world. He lifted his boot.

'Don't do it!' yelped Steeger, noticing. 'Bad scene!'

'Uh?'
'Yeah. Don't you know?'
'Know what, man?'
'Very uncool to kill cockroaches. There's a poor student, see, usual thing, and he's got a tough exam, things are getting him down. So he's lying there, thinking of the beautiful princess . . .'
'Way-waid a minute. Princess? Now where this princess come from?'
'Oh, he's hoping to capture her hand in marriage. But the deal is, he's gotta pull out the aces on the big exam or he's had it. And he knows he's gonna fuck up. So he's dreaming of this chick and he sees this mother of a roach waddling past and he's just about to crush the shit out of it, when he like, stays his hand. Or foot. Then, *bam!* The roach transforms, reveals itself as – *Buddha!* Buddha's so damn grateful the guy didn't crush the shit out of him that he guides his hand in the big exam. The kid gets the girl, Buddha gets another convert. End of story.'
'Yeah, man. But I don' believe in Buddha. So if I crush the roach, it don' apply.'
'Tell that to the Vietnamese,' said Steeger darkly. 'You crush a roach, there's a black wind blowin' the rest of ya life. Or what's left of it. Which ain't much. Lotsa bad shit dumped on ya, if ya crush a roach.'
'You live where I live, babe,' said Marco, 'you take an M60 to the fuckin' roaches.'
Steeger wasn't listening any more. He'd jumped back; was pondering the advisability of an in-depth trawl through dark waters.
'Maybe I oughta do the whole bit. Deep investigation. Right back, you know? To when the KMT jumped outta China in '49 and took over the Golden Triangle. There's a hell of a story there. Lotta threads to pick up, tie together. Our guys, Laos, the Chinese – the fuckin' Mafia, I'm tellin' ya! You know, the EnVees got a finger in that pie, piecea that action. Christ, they probably got an armful if the truth be known. Strange bedfellows.'
'Yeah,' said Marco.

'But then there's a lotta dough involved in horse,' said Steeger reflectively. 'Gotta be said. Millions. Billions. Fuckin' trillions when ya get right down to it. We're fightin' this war, right? And on the surface it's kill or be killed, and we're savin' the world from the Red Peril. But I'm tellin' ya, Marco, when ya dig deep there's some weird things going on. Know what I'm sayin'? Some very weird things.'

'Yeah.'

'And then maybe I oughta keep my nose clean, or maybe some fucker's gonna come along cut it off. And the rest of my face with it.'

Steeger's right hand twitched suddenly. His eyes closed.

The man called La Bête sat on the edge of the bed and sucked smoke deep into his lungs. The hand holding the cigarette was only millimetres from his mouth, but the smoke did not seem to be worrying him. He stared at it, unmoved. He seemed to have been turned to stone.

His companion gazed at him fearfully. As soon as he'd got a quarter way through his story he knew he should not have even started. He should have explained everything away as the result of an unfortunate accident. He should have paid the GIs off – the good God knew, he had enough money on him to cope with that – and simply reported André's death as an accident. That was exactly what he should have done. No one would ever have known the difference, and the GIs would not have talked.

Instead, he'd let it all come out, the whole story, and now La Bête was mad. He might not look mad, sitting there contemplating the smoke from his cigarette, but the man watching him knew different. He knew the signs. La Bête was *enraged*.

Suddenly, the Corsican spoke. 'Come here.'

His voice was rough, throaty.

The man slowly got up from his chair and walked across to the Corsican as though he was treading on egg-shells. He stood beside the bed.

'No. In front of me. Squat down. I want to talk to you.'

The man bit his lip, did as he was told. He squatted down

and the Corsican clasped him by the shoulder with his left hand, still holding the cigarette in his right.

'Now,' said the Corsican. 'You are certain it was the American?'

The man began to sweat. 'But yes. Certainly it was. I remember his face. André, too. He has not changed much.'

'*Pouf!*' said the Corsican mildly. 'It is only eight years.'

'Of course.'

'But you did not kill him.'

'It was . . . difficult. He had friends with him. He . . .'

The Corsican interrupted. 'But he only had two friends with him, as you described. And there were, it appears, seven of you. This is how you describe it.'

'Yes, but . . .'

'That was foolish of you, Jean.'

'He was incredible, I tell you! So fast, and . . .'

'No, no, no. I do not mean that. It was very foolish of you to tell me the truth, Jean, when you could so easily have told me the untruth. To save yourself.' The Corsican still did not take his eyes off the cigarette.

'But I thought you should know . . .'

'And now the American is still alive, walking the streets of Saigon. He will be wondering why he was attacked. He will be turning the problem over in his mind. He will be thinking: Who is it that so wishes me dead? He will perhaps have recognised you, and remembered. He will be thinking: Ah! Now why are they here, these men I last saw eight years ago? What are they doing? What are they planning? What are their reasons? He will be alerted.'

The man's knees were beginning to ache. Sweat was trickling down his face in a steady stream. 'No, I don't think so . . .'

'You don't think so? It doesn't matter.' The Corsican suddenly seemed to have lost all interest in the conversation. 'For you, nothing matters. Open your mouth.'

The man stared at him. 'What? Open . . .?'

'Your mouth. Open it.'

The man opened his mouth, his eyes narrowing in bewilderment.

The Corsican flipped the cigarette inside.

Instantly the man reacted, trying to spit it out, yelling as the burning tobacco seared into the roof of his mouth. The Corsican shot up from the bed, clutching at the man's jaw. He smacked his right hand down on top of the man's head with piledriving force and exerted pressure. The mouth snapped shut and the Corsican dragged the man over sideways. The man's legs kicked out, his hands tried to pull at the Corsican's wrists. The Corsican kicked him in the groin. The man could not shriek, except through his nose and from the back of his throat. It was a strange, birdlike fluting. The Corsican began talking to him, telling him what a fool he had been, what a crazy, stupid, brainless idiot. As he spoke he twisted the man's head in his hands and then sank down on one knee so that the man's neck lay across it. He squeezed and pushed and wrenched with his left hand until the man's jawbone cracked. The Corsican, still talking in a low voice, exerted more and more pressure on the man's neck. He twisted and twisted, and went on twisting long after the action was at all necessary.

IV

'The point is,' said Colonel Phil Esteban, staring down at his cluttered desk, 'there's just too damn much paperwork.' He looked up at the tall, lean dark-haired man lounging against the window, through which nothing could be seen but darkness. 'You must see that, John.' He was almost pleading.

Hardin dug thumb and forefinger into his shirt pocket and fished out a pack of cigarettes. He tapped one out and Zippoed it alive.

'Halderling promised me,' he said in a neutral voice.

'Well, sure! And for Christ's sake, John, you more than anyone ought to know he's a man of his word. Especially with you. I mean, I know you and him. You go back a whiles. Years. A decade or more. He's not going to fuck you around. You know that!'

'Yeah.'

Hardin's voice was low, colourless. He blew smoke at the window-pane in front of him and watched it erupt against the glass, obscuring his image against the blackness outside.

'It's just that it takes time,' said Esteban. 'Those guys you had with you on that last mission – I mean, they weren't regular grunts in the accepted sense of the word. No way were they! Christ! You had a rich mix in that outfit!'

'It wasn't a regular mission,' said Hardin dryly, 'in the accepted sense of the word.'

He turned from the window and gazed across the shadowy room. Esteban gazed back, blank-faced, and then went on, as though Hardin hadn't said a word.

'Dopers, killers, fraggers. . . .' He shuffled through papers on his desk and plucked one out, running his eyes down its contents. 'This guy Garrett – the EssVees are still raising a shit-storm about him, you know.' He mumbled his way through the words on the sheet of paper. 'My God! They're saying here that the only reason they released him into US military custody in the first place was because they assumed he'd be executed on the spot! For killing this old guy – whatsisname . . .' His eyes flicked down the sheet. 'Ngo Phanh. Some big political wheel with mucho clout.'

'Garrett says it was the son. The old guy's son. Paid him to do it. It was a job.' Hardin was staring out the window again.

'A job!' Esteban yelped. 'Jesus H. Christ, John – come on!'

'Seems Garrett was a hit-man for the Mob, back in the World. Then a deal backfired.' Hardin sounded almost amused. 'He joined up to escape, ah . . . mob vengeance.' He paused. 'I think that was the phrase he used.'

'God in Heaven,' muttered Esteban, hunching over his papers. 'Mob vengeance? Mother of Christ!'

'It's a weird war,' said Hardin.

'That's the truth.' Esteban slapped the piece of paper down on the desk and glared at it. 'But it's got nothing to do with the fact that the EssVees have somehow gotten wind of Garrett's continued non-extinction, and they're bitching to Command about it.'

'Probably the son.'

'Almost certainly the son! And if it's as you say it is, and the son was mixed up in it, I'm not surprised. He'd not like the guy he briefed to do the fell deed hanging around still! But that doesn't alter anything. You're now saying this Garrett should be given a medal and spirited out of Nam.' Esteban winced. 'Like I said, it's not going to be easy.'

Hardin turned from the window again, this time stepping across the room and leaning past the bent arm of the anglepoise lamp that hung next to Esteban's head, placing both hands squarely on the paper-strewn desk-top. He said softly, almost in Esteban's right ear, 'It's as easy as hell. You know it, I know it. It's done all the time, for one reason or another.'

Esteban scowled. He shuffled through more papers, sending some fluttering off into the darkness beyond the lamp's penumbra.

'Well, sure,' he muttered irritably. 'I know it, you know it.' He snatched at another document. 'Look! Look at this! This kid Vogt! He's supposed to be in the stockade for murder too! And Jesus, this is worse than some old goddamn slant-eyed politico on the crook – this is a goddamn sergeant in the US marines! Let's see – out in the field . . . battle situation . . . shot his sergeant – Christ! And you want a ribbon for him too! Honourable discharge! The works!'

Hardin dumped himself down in the swivel-chair the other side of Esteban's desk. 'That was a mistake.'

'What was a mistake?'

'Deep-sixing the sarge.'

'A mistake, you say!' Esteban was incredulous.

'Yeah. The kid got it all wrong. He thought the sarge was some kind of monster. The guy was about to knock off some little kid, so Vogt iced him. It then transpired the little kid was carrying a grenade to blow the sarge and his men out. It was a VC set-up. Vogt didn't know it. He fired first and got told the answers later. Happens all the time. You know it, I . . .'

'Yeah, yeah,' Esteban cut in tetchily. 'He's a fucking saint, I know.' He flicked through his papers some more, picked out another sheet. 'This guy Ronald Pepper – a medic. *He* didn't take the Hippocratic Oath, that's for sure!' He glared at the document he was holding. 'Running a goddamn junkie's supermarket chain, from what I can make out, then got busted by the MPs in some unsavoury situation or other. Mm . . . mmm – yeah! Picked up in some shithole of a hotel in Saigon where some turdbird newsman was OD-ing on rough-cut heroin.' He gazed across at Hardin in astonishment. 'And you want this guy *out?*'

Hardin smiled a private smile. He'd known Phil Esteban for a long time, and not just in Vietnam. Esteban, too, went back a long way with General Lewis J. Halderling.

He was tall and skinny with thinning hair. He wore rimless glasses and a worried expression; both sat naturally on his narrow, scholarly face. To look at him, one would think that here was a typical Remington Raider, desk-bound and safe at the rear and proud of it, contemptuous of the grunts and the boonierats who did all the actual work, waded through all the blood and muck and sweat of war, risked their lives, lost their lives. He looked to be the type who would scream girlishly and flap his hands if someone dripped blood over his highly polished shoes. Hardin knew better.

He recalled a night in Trieste when three Russians had made just such a snap judgement. They had lived to regret it.

Or, to put it another way, they had not lived to regret it.

Halderling depended on Colonel Phil Esteban. He was someone to be trusted implicitly. He kept his teeth tight-clenched when all around him were jabbering like monkeys.

'Yeah,' said Hardin. 'I want him out.'

'And look at this!' Esteban was waving yet another document in the air, his eyes almost bulging behind his glasses. '1st Sergeant Walter Olsen! My God, John – he fragged his own L-T in the field!'

'Way I heard it, the guy was an A-1 asshole.'

'A-1 asshole or not,' said Esteban sternly, 'he was an L-T and you cannot just go around blowing L-Ts all over the battlefield. Not your own L-Ts anyhow.'

'There's got to be something in the rule-book says you can't,' agreed Hardin.

He let his eyes drift round the shadowy room. There were tall dark green steel filing-cabinets everywhere; two of them were actually standing on their own away from the walls near the centre of the room. Most had at least one drawer fully extended, with card-files and loose papers spilling out on to the floor. Books, military pamphlets, box-files were double-stacked against the walls; in places, triple-stacked. Some of the piles leaned outwards so precariously that it looked as though just the sound of a snapped forefinger and thumb would send them crashing to the floor.

Hardin leaned back in his chair, extending his leg. His right foot snagged something in the darkness below the desk and a small avalanche of paper susurrated over his boot. He kicked it aside, knowing that whatever he did it would make no difference. Whatever was there, Esteban would find it if he wanted to find it. He had the knack of living in utter disorder and yet leading an astonishingly orderly existence. In this triumph of chaos and clutter, Esteban could lay his hands on a single document within seconds of needing it.

Although, more often than not, the thin man relied on his memory rather than records or documentation. Esteban's memory was outstanding, verging on the phenomenal. At any given moment in time, he knew exactly where all sections of General Halderling's heterogeneous Nam-based irregulars were to be found, why they were where they were, what they were doing, how they were doing it. He was rarely wrong. And when he was wrong it was because some numbskull wasn't doing what he ought to have been doing – and that wasn't very often. There weren't too many numbskulls in Halderling's outfit.

Out in the field was another matter, of course. An insertion-force into Laos, say, or North Vietnam itself did not – could not, by the very nature of the operation – follow the book, apart from the normal rules of survival that were learned by experience rather than from the pages of a military manual. Esteban could not be expected to know where guys were exactly, 300 klicks into Indian territory. But he usually had a rough idea. And he knew what they had with them, where they were headed for, what they ought to be doing. More important, he had more than just a rough idea of what to do if things went sour, for any reason – how many men to insert as a raid-and-rescue party, how many back-up, where to extract them from in the first place, how much materiél to throw into the field, where to get that materiél from at fifteen minutes' notice or less, how to bring all these disparate strands together so that a satisfactory conclusion was obtained. He was a logistics genius, and it was mostly done from memory.

Hardin had long ago decided that if it was true that most human beings utilised less than one tenth part of their brains, Phil Esteban belonged to that tiny – infinitesimal, even – minority who were able to use one and a half, and maybe as much as two, tenths in the normal way of things. Or the abnormal way of things.

Esteban said forcefully, 'You're damn right there's got to be something in the rule-book says you can't go around blowing away your own L-Ts. It's in the section under "Mutiny".'

'Olsen's a good man,' said Hardin mildly. 'Real Papa Sierra.'

'Yeah?' Esteban sounded dubious.

'Yeah. He's a fussy fucker. Like you.'

Esteban shot him a thin smile. 'Flattery will get you nowhere, buddy.' Then he said, 'Who else have we here?' As though he really wanted to know the answer.

Hardin frowned. 'We don't have anyone else. That's it. All the other guys got nailed.'

Esteban shook his head. 'Uh-uh. You've got an L-T here somewhere. Comeraro. Arthur Comeraro. From Chuck Welland's base at Pen Kho. Also another Top – uh, Sergeant Fuller. Joseph Fuller. Not forgetting that flyboy friend of yours Frank Marco.'

'Yeah, but Comeraro and Fuller weren't in the Dempsey business. They got pulled in for the Laos/Cambodia insertion.'

Esteban nodded thoughtfully. He picked up a pencil and tapped his teeth a couple of times. 'And because of that,' he said suddenly, 'they've become kind of like displaced persons, John. Fact is, you're all displaced persons.' He paused. 'The General runs this outfit without much interference from MAC-Vee in Saigon. You know the score there. We all know the score. They give him a loose rein, mainly because if they don't he goes down to Saigon and starts tearing Command apart with his bare hands.' He smiled faintly. 'He keeps saying he's going to retire imminently, but I don't think the old sonofabitch'll ever retire. And if he ever does, he'll no doubt go into the business of robbing banks. Or something like that. Keep his hand in. Anyway, this is all beside the point, which is . . .' and Esteban jabbed the pencil at Hardin as though he meant to throw it like a dart '. . . that MAC-Vee are grumbling and bitching about *you* – and even Halderling is finding it increasingly fucking difficult to keep them off your back.'

Hardin concentrated his attention on the green phone on Esteban's desk. He'd heard most, if not all, of this before. A number of times.

'There was the Dempsey business. There's no possible shadow of a doubt that Dempsey was up to his ears in all kinds of crazy shit. He had a hand in the Tun Phouc massacre, he was running a score of boom-boom houses, he was into dope in a big way, and best of all he was fraternising with the enemy to the point where he was about to blow some truly heavy stuff to them. Somehow you got involved. Somehow Dempsey got wiped. It's said that you wiped him.'* Esteban sighed, looked almost forlorn. 'I wouldn't know about that. No one tells me anything.'

Hardin gave a snort of laughter. 'I've heard some shit in my time, Phil, but that's gotta be the richest!'

'I'm just a desk-man,' said Esteban defensively. He waved a hand around him at the cluttered room. 'I sit here all day, all night, trying to make sense of this crap. I shuffle papers, I see reports, I get questions, I dictate answers. I'm the original man-in-the-dark.' He lit a cigarette. 'So. After the Dempsey business you were deemed to be a problem, one way or another. We then get this weird business up in Laos, where guys seemed to be deserting the ship to set up business on their own. Halderling threw you and what was left after the Dempsey thing into that and . . .'

'And I gave Halderling a sweet jumping-off point right in the heart of bandit country,' Hardin cut in, suddenly angry.

* See *The Killing Zone* by Jack Hamilton Teed.

He was tired of the whole business. The opium hadn't turned the plane-hitch from Saigon into a beautiful dreamer – he'd been too busy thinking about the fight in the bar. He hadn't slept at all. 'An impregnable valley with a natural chopper-apron and space for storing a whole fucking arsenal. On a plate. A natural HQ not only for monitoring the Ho Chi Minh Trail but sabotaging the hell out of it too. Our finest acquisition in the past five years. And all through me, and the guys with me – some of whom didn't make it back. Halderling owes me!'

There was silence in the room. Phil Esteban stared down at his desk-top, the cigarette smouldering between his fingers, its smoke, in the draught-free air of the little room, a thin grey-blue column rising into the darkness above the light-field of the lamp.

The blackness outside the window was, Hardin now saw, lifting a little, visibly shading into grey. Dawn was approaching, and with it the business of life and death that was the war in Vietnam, never wholly over even during the hours of darkness, would crank itself back into motion again. Esteban had his own personal schedule of toil, his own private time-zone. The main body of his work was done from 4 a.m. to 7 a.m. He said he operated better then. His brain was fresher. The cog-wheels meshed more smoothly. He was on the ball. 'You've heard of Dawn Man,' Lew Halderling used to joke. 'Phil Esteban's a Pre-Dawn Man. Which, I guess, makes him an anthropoid ape.' Right now, Esteban didn't look at all like an anthropoid ape.

'How long have you been with the General?' he said, still looking down at the desk.

Hardin chuckled, the tension easing out of him. 'That's a rhetorical question, Phil. Come on! You know damn well how long I've been in the SSG. It's in the files and it's in your head, and if it comes down to pinpointing a date I think I'd rather trust what's in your head than the files.'

'The trouble is, John,' Esteban spoke in a low voice now, quite fast, 'there's a good deal in the files. You've done a hell of a lot for the SSG and a hell of a lot for the good ole US of A in this fucked-up conflict, and elsewhere. But you've also stirred up a deal of shit, especially over these past two missions. Exposing Dempsey blew the covers off a fuck of a lot of people who had their hands deep in the till, right up to a couple of guys who were tight with President Thieu himself. Dempsey's files made interesting reading. Some of the stuff was so fucking hot a lot of people at the top actually expressed the opinion that sleeping dogs ought to have been left to lie. There was a CIA involvement, too, which created major hassles all round.' He paused, taking a quick drag at the cigarette. 'Command were pissed, rightly or wrongly. Their attitude was, maybe some of these things ought not to have been brought to light. Maybe it would've been better all round, because of the war, our relationship with the EssVees – that kind of thing. They didn't know what to do with you. So when that mass-desertion business came up they didn't throw up too many obstacles when Halderling pushed you into it. You can probably figure out why.'

'Sure,' said Hardin easily, 'they were hoping I wouldn't make it back.'

'Right. But you did make it back. And not only did you make it back, but you gave the SSG a beautiful present of a beautiful valley right damn deep in the heart of bandit country that a lot of guys'd give their nuts for.'

'Like the spooks,' said Hardin.

'Like the spooks, indeed. And talking of the CIA, there was a heavy involvement there too. As you're well aware, there was a rogue element from the CIA backing those sonsabitches, and a raft of documentary evidence to prove it. The guys in Thong Nhut Street were not best pleased when the General rode into town waving a satchelful of papers proving that certain agents in the CIA were financing a bunch of redneck deserters to maybe fire off a few nukes at China!'* Esteban raised his eyes to the ceiling. 'Jesus Christ! This madness has got to stop somewhere, but it never seems to.'

Hardin lit another cigarette then offered the pack across the desk. Esteban moodily shook his head.

* See *Fire-Force* by Jack Hamilton Teed.

'Tell me, Phil,' Hardin blew smoke towards the window and grinned. 'Can you figure out which of the elements in the CIA *isn't* rogue?'

Esteban shrugged wearily. 'God. I dunno. What kind of question is that?'

'What about our outfit, the SSG?'

'And what kind of a question is *that*?!'

'An academic one, I guess.'

'Yeah.' Esteban shrugged again. 'Who knows. It's all to do with power, I guess. We're all after power.'

Hardin nodded. It was a reasonable answer, not too far from the truth as he saw it.

'And trade-offs,' said Esteban, his tone suddenly more businesslike. 'Power and trade-offs. We have to go for what we think we can get away with, which isn't necessarily what we end up with.'

'Jesus, Phil, spit it out! What're you about to tell me? What weight of horse-shit are you about to dump on me? Where's the fucking trade-off here? Is Lew Halderling gonna throw me to the wolves?'

Esteban shook his head, smiled crookedly. 'He gave his word, remember? Like I said before. My own feeling is that in the end these guys you want out with ribbons will get out. With ribbons. But it's going to take time and effort. The General is pressing, but he's also busy with his new toy – the toy you gave him. He's seeing to it that that valley is made even more impregnable than impregnable. He's manning it. He's weaponing it up. And he can't be in two places at once.'

Hardin stood up. It was definitely lighter outside, with that strange dawn-light that turned this part of South East Asia into a wonderland out in the jungle. And that was where he wanted to be right now. Deep in the naked, primeval forest, where it was cleaner, sweeter, purer. And more deadly. You had to take the bad with the good out there. More trade-offs. But then that was a part of its strange allure.

Esteban was still talking. 'It isn't going to be easy. There are guys down in Saigon who want your head on a gridiron, and Halderling's truly doing all he can to fend them off. But you have a shit-hot record overall, and that tips the balance. Halderling's managed to finagle you and all those guys who got caught up with you into an extended R-and-R. That way, it gets everybody off the hook – sanitises the situation. You can go anywhere, do what the fuck you want. Until this business is sorted out.' Esteban looked at the tall figure across the desk from him. His expression was wary. 'There's just one but . . .'

'Okay,' said Hardin. 'Hit me with the punchline.'

'For Christ's sake – keep your nose clean.'

V

The Bell 209 AH-1G Huey Cobra didn't look like a cobra at all. It looked like a shark, a great white shark – or, more accurately, a great green shark.

It was chiefly the nose that did it, that extended snout sniffing at the air – that, and its long slim hunter-killer lines, its stripped-down-for-speed fuselage. Even when grounded, immobile, it looked like it was in the act of pouncing, although this romantic fancy – used to excess by the more excitable of descriptive journalists – was in fact due to an optical illusion. Seen from side-on, the nose looked like it was dipping; in fact it was angled upwards. It was just that the chin-turret, which carried a MiniGun capable of spitting 4000 rounds in less than sixty seconds, gave the impression of snout-droop, as though the chopper was lunging forward ferociously.

To firm up this evil impression, give it that extra amount of terror-clout, most crews painted teeth over and under the nose. The lips were an outline in black, curving up towards the tip of the nose, down towards the chin-port. The teeth were a chunky, claw-tipped white. Inside the teeth it was all red – red for danger and blood and disaster and death, but mainly because white fangs looked almost 3-D against it.

Most guys left it at that; it was warning enough. Some went further, painting great scarlet slanting eyes each side of the nose but back a little, under the co-pilot/gunner's canopy. But that was only effective if the bird was coming down at an angle – and if you could see it as it ought to be seen, see a single snarling eye so that it struck terror into your soul, it wasn't firing at you at all but at some poor fucker yards away. Which made it psychologically impractical.

The Cobra that was hurtling over the tree-tops at 300 km/h, heading in the general direction of the DeeEmZee, had a refinement: two front canines extending down over the chin-port, thick and sharp. Head-on there was no pissing around. It looked ultra-effective, real bad news – like it was Count Dracula lunging for your jugular.

Frank Marco, piloting the Cobra, gently took the bird a few degrees to port, chuckled into the intercom.

'So maybe I better stick around, huh? Keep a fresh box of Kleenex within easy reach. Dab that Durante whenever I see a smudge.'

Hardin was hunched down in the front co-pilot/gunner's seat. His eyes were taking in the view, watching the sun start to edge its way up over the horizon on his left, seeing a hard-edged brilliance wash across the jungle.

'"Durante?" For Christ's sake, Marco! Where'd you get that shit from?'

'I jus' makin' it up as I go along,' admitted the black, Tomming it. 'I kin do it cos I a eddicated nigra. I kin pluck dem con-tem-po-ray al-lu-juns outta the air.' He switched back to his normal East Coast-educated drawl. 'Hey, listen. They gonna be pissed if we take a tumble in the Big Green, this be a rec-flight and all.'

'Why should we take a tumble? Think positive. Any case, I'm just following orders. It's what Phil Esteban said. You're on R-and-R. Do what you like. Let the White House pay for your fun.'

'He say *that*?'

'Well, no. Not exactly.'

'He *mean* that?'

'Again, no. Not entirely. I'm interpreting the ground-rules very loosely. Being under a cloud has its compensations.'

'All I need,' sighed Marco. 'We goin' anyplace, or jus' burnin' fuel?'

'Burning fuel,' said Hardin. 'I'm watching the sunrise. I need the charge.'

'Hey!' Marco's eyes had caught at something out of place in the jungle-roof. 'Left, six o'clock.'

Hardin looked. Mostly the jungle was flat here, a green carpet that stretched away into the fast-thinning morning mists. To the left low hills began to obtrude, gradual stepping-stones up towards the high mountains that ranged into Laos. Near, a dark patch could be seen in the tree-canopy, a blackened hole in that sea of green.

'That's a flamer,' said Hardin. 'Circle it.'

Marco said, 'Man, this hell's graveyard. We got another one. Nearer. Three o'clock of that hill. I'm goin' there.'

Hardin stared down at the mess dispassionately. A dead chopper. It was no big deal. There were dead choppers all over Nam; enough wreckage to cannibalise into a whole new air fleet, probably.

This one had fire-balled in the jungle itself by the look of it; either been shot down or dropped out of the sky due to mechanical malfunction, then ripped itself apart. Closer to it, he could see bits of wreckage tangled up in the top-growth of the trees around the actual hole, which meant it had been shot at and had started to disintegrate before ground-eruption.

'Let's check out the other one. Nothing here.'

Marco shifted the cyclic, took the bird in a swooping dive across a mile or so north. Here, the hole in the jungle was directly in front of a hill and Hardin muttered, 'This one had it easier.'

There was debris scattered about here too, struts, bits of metal, but no fire-wash across the trees. The chopper could still be seen, mangled and buckled but still fairly intact; with its slightly longer and fatter body, recognisably a Huey UH-1D gunship/grunt-carrier.

'Take that back,' said Marco in his ear. 'No way did that bird have it easy.'

On closer inspection Hardin had to admit the truth of

this. This one had been flayed by rounds all along its body. It looked to have been a frontal attack, close up and savage.

'Lower,' said Hardin.

'Like, roost on the top stuff?' Marco was mildly sardonic.

The Cobra sank down and now Marco could feel resistance, the ground effect, as he edged lower. Hardin narrowed his eyes, the better to pick out the details through the whirling mess of leaves and torn branches caused by the rotor down-draught. The chopper had ploughed straight down, smashing in through the top branches of the trees, tearing its way down at an angle and nose-diving at the ground. Its greenhouse panels had gone – a combination of lashing rounds delivered, almost certainly, at point-blank range and the final impact into the trees – and the top canopy had been thrust back almost to the rear of the main cabin, opening up the Huey like a sardine-can.

Hardin could even make out the sardines. Or what was left of them. It didn't look to be a hell of a lot.

'This is recent,' he said. 'Like, within a day or so. You see any reports of action in this area?'

'Uh-uh. I looked. Clean sheet up to last night.'

Hardin nodded. He knew that Marco would have checked automatically, after he had contacted him earlier that morning and suggested a flight that would be logged, loosely and truthfully, as a 'patrol'.

'So what we have here,' he said thoughtfully, 'is a confrontation with the enemy, size of force unknown, that resulted in two of our machines being knocked out of the sky.'

'Affirm on that.'

'And nobody *knows* about it?!' Hardin was incredulous.

'Maybe the cavalry on their way?' said Marco, feeding him. 'You know, man, they hackin' a path through the jungle, uh . . . e'en now.'

'Where from? Nearest base is our base, Do Thon, and there were no reports filed of action in this area. We've already established that. But these guys must've yelled for help to someone on the net. You don't get jumped by Charlie and not report back damn fast. Faster the better.'

Hardin stared down at the wreck. 'Any case, this didn't just happen last night, or even early this a.m. The burn-out'd still be smoking. I'd say twenty-four hours, top – plenty of time for rescue parties to have been and gone. And a Sky-Crane would've pulled this one down here up and out; plenty to be salvaged.'

Marco was getting the drift of all this. He'd known Hardin now for long enough to be able to attune to the way his mind was probing.

'So, in four words,' he said, 'you don't like it.'

'Roger that.'

'An' in another three words, you' goin' down.'

Hardin chuckled.

'You wanna rappel, or climb down like a gentleman?' asked Marco.

'I'll throw out the ladder. Just keep her sweet and steady.'

'Yo life is in mah hands,' Marco intoned.

He eased the bird round to a better position and watched as Hardin threw up the side-canopy and began fixing the rope ladder prior to hurling it out. Then he switched into the net.

'Barnyard, Barnyard – Eagle Three. We got us a coupla nose-dives.'

The Do Thon op's voice grated back across the mush. 'Give us your position, Eagle Three.'

Marco verbalised the coordinates. 'Better send us a hunter-killer tandem, Barnyard. It look clean out here, but ya never know.' He watched Hardin, assault rifle slung across one shoulder, climb up out of the cockpit and disappear over the side. 'I have an observer on recon.'

'Physically?' The Do Thon op registered surprise.

'Roger.'

Now the op sounded pissed. 'Eagle Three. Pull him back. Got no business to do that.'

'Difficult, Barnyard. He already gone. Not to mention he outrank me.' Marco's eyes suddenly took in the fact that he was no longer alone – or, at least, such was going to be the case within seconds. A Huey was racing low towards him from the east, sharply outlined against the light from the rising sun. 'Hey, Barnyard! Now that right fast! That *reel* special delivery!'

'Say again, Eagle Three.'

The Huey moved in and around Marco, circling. Marco waved a gloved hand. The Huey pilot did not wave back. Marco could see other figures, peering out of the gunship's side.

'Say *again*, Eagle Three.' The Do Thon op sounded even more exasperated.

'Barnyard, I said . . .'

The Huey swung lazily away from him, sideways on, then shifted round in a tight semi. Its four 7.62mm M60s suddenly opened up, a withering spray of fire that lashed the Cobra's fuselage. The bird shook, juddered as though it had the ague, or as though some mighty hand had clasped it and was shaking it furiously. Glass shattered, metal buckled and tore; rounds savaged the body, erupted out the other side.

'*Fucker!*' screamed Marco into his mike.

'Eagle Three . . .'

'I'm takin' fire! The mother opened up on me! I'm hit! Takin' fire!'

As he howled this at Barnyard Marco sent the Cobra out of hover and forward. But he knew there was no hope. He could feel the massive power-loss under his fingers, as though the bird had gained an incredible weight on its back, or very suddenly grown very old.

By a miracle not a bullet had touched him, not one single round had even passed through his clothes or boots, but the radio was dead and above and below there was only a shambles of ripped metal, smashed glass and struts, trailing wires. There was smoke too, thick and black, pumping at him it seemed from everywhere all at once and sent swirling around him by the rush of air through the shattered windscreen. He was almost at tree-level and he didn't know what the hell had happened to Hardin. That dude would have to look after himself. There were other things to think about – a million other things. Or maybe just one. He yanked the Cobra back to hover then cut the power stone-dead. He felt the bird buck and bump as its belly dragged through top-growth and he brought his arms up and over his head and thought, 'Oh fuck this, man . . .'

Seconds before Marco killed the chopper's power Hardin was just about fighting his way out of near-terminal shock.

Clinging to the rope ladder as it twisted and turned in the air, its tail dragging in the trees, battered by the rotor down-blast, and deafened by the Cobra's roar, he'd been too intent in any case on the wrecked chopper below to notice the second gunship as it homed in on Marco and circled above.

The first inkling he had that the situation was way out of kilter – about to tip straight down the tube, in fact – was when the shattering sound of four M60s cut through the clamour of Marco's rotors and the rope ladder began jerking madly as the Cobra shook with the hammering impact of point-blank fire.

Hardin jerked his head up and gazed uncomprehendingly at the newcomer, just glimpsed beyond the Cobra's belly, and the tracer that was lashing from its guns, then his stomach lurched sickeningly and his gloved fingers were instinctively clamping themselves round two rungs of the ladder as the Cobra plunged forward drunkenly, juddering and shaking, its engine vomiting smoke. The bottom of the ladder was snagging at the trees as the chopper staggered through the air on its drunken dying run, shredding leaves from top-growth, tearing branches off wholesale.

The thought that raced through Hardin's mind at that instant was that nothing was going to save the Cobra. Not Marco's renowned skill as a pilot – which might now be precisely nil anyway, depending on how badly he'd been shot up – nor anything else save an act of God. And Hardin didn't believe in God.

The Cobra was truly doomed. Any second now and it was going to belly-flop into the jungle and a few hundred tons of dead metal were going to be smashing straight down on top of him. There wasn't going to be enough of him left after that to fill a soup-plate.

And at that exact moment in time, as that thought hit him, he came out of shock and began to whip his head together.

He didn't understand what the hell was going on, and he didn't bother to give the problem even a moment's consideration or analysis as he clung to the wildly swaying ladder. All that could sort itself out afterwards. For now sheer survival, with as few broken bones as was humanly, or inhumanly, possible was what filled his mind.

There was only one way of getting out of this one, and yet that was so hairy he almost baulked at it, rejected it utterly then and there, stayed where he was. Almost.

But not quite. The Cobra was floundering now, its rotors rattling, its engine hawking and coughing and spluttering. Any moment now and she'd be dead, and so would he. Hardin's eyes locked on to one tree ahead that fingered the sky above the rest of the foliage by three foot or more. Taking his feet off the rope-ladder he unclenched his hands and let go completely, closing his legs as he flew into the tree. He curled his left arm around the top-growth, his eyes tight shut, his chin thrust down into his chest as far as he could shove it, as though he was trying to burrow his way into his own gullet. The slender tree-top bent wildly with the impact of his hurtling body and pain shot up his arm, bit savagely at his shoulder. But now he was swinging around, held to the tree by the crook of his arm and his right hand, which was scrabbling at twigs and leaves, anything that could be clutched or clawed at. His legs were at right angles to the tree, his body had almost become a whirling rotor itself. His legs curled round like an acrobat's, his body slamming into the wood which crumpled and snapped off. Then he was plunging down into the tree, his gloved hands wrenching at branches then letting go almost as soon as the fingers had made contact, simply to break his tumbling descent without dislocating his arms completely.

He winced his eyes open, glimpsing a whirling kaleidoscope of all shades of green as he bucketed onwards and downwards. Boughs smacked into his legs, his thighs, his arms, his chest; branches, sharp twigs raked at his face, tore at his hair. The noise of his crashing descent deafened him; it seemed to be the only sound in the world. Nothing else had any meaning.

Yet he was slowing down. Each desperate grab for a passing bough, each jolting thump to his body from branches he still didn't see, was throwing the brake on his careering, avalanching descent. His mind was still working on full gas, his instinct was still gauging his rate of fall; and both suddenly screamed at him to do what he had to do, what he must do, *now*. Or don't bother. Just forget it.

His hands caught at a branch, held fast, his legs curled up and round. He thudded into the bole of the tree and clung on with a desperation that tolerated no opposition. Even if the tree had suddenly, fantastically, come alive and tried to hurl him off, still he would have clung to it as though it was a part of his own body.

He opened his eyes. Looked down.

Below were bushes, flowering shrubs, undergrowth that was thick and tangled. The forest floor. Just a dozen feet below him; no more than that, possibly even less.

'Skate,' muttered Hardin, grinning a twisted grin. 'Real skate.'

His eyes took in the terrain, quickly and professionally. As far as he could see there was forest and only forest. No human presence could be immediately discerned. Nevertheless he eased himself down the trunk of the big tree warily and, on hitting ground, crouched, the assault-rifle jutting out from him as though it was an extra limb.

The chopper that had attacked was still racketing around overhead and Hardin glared up at the tangled green ceiling of the forest roof. He had half a mind to climb back up the tree and try to nail the bastard. All it would need was a quarter of the mag into the rotors. Not even that – but that amount of rounds would ensure a knockdown and the way he felt now expending that much ammo would cauterise the supreme insult of being shot down the way he had been shot down.

But there was so much else to do.

Where was Marco? He'd heard no sound of him impacting

into the jungle, but that was not so surprising – the noise he himself had been making in his wild plunge down eighty foot or more of thickly enfoliaged tree would have cut that off. Still, there'd been no explosion – no fuel tank blowing itself out – and that he would most certainly have heard. Which meant that Marco could be alive and marooned in the top-growth – maybe, he reckoned quickly, a half a mile or so ahead. Not much more than that.

One option open to him, therefore, was to head for where the Cobra was.

On the other hand, somewhere behind him – and not too far behind either – was the downed Huey, and that bird had to be investigated too.

And then there was needed a minute or so – or probably a good half-hour, such were the possible ramifications behind the deed – to reflect upon and sort out the whys and wherefores of the fucker who'd apparently appeared out of nowhere and blown them out of the sky. Who was he, why had he done it, who was behind him; was he simply Nam-crazy or were there far more sinister undercurrents to his action.

Hardin's mind flashed back to the renegades he thought he'd destroyed so recently. Was this another outbreak of that same madness, or something else entirely? Some other madness? Did it have anything at all to do with the attack in the Saigon bar?

And then he thought: Fuck that.

That was something to be pondered while sitting in an easy chair back at Do Thon, rapping it out with Phil Esteban, say, or General Halderling. Thoughts of that nature had no business to be drifting around his mind as he crouched in dew-slick bushes in the middle of bandit country.

For now – just like when he'd been clinging to that wildly swaying rope-ladder only minutes before – survival was the name of the game. Whatever, whoever, however – he was in deep shit.

He was in the act of rising to his feet from the crouch when he froze, all aches and pains vanishing in the flicker of an eyelid, all senses on hair-trigger alert.

Without warning, a man had suddenly appeared on the other side of the bush-screen. He wore khaki shirt and pants, a stained pith helmet on his head, full pack and webbing, a cloth rice-tube slung crossways, over and under. In his left hand he held an AK-47 assault-rifle.

He stood motionless, as though sculpted into position. Then his head moved, slowly, warily. He was half-turned away from Hardin and Hardin frankly didn't know how the hell he'd just popped up like that.

He watched as the man's head slowly turned. He seemed to be sniffing at the air, and that was just precisely what he was doing. He was alert, suspicious. Hardin knew the feeling exactly. He'd been in the same position a hundred times; a thousand times. An almost psychic awareness of unseen danger. Something, the EnVee would be thinking, was not quite right . . . not quite tight . . . not quite as it should be.

All he has to do, thought Hardin, is turn his head just about another half-inch and that right eye is going to catch a glimpse of me, the merest flash. But it'll be enough. The guy will turn and fire in one fluid zip because he's got the drop on me right now and no way am I going to be able to move fast enough to nail him before he nails me and I am paddling up shit river and the goddamn boat's sprung a leak.

Hardin stayed as frozen as the EnVee, calculating times and distances. Then just as the EnVee's head came wholly round it suddenly flicked back again.

Hardin too had heard the sound, the crack of a twig. He wondered if it was Marco, then saw the EnVee make an underhand gesture that was typical of the Vietnamese, an almost secretive flapping of the lowered fingers. He ducked down in that same instant, his right hand now clamped around the assault rifle he held, forefinger curled off-trigger.

He was now in a good position, could see through a narrow gap between branches of the bush-wall. The EnVee turned his head again, staring directly over the bushes behind which Hardin crouched. Hardin could see his eyes, darting to right and left in nervous expectation, trying to penetrate the undergrowth all around, still not entirely satisfied that nothing was amiss.

Hardin grinned darkly to himself as he watched. The time to hit him was now, because now the EnVee's nerves were on a hair-trigger. The snap of the twig had disoriented him. He'd had to relax in order to gesture at the unseen man behind him, then pitch himself right back up again to carry out his final eye-recon. Hardin knew that if he simply stood up and waved and said 'Hi!' all in one movement, the EnVee'd probably have heart-seizure.

A baffled frown crossed the Vietnamese's features. He relaxed, slowly turned away – then snapped his head back round again. Hardin almost chuckled out loud. The guy *was* good. It was going to be a shame to waste him. Except he was so good he *had* to be wasted.

The EnVee truly relaxed now, let his breath go, let his shoulders sag. He turned away once more, gestured with his right hand, this time a forward flapping of his fingers. Three more EnVees, similarly dressed, emerged from the bushes and into Hardin's line of sight.

They began muttering. Hardin listened, suddenly aware that the chopper was now just a fly's buzz in the far distance. The thought crossed his mind that those guys up there, unlike the EnVee, weren't at all professional, because they ought to have made sure of their kill before exiting, then he concentrated on the North Vietnamese just beyond the bushes.

Hardin could speak Vietnamese like a native, almost as though he were speaking English. He could think in Vietnamese. Even so there were odd references he did not understand, allusions he could not quite grasp.

They were discussing the Huey, the one that had been shot down the day before. They knew about it, yet it was clear from what they were saying that it had not been downed by North Vietnamese fighters or gunships. They had to search it; there was some object they were after in particular. A bag. Something else, too. Or maybe something in that bag.

Hardin tried to translate phrases that he heard back into

English but it was no use. Apart from anything else, the men's voices rose and fell; much of what they were saying was lost. But in any case, it was all very academic because none of these guys was going to leave this spot alive.

There was no moral problem about this. He had to kill them all. Not for the sake of killing, because you didn't act like that in the jungle: it could backfire on you a thousand ways. But because at some time or other one of them was going to spot the tree he'd fallen down, notice the broken branches, the torn foliage. Then he would remember the circling chopper, put two and two together and start looking for a body. And when he discovered that there was no body, the hunt would up.

They had mentioned back-up. And although this back-up was a day away, he could not afford to let any of these guys survive. He had to get back to Do Thon. Not to mention find Marco, see if he was still kicking, and get him back too. And that was going to be no goddamn picnic if a bunch of EnVee regulars suspected their presence and started a bush-by-bush search-and-destroy.

They all had to die and their bodies all had to be hidden away in such a manner that it would take days before they'd be discovered. Let the back-up wonder, try to figure out what had happened. By that time he and Marco would be well away.

He was still in the half-crouch that he'd fallen into five minutes or more before. Now he eased himself slowly forward on to his left foot and inched the barrel of his assault rifle towards the gap in the bushes.

Too fucking late.

The first man suddenly shifted to the left, out of sight, followed by two of the others. In his mind Hardin howled with fury. One burst would have taken them all out, and now it was going to be messy and complicated and . . .

He reversed his decision fast. He'd left it a fraction of a second too late, but a fraction of a second was as good as an hour in this situation. He'd blown it. What was worse, they'd left the fourth man as guard and this one was now leaning back against a tree, facing him, gazing over his hide.

Hardin knew he could not be seen through the bushes. He was wearing tiger-stripes, and this was camouflage that in the jungle gloom could not be penetrated.

Gently, millimetre by millimetre, he lowered the assault rifle to the ground. It took slightly under three minutes, at a count of one-thousand for every second, for the rifle to be dropped just about fourteen inches. Sweat dripped down his face; the muscles in his arms, thighs and at the back of his legs were stiff with tension. Then his right hand crept up and round to the knife at his belt, thick-bladed but perfectly balanced.

The EnVee seemed to be staring right at him, watching his every movement, following each tiny agonisingly slow-motion quiver that he made. Hardin began to wonder if he was not himself hallucinating. It was crazy. The guy's eyes seemed to be locked on to his, were growing larger . . . larger . . .

It was absurd. It was the tension that was knotting up his mind. With an effort of will he wiped his mind clean, concentrated on killing. When the need arose, Hardin was an excellent killer.

He slid the knife out of its sheath, hefted it gently in the palm of his hand. He still kept his own eyes on the EnVee's face, waiting for that one optimum instant when nothing the guy could do would save him.

It came – an eye-flicker to one side, a micro-second's lapse of attention – just as a soundless psychic siren shrieked in his mind that unless he moved that split-second he was dead.

Hardin didn't hesitate. *Someone was behind him, closing in.*

He rose like a startled bird, rocketing upwards from his toes. He hurled the knife and in the same moment, so that the two separate movements became one, plunged at the bush-screen in a long curving dive that took him almost over the top. It was the kind of high-dive one took preparatory to executing a double-somersault in the air, and Hardin nearly made it. Only his knees tangled in the top-growth and he pitched forward, head-first, arms flailing, on the other side of the bushes. But even as he felt the ground come up at him, hit him, he was back in control, rolling across the intervening space towards the EnVee, his hands scrabbling for what, unless his skills had totally deserted him, ought now to be lying in the grass at the Vietnamese's feet.

His fingers touched steel, clutched at it, slid down and along it until the feel was exactly right, until his grip on the object was utterly natural. This did not take even as much as two seconds. Holding the fallen Kalashnikov AK-47 he screwed round on the instant and dived another three feet into the grass, firing to his left as he did so, spraying the bush-screen that only seconds before had been his hide with a devastating burst of rounds. He flayed it, left and right and back again, the distinctive high-pitched chatter of the Kalashnikov ripping the jungle silence apart shatteringly.

The mag emptied itself and Hardin, still clutching the AK, jerked into motion again, sliding through the grass in fast slithering dives, propelling himself along by his boots and elbows. He found a thick tangle of undergrowth and crouched behind it, suddenly still.

All other movement ceased; squawks of outraged birds died into the distance. He stared at the surrounding jungle wall, seeking leaf-flutter, branch-quiver, anything at all that would tell him that someone was still on his feet, still dangerous. He saw nothing.

Slowly he rose to his feet, ramming another mag up into the AK. He began moving through the undergrowth stealthily, in a wide circle, until he reached to within fifty yards or so of the spot he'd so swiftly vacated. He gently pushed his way into a thick maze of rhododendron, to the centre, then counted sixty and, right hand still gripping the AK so that it pointed forward, the butt into his side, used his left hand to part the leaves and creepers.

Beyond two men lay, two North Vietnamese, just behind where he'd been crouching. Both were dead, no question. One seemed to have walked straight into his fire face-first. There was a lot of blood and fractured bone and mush and the guy's mother would not have recognised him. The other lay half on his side, twisted round, his back towards

Hardin. This one must have been caught twice, hurled round by the hammering impact. His shirt was all chewed up to shreds. There were irregular blotches of scarlet across his upper back and then lower, running along his kidneys.

But that left the third man. Where the fuck was that one? Hardin let off a controlled two-second burst at the matted foliage behind the two sprawled men then jerked his head forward, wincing, concentrating. The echoes died away. To nothing. No other sound.

Hardin cautiously backed out of the bush, sideways, one eye alive for movement to his right, the other for movement to his left. Nothing showed. He slid back round to where the fourth man was, the guard.

He was still there. Approaching from the rear, at an angle, part of him could be seen round the tree's trunk. He looked as though he was lounging back against the tree, one hand – the hand that once had held the AK – negligently drooping against the bole. Hardin knew better.

He could smell nothing suspicious in the immediate vicinity, but still he was wary as he edged his way to the space in front of the guard. The man was skewered to the tree. Such had been the tremendous force of the throw that the knife had sunk into the man's throat almost to the hilt, severing the jugular, shearing through the oesophagus a fraction under the chin-bone. The EnVee stared blankly into the far distance, his head held up almost proudly, the point of his chin resting on the flat of the blade and the hilt. Down the front of his khaki shirt a rich river of blood had flowed, staining the material blackly, and the arteries were still, even now, pumping feebly.

Hardin reached up, tugged the blade smoothly out. There was a wet, gulping sound and the man's head rocked forward, his body sliding down the tree, catching on a root and tumbling to the ground in a huddled heap. Blood stained the grass. Hardin wiped the blade carefully on the man's pants, re-sheathed the knife.

He returned to his original hide and retrieved his own assault rifle, like those of the Vietnamese a Kalashnikov. It was the weapon he preferred above all, certainly over the normal US army issue M16 rifle which was altogether too delicate, too fragile a piece of machinery for the kind of rough handling you had to give it out in the jungle. The Kalashnikov AK-47 assault rifle could take a beating and you didn't need to treat it like it was a new-born baby, although Hardin took great pains to keep his own piece in prime condition.

He checked through the dead men's equipment, gathering spare mags and spring-checking them. You could never have enough spare magazines in a hot situation, and with EnVee back-up heading in this direction and one guy still on the loose the temperature on this one was definitely sliding upwards.

He checked his watch, raised an eyebrow. Still, after a decade-plus in a dangerous business, it never failed to surprise him how time seemed to slow down when life was at maximum risk and death was tapping on your shoulder with a bony finger.

He stiffened suddenly, his eye catching a flutter of movement through the shifting of branches in a sudden breeze, high up and some way away. He ducked down, began to move swiftly in its direction, threading his way past bushes, through thick elephant grass.

As he moved so he began to hear sounds – the clinking of metal on metal, hurried scrapings, someone working in feverish haste.

The answer came to him in a flash. The downed Huey. The fourth man. He began to move faster.

Which was a mistake. His right boot snagged at a rotten branch lying on the ground. It cracked loudly. Instantly, Hardin threw up the AK and fired. He was still on automatic; the short burst flayed the bushes he fired through. He ceased firing and listened – listened to the echoes merging into the distinctive sound of someone running, madly, desperately; the crackle of twigs snapping, the crash of trampled undergrowth. That, too, died into the silence.

Hardin cursed, then shrugged. The one that got away. And it would be foolish to pursue him. He moved on quickly until he emerged into a small clearing, across which the wrecked Huey loomed large, jammed into the trees, its nose almost touching ground.

Another sound disturbed the silence, more cracking noises. Hardin jumped for a tree cursing even more savagely, but this time in his mind. Was there, for Christ's sake, a *fifth* man?

A voice, flat, low-pitched, said, 'Hardin?'

Hardin snorted.

'Come out! You nearly got your head blown off, you black fucker!'

Frank Marco limped into the clearing. There was a line of dried blood across his forehead, his left eye was swelling, his clothes were torn. He grinned.

'Ain't no way to talk to me, honky.'

'You and your tumble in the Big Green. You bad-mouthed us. Put the fucking hoodoo on.'

'The way it go, man,' shrugged Marco.

'Shit, Marco, this is no fucking joke.'

'Negative, bro. *Everything* a joke after what I been through. Took a dive into the trees, straps snapped, went out through the greenhouse, through the fuckin' trees.' His voice curved up softly, his eyeballs rolled, exaggerated, flipped-out. '"Lak a rubber bah-owl Ah come bouncin' back to yew-www!"' He slumped against a tree. 'Shit, man. Like they useta say, this coon am fucked.'

Hardin glanced around the clearing, still alert. 'Where'd you land?'

'Bush. Ass-wise first. Dig?'

Hardin chuckled. 'Yeah. Was it exactly like that?'

'Uh-uh. Jus' feel like it. The bird took most of the shit. She slid into stiff opposition. Trees 'n' stuff. Straps popped after we hit. I jus' slid out frontal. No big deal. Crawled down, jumped into a bush with plenty flowers. It took my weight. There was a bad smell of fuel – ba-a-ad. So I lit out. Heard the bangs. Follow the trail of stiffs.' He O-ed the forefinger and thumb of his right hand which, Hardin now saw, had blood all over it. 'You still a killer-diller, man. The score look good.'

Hardin said, 'I missed one.'

'Tough. Still, three outta four get you a Tootsie.' Marco yawned. 'Now I fucked. What happen to you?'

'Fell down a tree.'

Marco cackled. 'Hey, ain' you done that before? You land in a whole heap of EnVee shit, right? You land on the regimental crapper, I heard.'

Hardin nodded. 'This time it was clean.'

'Like the Buddhists say,' remarked Marco, 'it' gettin' better all the time.'

Hardin moved across to where the Huey lay slumped across the trees. Its nose was almost kissing the ground except it had no nose; cannon-fire had shredded that and the plexiglas windscreen, and savaged the top canopy which had in any case ripped back almost to the main-cabin rear by the impact of the final crash. The bulk of the machine was jammed down tight in between thick curved tree-boles that took the weight. A piece of rag from somewhere was flapping in the light breeze, caught on the end of the shredded tail-boom; it was that which had attracted Hardin's attention through the trees.

'Hey,' said Marco. 'Civileens!'

He was peering into the interior of the chopper from the port-side door. Hardin went past him, climbed up into the bird. There were creakings and raspings but the wreck stayed where it was. The thought went through Hardin's mind that even a CH-54 Tarhe Sky-Crane was going to have a problem with this baby; it was firmly gripped, the trees were not going to let it go without a struggle.

The pilot's area was a shambles. No one could have survived the terrible onslaught of virtually point-blank cannon-fire or the subsequent smashing dive into the trees. He looked to his right. There were only two stiffs that he could see, although there would have been a couple of MG-gunners at least on the flight. Probably flung out on impact, their bodies would be somewhere in the trees.

He moved through the debris, stepping over spilled shells from burst ammo-boxes, avoiding a tangle of wires and cables, crunching through broken glass. The two men were certainly dressed in civilian clothes, although that did not necessarily mean they weren't military. Both were very dead; he didn't recognise either of them. The strong steely stink of recently-spilled blood still lay heavily on the air.

One had been caught by cannon-fire in the chest and was lying all twisted up in a blackened and tacky pool of his own blood. Flies feasted greedily and Hardin swatted them away, a slight revulsion in his gut. It was about the only thing that truly sickened him about the actual state of death, the filthy carrion that fed on it. The flies were fat and torpid; they had fed well here.

The second man was hunched up on his right side in one corner. Part of the chopper's rotor driveshaft assembly, which had snapped off, was pinning him to the floor. It had clearly smashed through the roof at an angle on impact, possibly killing him before trapping his body; the back of the man's head had caved in due to some fierce punching crack from behind. The flies were here, too. Not to mention the ants.

Hardin went back to the first man, began methodically going through his pockets. He frowned. There was something wrong here. He returned to the second man and searched him. The result was the same.

They had cigarettes, lighters, combs, packets of paper Sneazies, pens, pencils, key-rings, money, both paper and coin, piastres and dollars. The man who'd been shot had a packet of condoms in a jacket pocket. The man with his head stove in had a fold-up metric rule and a small pair of nail scissors. But there was no documentation whatsoever. Of any kind.

No IDs, no military or civilian passes. No letters or old envelopes. No cards, credit or otherwise. Nix. Zero. Nothing to identify them in any possible way.

He stared down at the man with the caved-in skull and suddenly realised that there was something else – something about this man in particular he hadn't noticed before.

'Hey, man. You hear it? That muted thappa-thappa in the air?' Outside Marco was whooping with glee. 'You recognise that engine-hum? That our boys, they come to collect us. Bout fuckin' time too, man. I told the sonofabitch back at Base I was takin' fire. It take 'em twenty fuckin' minutes to bounce. Can you believe it? Rascals!'

The man with the caved-in skull was missing a hand.

VI

Halderling said, 'Damn it, John, you'll get me to thinking you got a hoodoo on you or something. I mean, what is it with you, for Christ's sake? Someone got a book on you discovering the weird and the wonderful? Is that it? Jesus! I mean – a hand? The guy was missing a *hand*?'

He turned back to the window in disgust. Outside, rain clouds were scudding in from the west, from the high mountains. The day was darkening.

'The left hand,' affirmed Hardin. 'Hacked off at the wrist.'

General Lewis J. Halderling snorted. He was tall, thin, almost emaciated. His hair was close-cropped, white; his face was deep-tanned, the colour of old parchment.

He was wearing army casuals and he had his hands thrust deep into his pants' pockets. He was sixty-one and he looked, and was, craggy. In fact he was the toughest old bird Hardin knew, and Hardin had been working for him for a long time. It sometimes seemed to Hardin that he'd been working for Halderling, one way or another, for centuries.

He felt in his pockets, pulled out cigarettes, lit one. He gazed around the room.

Halderling's desk-top was neat, orderly. A blotter lay in the centre; there was an intercom system and three phones, each with a scrambler attachment. In a large glass ashtray there were tobacco grouts and shredded dottle, piled high. Halderling smoked a particularly vicious brew he cultivated himself back in North Carolina, the kind of tobacco the analysts of the Surgeon General's department might well prohibit utterly as being of use only to aspiring suicides. Next to the ashtray was a framed photograph of Halderling and his second wife, Annette. Annette Halderling was French, twenty years Halderling's junior, two-thirds his height, much prettier. Hardin had long since figured out that this relationship was what kept Halderling up to top crack. At sixty-one anyhow the old man was hardly ready to be put out to pasture, but he had the energy and the keen, incisive intelligence of a man ten or fifteen years younger. He had his fingers on every pulse that mattered, and a few that did not matter but might do in the future; he had the ability to outsmart just about anybody in the military hierarchy, over here or back in the World, and frequently had to and nearly always did. He was on a tight-rope the whole time, and undoubtedly thrived on it. Hardin put most of this down to Annette, as the electrical charge Halderling needed.

He idly wondered whether Annette Halderling knew all there was to know about her husband. It was a subject which fascinated him.

Did she know, for instance, that Halderling's personal body-count ran into scores – and that was not including the normal business of war-killing. Halderling had fought with the International Brigade in Spain and had spent most of World War Two shaping up behind-the-lines guerilla squads in the Philippines. But you didn't count that; that was regular. It was the post-War, highly unorthodox, downright *irregular* stuff about which Hardin pondered. The hits, the assassinations, the de-stabilisations; all planned and set up by Lewis J. Halderling and carried out, for the most part successfully, by the SSG, the group he had created way back at the time of the Korean conflict and still ramrodded today, even to the point of actually going out into the field himself when it was necessary.

Indeed, only eighteen months before, Halderling, at the age of fifty-nine, had calmly seated himself at a street-table of a restaurant in Taipei on the fortress-island of Taiwan simply to flush out a prime target who happened to know Halderling by sight and whose nuisance-value in the political arena of South East Asia was getting to be way out of proportion to his power and the number of men who owed allegiance to him.

The bait had been eagerly grabbed. Minutes after Halderling had sat down, and while he was thoughtfully pondering the stock-market reports in the *New York Times*, a car had driven up. Stopped. Shots had been fired. Halderling had slumped to the ground.

What his attackers, however, had failed to notice in their haste was that Halderling, a spare, gaunt figure normally, had somehow put on weight overnight, become suddenly quite portly. This was due to the double-density body-armour he was wearing under his shirt. The bullets dented it, gave the old man a couple of bruised ribs, but otherwise left him unharmed. The same could not be said of the hit-team, whose front tyres were abruptly blown out by an unseen marksman and who themselves were quite suddenly yanked out of their car by heavily armed men with stony expressions, hustled into a shabby panel-truck nearby, and driven off at high speed.

Hardin knew all this because he had fired the two shots from a second-storey window which had disabled the car. But, he wondered, did Annette Halderling know that her husband was often involved in such strange and stark activities?

Halderling was a hero to his men, detested by his rivals (notably the Langley crowd), and endured with gritted teeth by the upper echelons at the Pentagon, and thus the White House, who bad-mouthed him regularly but who often had to go to him virtually cap-in-hand and put it to him that they, personally, believed in him utterly, whatever might have been said in the past, and whatever the scuttlebutt drifting around the corridors of power, and he was really the only man who could, uh . . . sort out this, uh . . . little problem that had suddenly, uh . . . come up.

The Strategic Studies Group had solved a great many little problems, most of them extremely large. And yet it had no actual existence, as such. Its funding was spread out over numerous government bodies and corporations, all of them innocuous: dairy farming agencies, tree-conservation committees and the like. Even if some shit-keen investigative journalist had been given the merest hint of its existence and had smelled something that seemed not quite right, pursuing the tortuous, labyrinthine trail to the very heart of the matter, Halderling himself, would have been akin to tracking a will-o'-the-wisp, or trying to recall in detail a dream, however initially vivid, on waking. In any case, officially Halderling had nothing whatsoever to do with the SSG. Officially he was just some tedious old fart who administered a minor US Army pension scheme for disabled officers. He even gave public lectures on the subject, suitably primed by Phil Esteban. The lectures were seldom well-attended.

Hardin stared at the photograph of Lewis and Annette Halderling. It mesmerised him. It was so fucking *domestic*.

He was suddenly aware that Halderling had turned from the window and was looking at him.

He said, 'How's Annette?'

Halderling shot him an odd look. 'Fine, fine. How's your wife?'

Hardin was momentarily perplexed. 'Uh . . . I don't have one, General. You know that.'

'Of course I know that!' snapped Halderling. 'You ask me a dumb question, I reply with one that's equally dumb.'

Hardin grinned apologetically. 'Yeah, okay. I was somewhere else.'

'Other side of the fucking galaxy I should think,' growled the older man. 'What's my goddamn wife gotta do with all this, anyway? You suddenly got the hots for her or something? Lay off, son, or you're liable to wake up in a back-alley with no fucking legs. I may be sixty-plus, but I still got *cojones*.' He frowned suddenly. 'Leastways, I think I have. What I've been told, anyhow.' He grinned darkly.

Hardin relaxed. 'All I was wondering was how much Annette knows. It was a random thing. Drifting around my mind.' He gestured at the desk. 'The picture. I've seen it a thousand times. You have copies in every office you have in Nam. I've seen you together, parties, that kind of shit. I've stayed at your farm in the Smokies. It's the domestic bit. It's not that I don't understand, can't figure it out, it's just that it suddenly hit me – how much does she *know*?'

'Everything,' said Halderling easily. He did not enlarge on this, just watched Hardin, his head slightly cocked to one side like a wise old vulture. He was wondering what to do with the younger man.

Halderling genuinely liked Hardin; more than that, even. He certainly admired the younger man, knew that Hardin, all things considered, was one of his finest operatives. Hardin thought about things.

It was generally considered that thinkers were no damn good in Halderling's line of business – which took in subversion, counter-revolution, sudden death, in all their various forms and aspects and to all their various degrees. The best killer, it was said in the manuals, was the guy who didn't think, who didn't argue, who just did it and forgot about it, didn't ever let it cross his mind again. Halderling didn't agree with this, and had never agreed with it. He preferred a man with a Jiminy Cricket in his head, with a certain amount of conscience; a man who, like Hardin, did on the odd occasion wrestle with devils in his mind. The man who did a dirty job without a thought about it, about the whys and wherefores, about the implications of what he was doing, was an automaton, and Halderling didn't trust automatons. Automatons were liable to short-circuit, blow a fuse just when you least expected it, or needed it. Automatons were dangerous, and in a high-risk business you could do without the extra worry.

Halderling had spotted Hardin as far back as 1957, although Hardin didn't know this, and had tagged him shortly thereafter as a non-automaton. Halderling knew a great deal about Hardin that Hardin didn't realise, and it was going to stay that way. Halderling, for instance, knew for a rock-solid fact that Hardin had been in Cuba in 1957–58, had joined the rebels in the Sierra Maestra, had fought alongside Che Guevara in the Palma Mocha River encounter, and had been one of the eighty-odd men who had followed Castro in his assault on the army barracks at the Battle of El Uvero.

That would not have looked too good on Hardin's record, all things considered. Which was precisely why, courtesy of Lewis J. Halderling, it was not on Hardin's record.

Hardin was not a communist; in fact he disliked the philosophy intensely, mainly because it seemed to him to be an arid one, utterly unworkable in the real world. He had been drawn to the rebels' side by the excitement of danger and his loathing of the corrupt and vicious Batista regime, and had drifted away from Cuba when it became clear to him not only that Batista was on the run but also that Castro, ideologically, was no angel, and that an immoral and detestable dictatorship was about to be replaced by a regime that might be rather more moral but was a dictatorship nonetheless. For Cuba, a case of out of the skillet of corruption and greed and into the purifying flames of Marxism. It was a toss-up, for the people of Cuba, as to which was the best. Certainly it led to a deal of disenchantment as far as Hardin was concerned.

Halderling understood this, and was not censorious. He had himself fought with the communists against Franco in the Spanish Civil War and didn't give a damn who knew it. It had led to problems in the fifties, when the McCarthy witch-hunts were in full spate and when, at one time, he had been in some danger of being dislodged from the power-base he had erected for himself, but Halderling had a short way with people, of whatever persuasion, who threatened him.

Ever on the lookout for recruits, for men who measured up well to his own extremely high standards, it was not surprising that the young John Hardin should have drifted into his sphere of influence. Halderling had watched him from afar, gauging his value, his capabilities, his fitness for recruitment into the SSG. Through trusted intermediaries he had used Hardin as an unofficial courier at first, sending him all over the globe on message-carrying missions of increasing importance and delicacy, gradually drawing him deeper and deeper into the shadowy world over which, Pluto-like, he presided. In the early sixties he had then employed Hardin on a freelance basis, as guard, insertion-agent, mercenary, at times assassin. He had thrown Hardin into Russia on several occasions, sent him into just about every country in South America, plunged him into the cauldron of South East Asia. Finally he'd pushed the younger man into the army, let him find his feet over a period of twelve months, then snatched him back and enrolled him officially into the SSG. After that Hardin's promotion had been rapid.

In the Vietnam conflict he had proved his worth time and time again. He had twice been to Hanoi, had carried out a two-month surveillance mission operating from an island overlooking the port of Haiphong, had even penetrated into China, where he'd holed up in a friendly village in Yun Nan province charting the political temperature in the Chinese boondocks for six months. For that, Hardin had been made a full Colonel at the age of thirty-two.

And through it all, Hardin had remained his own man utterly, had gone his own way, trodden his own path. Halderling liked that. It was exactly what he did.

It was unfortunate that because he was a loner in the larger sense and got solid results, Hardin had acquired a fierce rep, and as a consequence a hell of a lot of enemies, especially amongst the bureaucrats in Saigon. Too, Hardin had tried conclusions with the powerful CIA on a number of occasions and come out on top. This made him a marked man, however many important hits he'd made, or missions he'd successfully carried out, and however much his talent for gathering intelligence had turned him into an operative who was almost indispensable. And in the past eight months or so, the pigeons had come home to roost. With the Dempsey business he'd not only stirred up a great deal of shit but had put himself out on so dangerous a limb that even Halderling had had to sweat a little to stop him falling off. In the case of the fake renegades, Hardin had pulled off a masterstroke for Halderling and the SSG by handing over a totally secure jumping-off point deep in the heart of bandit territory, but in the process hadn't done himself an awful lot of good since, at the same time, he'd exposed the activities of a rogue element in the CIA, and the CIA, of all the intelligence agencies, was not one to forgive and forget.

At the moment, Halderling had been forced into a position where he was keeping Hardin on the back-burner. He didn't like doing this – apart from anything else, it was a waste of a good man – but he had no choice: there was such a thing as keeping the peace. Halderling didn't mind internecine squabbling or even downright warfare; he thrived on it. But right now he could do without it. Right now he was too bound up with his valley-HQ, chopper-hopping materiél and men up there, securing the caves against air-attack, setting up artillery and missile-silos. All this took time. The Hardin problem – what to do with him until the flak died down – was secondary.

And now, goddamn it, Hardin had by sheer fucking chance tripped over something that looked to be explosive!

Halderling stepped away from the window and slumped down into his chair.

'Forget about the domestic bliss shit,' he said, 'and think about this. I come back here on a flying visit and discover that the guy I forced Command to let me throw into an unlimited R-and-R has gone sightseeing in the fucking jungle, has got shot down by one of us, and then discovered something that's causing goddamn migraines already all over fucking Saigon.'

Hardin said tiredly, 'As opposed to simple headaches?'

'Right!' snarled Halderling. 'Take these two downed birds you found – no one knew about them until you tripped over 'em. Why the hell not? They must've taken a nose-dive all of twenty-four hours ago.'

'Yeah, Marco and I figured that. And if they were attacked by Charlie they ought to have pushed the panic-button. They ought to have been patched into the net and screaming blue murder. *Something* ought to have been bounced for them.'

'And not only that,' growled Halderling. He jabbed at a button on his intercom system and barked, 'Phil!'

Hardin sat back in his chair with his legs out. Hurried footsteps could be heard in the corridor outside. There was a double-tattoo on the door and Phil Esteban entered. He closed the door behind him.

'Let's have it,' said Halderling, scowling. 'All you've got so far.'

'It smells,' said the scholarly man to Hardin. He looked tired. 'We've had a team out there all day. First thing, we brought the bodies back from the unburned chopper. We've identified all of them, and it doesn't make sense. The pilot and co-pilot were both Air Cav from Da Nang, one of the gunners was from Da Lat, the other Kontum. The two guys in the rear . . .' He shrugged expressively. 'Not too difficult to place them, although I don't know them personally. But no one's talking. I tried five sources, but got nothing, either hard or soft. I doubt that we'll get any further. The chopper was from Long Binh, supposed to be in for repair. They were very surprised when I told 'em it was downed up here.' He gave a thin smile. 'They called me a liar, then phoned back later and apologised. They were perplexed. Not to mention pissed. Couldn't figure it out at all.' He turned to Halderling. 'I know I've only been on this a few hours, but I have a gut feeling that even if I take a month I'm not going to be able to take it much further.'

'And you don't have to tell me,' said Hardin, 'that no one knows anything about any goddamn chopper that was barnstorming around knocking the fuck out of Marco and me.'

'If that's a question, it gets a negative.'

'What I thought.'

Halderling brought his pipe into play. He scooped it up from the desk-top and pointed it at Hardin. 'You didn't see any markings on the bird that jumped you?'

'I was too busy trying to save my ass! You feel kind of vulnerable hanging on to a rope-ladder eighty foot above the ground and some guy's trying to shoot you down in flames. Cool professionalism only extends so far. That chopper could've been covered with every fucking identification decal in the army, navy, airforce, and I wouldn't have noticed shit!'

'What about Captain Marco?'

'Again, he wasn't looking for anything out of sync. He'd just radioed in with the bad news and a chopper arrives. Sure, he didn't think the guy was from Do Thon, but the way he told it to me, it was someone else on the net who'd picked him up and come looking. You see a hundred birds a day in the sky, you don't bother to check out every goddamn one.' Hardin leaned forward, stubbed out his cigarette. 'And when the guy opened fire Marco was like me, too busy trying to save his balls to worry about inessentials.'

Halderling began to fill the pipe, plugging coarse black tobacco into the bowl as though he was trying to choke it. 'Saigon,' he said carefully, 'are gonna say that you could've made a mistake. That the chopper could've been EnVee. That in your panic you mistook a North Vietnamese gunship for one of ours.'

'Look,' said Hardin dangerously, getting to his feet.

Halderling flapped a leathery hand at him. 'Siddown, John, for Chrissakes. *I'm* not saying that. I'm just telling you what Saigon are gonna be saying.'

'Saigon,' said Hardin carefully, 'are a crock of shit.'

'That is a not very helpful remark,' said Halderling heavily. 'Under the circumstances.'

Hardin subsided. He grinned suddenly. 'Funny thing is, it's not the fucker who blasted us I can't get out of my mind, it's the guy on the ground with his hand off.'

'This is all I need,' said Halderling sourly. 'This is trouble. This is phone-calls, paperwork, six-hour rap-sessions with Command. Look,' he appealed to Hardin, 'what's so big deal about a guy down in the forest with his hand sliced off anyway? Some of our guys out there collect ears and noses, don't they? Jesus, some of those animals collect fucking dicks! So we got Charlie the Freak who gets off on hands. Maybe he's gonna embalm it, stick it up on his hootch-roof to show him which way the fucking wind's blowing. *I* don't know!'

Hardin shrugged and said, 'Sure. And maybe what that hand was holding was so goddamn hot that it had to be attached to the wrist with a security chain and Charlie was trying to break the chain then heard me coming and thought the fuck with this and zipped the whole thing off with his machete.'

'Well, Jesus,' said Halderling, heavily sarcastic, 'I figured that out.' He blew smoke into the air, his expression sour. 'So it was a bag. So what was in the bag?'

'Papers?' Esteban shrugged, open-handed. 'Plans? Meat-loaf on rye? Maybe Charlie just took it with him because it looked interesting. If it was chained to the wrist, it wouldn't have been a dime-store lock on the bag or he'd've just ripped the flap up and grabbed what was inside. Charlie's no fool. Something like that, he'd know it was good.'

Hardin stared at his finger-nails then glanced up at a map on the wall. His eyes took in the area where the gunship had crashed. Shaking his head he said, 'No.'

Halderling looked up again, but this time he was tense. Esteban stared at Hardin then at the Old Man. Then he walked over to a chair and sat down carefully, his eyes back on Hardin.

'Okay, John,' said Halderling. 'Tell us the worst.' His voice had lost all trace of amusement or irritation.

'They knew the chopper was there,' said Hardin flatly. 'Not only that, they knew what was in it. They wanted everything they could lay their hands on, sure, but there was something definite they were after. Something they'd been told about. Something specific. They actually mentioned a bag. Another thing. From what they said, it wasn't hit by them. The chopper. They didn't make any comment about who did nail it, but whoever it was, it wasn't Victor Charles.'

Halderling began to doodle on a pad with a pencil. His pipe was clamped between his teeth. 'You were where?'

'Other side of a bush. They were chewing the fat and I was just about ready to knock 'em off when the moment passed. One of the guys, the honcho I guess, was suspicious. He didn't know where I was, but he knew I was somewhere.

He must've told his men to roust me out while he went to the chopper, got what he came for. Things became kind of heavy after that.'

Halderling sighed, a long drawn out 'Ohhh.' Then he said harshly, 'Fuck it. It fits. Something's up.' He nodded to Hardin. 'What d'you think? Someone our side ferrying stuff up to the EnVees? Is that it?'

'Crazy way of going about it if it is. Why the weird mix in the chopper's crew? It wouldn't be very secure to man up a gunship, which in any case you've borrowed from a military repair yard, from all over Nam for that kind of operation. And you're not gonna tell me all those guys were in it, whatever it is.'

'Why not? They were in *something*, for Chrissakes!'

'Yeah, but not something as deep as spying, or any kind of real treasonable activity like that. Sure they were in it, but I'd guess they didn't know too much about exactly what they were in. Maybe they were just paid to do the job, keep their mouths shut. A sweet little number on the side.'

'There's a lot of it about,' mumbled Esteban. 'Pity you iced 'em.'

Hardin grinned with his teeth. 'If I hadn't of iced 'em, I wouldn't be here now. No way. All I had in my head was find Marco and get the fuck out in double-time.'

Halderling said, 'Let's toss this around some more. How about if these guys are born-again renegades? How about if we didn't clean up the nest properly and these sonsabitches are holed up somewhere waging war on all and fucking sundry?'

Hardin shook his head. 'Could be, but I just don't think it is. It doesn't add up right.'

'More to the point,' offered Esteban, 'and getting right down to the nitty-gritty, however unpleasant it may be – how about if these dudes just didn't like *you*? How about if *you* were the target? How about if the word's gone out from on high: Nail that bastard Hardin, and nail him good.' He shot a lop-sided grin at Hardin. 'You don't exactly have no enemies over here.'

'That vote of confidence warms my heart,' said Hardin.

His mind was flicking back to the resurrected nightmare of the previous evening. He looked up at Halderling. 'Funny thing happened to me last night.'

He told them about it, including the gossip from Steeger.

Halderling said, 'Christ, and you think that the big guy could have been Guerini?'

Hardin said, 'I don't think anything! There must be a billion guys that look like gorillas in the world, but the attack in the bar for no reason at all from guys who looked very much like they ought to have been associated with that mad fucker makes one, as they say, to think.'

'Well, as I recall, he sure didn't love you.'

'I carved him up some. He bounced me around a little. I have no reason to love him.'

'Guerini,' said Phil Esteban thoughtfully. 'Henri Guerini? French Corsican? The Algerian business? A little before my time, but I seem to remember an old file. Wasn't he SDECE?'

'SDECE,' said Halderling expansively. '*Service de Documentation Exterieure et de Contre Espionage.*' His French accent wasn't at all bad. 'Nah.' He suddenly shook his head. 'He was SAC mainly. He took the blood-oath, you betcha – the hand on the knife, the Cross of Lorraine, the darkened room, the whole bit. He might have been recruited by the SDECE originally, but he ended up in de Gaulle's hit-squad. Bunch of animals. Jesus, even *I* think those guys were the pits.' He looked up at Hardin. 'You got blown out of the villa in the big one, didn't you.'

'Yes,' said Hardin in a neutral voice.

'Lucky for you,' commented Halderling. 'As I recall, they were pulling your teeth out one by one, weren't they?'

'Yes.'

'I had an interest in one of the OAS brass,' Halderling said to Esteban. He waved a hand dismissively. 'It was complicated. The French grabbed him, but John sprung him. Unfortunately, the SAC tagged John, we never did quite figure out how. They had a place in Algiers, a villa in the El Biar district. Guerini was in charge of the cellars. Luckily the OAS decided to cream the villa. Nothing to do with me. But they didn't piss around – blew the whole fucking place sky-high. John beat it in the confusion.' He turned to Hardin. 'You stuck a knife in the big guy, didn't you.'

'Right in.'

'Mmh.' Halderling pondered this. Then he said, 'Too many maybes here. You think there's a link between whoever nailed your chopper and whoever jumped you in Saigon?'

Hardin shrugged.

'Or d'you think it's something else entirely? The chopper business.'

'More likely that. I'll tell you what I think – we got bounced because we were sniffing around those two wrecks. Forget about Saigon. That may have something to do with it – or it may just be a wild coincidence. It's those choppers I'm more interested in.' And as he said that he suddenly realised he *was* interested – more than interested, in fact. 'Here's a scenario. There's a chopper. It has something important or valuable, or both, aboard. It gets bounced by, say, a couple more choppers. It manages to shoot one down, then gets shot down itself. For one reason or another, whoever's left can't do anything about the important or valuable cargo right then and there. Maybe there's a time-element involved. Whoever's left, however, can come back again, some time next day. He knows no one'll come looking for the two wrecks because no one *knows* about the two wrecks. Radio-silence, right? He comes back. He sees *us* there, nosing around. He doesn't think twice. He shoots *us* down. Then he takes a powder because he can't be sure we didn't yell for help before the crash.' He appealed to Halderling. 'What d'you think?'

'Fine, fine. So what're you gonna do about it?'

Hardin gazed at the older man impassively. 'Is that an order?'

Halderling gave a shark-like smile. 'Well, it solves one problem. It gets you outta my hair. You and that buncha brig-trash who keep drinking the Do Thon club bar dry every goddamn night.'

'What about Command?'

Halderling scowled. 'Ah, fuck 'em. They wanna yell, let 'em yell. I'm going back into Laos anyhow. Phil can take the flak.' He grinned at Esteban, then jabbed his pipe at Hardin. 'I'll tell you what I suddenly want to know,' he said. 'The contents of that bag, case, satchel, trunk, whatever. And I'll tell you something else I want to know – how Charlie jumped in on the act. I very much want to know that . . .'

VII

Lieutenant Arthur Comeraro was aware that the decibel-level had risen around him, but only in as much as someone might be vaguely aware that a thunder-storm was approaching and it might be as well to seek shelter in, say, ten or fifteen minutes' time. No more aware than that. In any military club anywhere in South Vietnam where a good deal of serious social drinking was done the noise-level was pretty fierce. You got used to it after a while. After a very short while.

He glanced up, reached for his beer. Across the table from him Garrett was arguing with Doc Pepper. They looked an odd couple to Comeraro, although he could not for the moment say why. Garrett was solidly built with a mean face and close-cropped reddish hair; Pepper was tall, skinny, gangling. And relaxed. Even when he was arguing, Doc Pepper looked at ease with the world, as though he didn't give a shit how things went, what happened to him. Comeraro could not be sure how much of a pose this was. He'd only known Pepper for a short time and had not seen him get truly wired up about anything. But you never knew. Strange and violent emotions could well be lurking under that calm and laid-back exterior. Garrett, of course, was strange and violent most of the time.

Next to Garrett sat Sergeant Olsen. He was solid too, but

looked more like a friendly bear than Garrett, who invariably looked, and acted, anything but. Sergeant Olsen was chugging Bud thoughtfully, in a considered kind of way, as though he was checking it out for an opinion poll on beers. Every so often he would exchange a serious word with Sergeant Fuller, who sat next to him on Comeraro's left. Sergeant Fuller was playing solitaire with a well-used pack, and he would nod grimly at what his colleague said, mutter in agreement, only briefly taking his eyes from the cards set out neatly in front of him on the red formica-topped table.

On Comeraro's other side sat Leroy Vogt, who was leaning forward, his elbows on the table, glumly drinking Millers High Life and listening to Garrett and Doc Pepper. A couple of nights before Vogt had confided to him why he always drank Millers. It seemed that some English guy he knew, back in the World, had said that the Millers TV ad – slow motion sea-gulls in close-up drifting over spume-tossed rocks on the Maine coastline to the sound of sobbing guitar licks – was the only ad worth looking at of the entire ad-output of the whole of American TV, apart from the one about the New York used-car salesman who nearly gets killed in the opening seconds by this idiot driver who only just throws out the anchors in time, sticks his head out of the car, and bawls 'Hey Jer-ry! What's the stor-ry?!' So Vogt always drank Millers. Comeraro could not tell if Vogt was taking much in, or whether he was simply using Garrett and Doc Pepper as background music. Vogt was only a kid – at twenty-four Comeraro could think like that; at twenty-four he was close to the grave in some guys' eyes – and it was often hard to tell what was going on in his head. Five or six years was a generation gap that was as wide as the Grand Canyon was long. Out here it was, anyhow.

The Doors were coming through the speakers behind the bar at the end of the long, tawdrily-decorated room, full pelt – an icy, uncompromising sound, an Arctic wail that chilled the mind.

'Well, fuck it,' Garrett was saying. 'I don't give a rat's fuck what you say, Pepper. They sound like a buncha wimps, they *are* a buncha wimps.'

'Listen, man, you really don't know what you're talking about.' Doc Pepper was grinning almost affectionately at Garrett. 'These guys are truly outta sight. Beyond. I mean, listen!'

'You listen, Doctor Dummy.' Garrett had an ugly expression on his craggy face. 'You ain't nothing but a jacked-off junkie. These guys are goddamn perverts. You can tell. Coked up to the fuckin' eyeballs. Perverts!'

'Look, man,' chuckled Doc Pepper, 'you're outta sight yourself, you know? I mean, you just can't say that, man . . .'

'Don't tell me what I can't fuckin' say! I just fuckin' said it! *Perverts!*' Garrett put his arms out and began to flap them slowly, more like a belly-dancer than a bird on the wing. He screwed his face up into an expression of hideous idiocy. 'Ooo-eee-ooo-eee-ooo-eee – *shit!*' He turned and bellowed down the room, 'Hey, jarhead! Put some fuckin' music on! This shit's dickin' me off!'

This was greeted by yells of approval from chug-a-lugging rednecks, howls and hisses from the cooler set. Lorenzini, the barman, took no notice; in any case he was too busy ripping tabs from cans and arguing with a small group of Chicanos. Garrett poured more Bud down his throat and continued to trade insults with Doc Pepper.

Comeraro lit a cigarette and gazed round the room, not really focusing on much at all, simply taking in the sights. There were maybe eighty to a hundred guys in the room and the smoke-count was high; it shifted and billowed whenever a door was opened either end of the long room, but otherwise formed a thick fog clinging to the ceiling. Groups filled, expanded, touched other groups, coalesced, drifted apart. Men moved from one group to another then back again, or onwards to fill spaces left by others doing likewise. There was continual movement, even with those sitting down at the small tables placed haphazardly round the room. Men drifted out into the night, returned, did not return. There was laughter, singing, cheers, shouts. It was mid-evening at the SSG base-camp at Do Thon, so near to the DeeEmZee you could almost spit at the cadres indoctrinating the forward troops across the line.

'Gotta light, mate . . ?'

Comeraro turned. Behind him a big, rawboned Australian in patched and faded jungle fatigues leaned over. Comeraro now recognised the source of the real noise in the room. Here were maybe a dozen Australians whooping it up for some reason. Or maybe not whooping it up at all. Maybe just drinking in the Australian manner which, Comeraro had to admit, was fairly spectactular. No one was talking, all were shouting, as though each man was separated from the rest by the length of a street block. Beer was disappearing down throats that seemed not to have experienced alcohol for a couple of decades. The laughter was raucous but, Comeraro decided, essentially without humour. They looked rangy, brutal, dangerous. When you got right down to it – crazy.

He struck a book-match, held it up. The Australian leaned down, sucked greedily at the flame through his cigarette.

'Ter.' He nodded, then waved a big-fisted hand at Garrett. 'Agree with yer, mate.'

Garrett stared at him as though the Australian had just spoken in Bomongo. 'What the fuck is this? Agree? With what?'

The Australian gestured vaguely with his hand, the fingers open, loosely extended. The gesture took in the entire room. 'This dog-piss. Real puke. Buncha long-haired fairies, mate, and what the fuck are we doin' listenin' to a buncha long-haired shaggin' fairies?' He stabbed an accusatory forefinger at Garrett, as though condemning him to death. 'Me, I like a bouncy tune.'

Garrett glared at him. 'Yeah? Bouncy fucker, huh?' He turned to Doc Pepper and snarled, 'We got us a real bouncy sonuvabitch here, Doctor Dumb.'

'This piss,' said the Australian, waving his hand again. 'Christ, a buncha pansies.'

'Yeah?' grunted Garrett. 'I've heard worse.'

Comeraro could see that Garrett was getting mad. There was no reason for this; it was simply Garrett's perverse attitude to life. He might – and frequently did – insult Doc Pepper about the kind of music Doc Pepper liked, but if some character barged into a conversation and started doing likewise the odds were high that Garrett would take an instant dislike to the guy (and Garrett's dislikes amounted to pathological hatreds), and switch to the opposition. What it boiled down to was that Garrett detested people agreeing with him, for no other reason than that he positively enjoyed argument for argument's sake.

'Ah shit,' said the Australian who, it was now clear to Comeraro, was very drunk indeed. 'Come on, mate. Gotta be jestin'. Rat could fart better'n this buncha fairies.'

'Oh yeah?' said Garrett dangerously. 'Well let me tell you, *mate*, let me just fuckin' set you right on a few fuckin' items, *mate* . . .'

Comeraro slid the comic book he had been reading on to the table. It was the pulse-pounding premiere ish of *Conan the Barbarian*, a new one on Comeraro who, despite being a 1 L-T, was a comic book freak, but there was hooded rage in Garrett's eyes, and it was clear he was going to blow any second. Comeraro had seen the signs before.

Garrett said, 'Only fuckin' thing I know about Australians, they fuck sheep. Ain't got the whip to fuck anything else.'

Comeraro glanced over his shoulder, turning his head as far as he dared without making too much movement. The Australians behind, most of them anyhow, had stopped yelling. That was a bad sign. Comeraro's gaze flicked back round his own table. Vogt was gaping up at the big Australian, who was clearly trying to articulate some truly vicious insult but was having trouble because he was too drunk to do it properly. Under the mistaken impression that Garrett was not looking at him he was trying to attract the big American's attention.

'Lis'n,' he managed to get out, loudly. '*Hey!* Lis'n. You.'

Doc Pepper was glancing round the room, almost certainly looking for an easy escape-route if things got heavy. Olsen was staring straight up at the Australian in a thoughtful kind of way; weighing him up, maybe even measuring him out. Fuller was smoothly gathering in his cards with a poker-face, as though nothing at all was happening within a thousand miles of his chair.

'*Hey!*' The Australian was still trying to translate images in his mind into cutting phrases. 'Hey, lis'n. You. Fuck. *Lis'n!*'

'Ya can't talk properly,' said Garrett in a chilling voice, 'ya wanna close down.'

'Suck . . . dinks' . . . dicks . . .' the Australian suddenly announced, very slowly and very clearly. 'Thass *you!*'

Garrett reached up and grabbed at the Australian's head with both hands then jammed it down with incredible force. The Australian hit the table-top face-first and Comeraro heard the crack of bone as his nose went, and probably – Comeraro couldn't see clearly – some front teeth as well. The Australian gave a howl of pain and rage and his left hand was suddenly holding a knife.

Comeraro shifted into top. His elbow smacked into the Australian's side, just below the rib-cage. The Australian honked, let go the knife. Comeraro shot up from his seat and grabbed a handful of the Australian's clothes, anywhere, any grip. He heaved upwards and the guy shot across the table, past Garrett who had let go of his head, and off into the air like a launched missile. Arms flailing, he smashed into the back of one of the chairs at the next table.

Garrett said, 'Now that was right useful, Lootenant, right smart thinkin' – *watcha back!*'

Comeraro ducked and felt the wind of something whirling over his head. Glass smashed. Something heavy descended on his bowed back and he heaved at that too, and sent a man pitching over on to the table where Fuller was already reaching out, grabbing, hurling him off in another direction.

Sergeant Olsen was bawling 'Stop that! That's enough! Goddamnit, you drunken prick!' but the stocky Australian who was lunging at him with a bottle in one hand didn't seem to be taking any notice of this at all, so Olsen slid off his chair, gripped the front legs and simply lifted it up so that the solid back-rest took the Australian under the chin with such force that he was thrown back four or five feet.

Men cannoned off men or chairs or tables and bounced into other men or chairs or tables. The fighting became general. Mostly the Americans – black, white, all shades, all hues – were bent on destroying the Australians, whom they'd never cared for. The Australian Special Forces set themselves up as the hardest-nosed, hardest-assed, meanest buncha heroes in the whole of Nam, which was by no means the opinion of the Americans.

But other scores were being settled under cover of the general mayhem and confusion. Comeraro saw a big black sock another black in the back of the neck with a rabbit-punch that floored him. A white named Jago, stocky with a thick moustache, sent another white man, name unknown to Comeraro, lunging for the floor with a bottle-blow to the back of the head.

Up the far end of the room Lorenzini was defending his bar against all comers with the Doors wailing him on. He stood on the bar itself yelling, lashing out with his boots at anyone who came within kicking distance. Three of the side-lights went, plunging half the room into a murky gloom; a window shattered.

Olsen grabbed Comeraro by the arm and bawled, 'The kid! He took one to the jaw!'

Comeraro struggled through the mass of milling bodies and he and Olsen reached down for Vogt, who was moaning and mumbling incomprehensibly under a table.

'You take his legs,' directed Comeraro, grabbing for an arm. They half-lifted, half-dragged the mumbling Vogt towards the nearest door, bumping into Garrett on the way.

'Out!' snarled Comeraro.

The big man shrugged. He was kicking at the prone figure of one of the Australians, helped in this by two other men Comeraro couldn't identify in the gloom.

'Just one more rib-tickler,' he said. 'Just fuck up his rib-cage some more.' The boot went in again.

'Out!'

Doc Pepper had the door open and Sergeant Fuller was cursing and clearing a path to it, yanking men out of the way with his bare hands and using his fists like sledges if they tried to fight back. Comeraro and Olsen skidded through the door just as a flying chair burst apart against the wall to one side, richocheting off into the crowd. Pepper was already through. Garrett followed and Fuller kicked someone out of the way and heaved the door closed.

'Jesus,' muttered Vogt. He staggered to his feet. His head hurt and the whole of one shoulder was throbbing with pain. 'Some sonuvabitch thought I was a football. Jesus. You know, sir?'

'You're a stupid fucker, Garrett,' said Comeraro through his teeth. 'Someone's gonna nail you to the floor one of these fine days.'

'Take some fuckin' doin',' said Garrett. 'Sir.' His face was a mask of blood but it looked like none of it was his. He wiped an arm across and took away most of it on the shirt-sleeve. 'Tell ya, Lootenant, them Australian fucks really get up my nose. They been gettin' up my nose for too long. Reckon I broke *his* fuckin' nose.' He nudged Doc Pepper in the ribs and shot him a grin that didn't last more than a nano-second. 'How bout that, Doctor Dummy. Settled his nuts, hah? Won't go round trashin' good Yankee fairies any more.'

Doc Pepper, still breathing hard, raised his eyes skywards.

They stumbled through the streets of Quonsett huts and hooches. Lighted windows were a random patchwork against the deep black of the night. Sounds of hard rock spilled out from open windows, heavy guitar licks sliding up in dirty, gutsy runs. Voices called out; other voices answered. The thunder of the fight in the club receded behind them.

Comeraro thought: What in Christ's name am I doing here anyway? What's going on? I get dragged into some utterly fantastic situation in which I'm killing guys who are supposed to be on my side, and when that's all over I get thrown into this goddamn camp on the EnVee border and told to take a sabbatical. This involves drinking with a psychopath most nights, a stoned-out freak, a dumb kid, and a couple of Papa Sierras whose conversation is not a hell of a lot more than nil.

Comeraro felt as though he'd been tried *in absentia* and he was now serving time, although he didn't quite know what for.

'Shit!' he suddenly said.

'Watsa matter?' asked Garrett. 'Sir.'

'I know you're not going to appreciate the finer points of my distress, Garrett, all things considered – but I left a copy of *Conan the Barbarian*, premiere ish, in the fucking club.'

'Premiere ish, huh. That means it's like, number one.'

'You got it, soldier.'

'It's like, the first of the run.'

'In a nutshell.'

'So that means it could be worth dough, in years ta come.'

'In years to come,' said Comeraro suspiciously, 'yeah.'

'Because it could be a try-out, right? I mean, I don't know what the fuck kind of figures comic books run to these days, like how many they print, ya know? I ain't touched a comic book since *Creepy Crappies* in 1954. But I figure a comic book don't get to be popular, like kids are buyin' it in their, I dunno, thousands, until like it's been goin' for maybe a year or more. So the early ones got to be kinda rare, right? An' that means the number one's a shit-hot number, because they maybe didn't print a half of what they'd print later if it goes over big.'

Comeraro stared at the big man. Garrett stared back. He seemed perfectly serious.

'I didn't know you had such a grasp of the subtle economic realities of monthly magazine publishing, Garrett.'

Garrett said, 'You think I'm some kinda dimbo. You think I'm the kinda guy reads the funnies with his lips movin'. As a matter of fact, I usedta move in real high-power circles, collectingwise.'

'You did?' Comeraro was fascinated.

'Sure. You remember the Rothstein kidnapping?'

'Uh . . .' Comeraro pushed his mind back seven or eight years. 'Yeah. Vaguely. There was a kid involved. The old man was a millionaire, he was into antiques . . .'

'Uh-uh.' Garrett shook his head. 'Pictures. Paintings. What they call "Old Masters". An' he wasn't a millionaire, he was a fuckin' billionaire. He had almost as much jack as Howard Hughes. But he was mean. The guy I was working for wanted a quarter-million for the kid. He wasn't greedy.

But the old man told him, fuck off. So we sneaked in past the cops one night – they were like, you know, guardin' the place with pump-guns, billy-clubs, flame-throwers, the whole bit – and stuck the old fart up. Threatened him, you know. But the fucker still didn't take us seriously.' Garrett stopped, lit a cigarette.

'So what happened?'

'So we ripped a buncha pictures up. Took us seriously then.'

Comeraro stared at him, open-mouthed.

'He had some, you know, black an' white pictures. Prints. French. Worth ten grand apiece. But not when we'd finished with 'em.' Garrett cackled triumphantly. 'So ya see, I've been a high-flier in my time.'

'Yes,' said Comeraro carefully. 'I can quite see that.'

'And then there was the time we hadda bomb a bookshop,' said Garrett, evidently in a reminiscent mood.

'*Bomb?* said Comeraro. 'A *bookshop*?'

'Yeah. The guy was gettin' to be a real pain in the ass, so we had to, like, teach him a lesson.' Garrett pondered this for a moment, clearly reliving the past. He shook his head. 'That was a tough one.'

'A tough one?'

'Yeah.' Garrett turned fully towards Comeraro and wagged a stubby forefinger under the Lieutenant's nose. 'You wanna bomb a bookshop, you'll find out how tough it is. It's a hell of a lot tougher than you might think.'

'Is it?'

'Affirm on that.'

'Books don't burn easy?' hazarded Comeraro.

'Nah!' Garrett was contemptuous. 'They say it's difficult to burn books because they're so thick. But it's no big deal. All you need's a lot of petrol.' He nodded to himself, a serious expression on his lumpy face. 'No, the real pisser is, ya gotta *open* all the friggin' books. It's a question of air, see, Lootenant. Ya gotta let the air get to the paper. *Then* they burn. But that takes time an' the fuzz could be on their way. S'why it's tough.'

'Mmh.' Comeraro nodded thoughtfully.

Garrett suddenly jabbed his forefinger at Comeraro again, as though galvanised.

'But I'll tell ya the best burners!'

'Oh?'

'Softbacks.'

'Oh.'

'Yeah. It's them cheapskate publishers, they use cheap paper. I learnt that. Ya learn a lot in my trade. It's not all just goin' up to guys, blowin' their friggin' heads off, ya know.'

Comeraro was saved the near-impossibility of making any kind of adequate response to this by a figure materialising out of the darkness. It stepped into a pool of light thrown from a nearby window. It was Colonel Hardin.

'What the hell happened to you?'

He stared at the blood-smears on Garrett's face, the wincing features of Leroy Vogt, the generally damaged aspect of the others.

'A minor skirmish, sir,' said Comeraro.

'You should see the other guys,' leered Garrett.

Olsen said loyally, 'With all respect, Colonel, something's gotta be done about the Australian contingent in this camp. They're frankly getting to be a pain in the butt, sir.'

Hardin brushed this aside. 'Get your gear together. Report to the armoury on the north side. Then assemble for a briefing in the low-level complex, Room 16C. Forty minutes.'

Sergeant Fuller said eagerly, 'Is this something big, sir?'

Hardin let him have a frosty smile. 'It's a sortie, Sergeant. But it could get out of hand.'

VIII

Hardin stared over Frank Marco's shoulder through the plexiglass windscreen of the Huey and noted with satisfaction that there was plenty air activity right where he wanted it. Choppers buzzed over and around the two holes in the jungle top-growth like wasps round a nest; all kinds, all sizes. Prominent was a huge CH-54 Tarhe, the 'Sky Crane', looking, with its long flapped-out wheel-arms, and its cutaway profile which made its nose its most conspicuous feature, like a vast frog about to gobble up some juicy morsel – although right now it was having problems. The morsel, as Hardin had suspected when he'd been on the ground, didn't want to be gobbled – or, at least, the surrounding trees had gripped the morsel in question too well; they weren't about to let it be gobbled.

A tiny little OH-6 Loach, two-manned, darted past the Huey's nose, streaked low over the jungle-roof to the north, spotting. Cobras raced around a wide perimeter, patched into the Loach scout and others, on the watch. Above, Hardin could see a couple of Kiowas circling, holding a watching brief too, but high, for all-round surveillance. Above the hole where the wrecked but unburnt Huey lay, clutched to the bosom of the forest, several UH-Ds circled and hovered. Even now men were climbing down from rope-ladders, disappearing through the top-growth. To the east, Hardin could see patrolling Sky Hawks and Cessna Dragonflies.

'Lotta firepower,' said Marco through the intercom.

Hardin, linked up, nodded. 'Needs it.'

'But they havin' a hard time pullin' that mother up,' Marco went on, skilfully avoiding a Loach who'd gotten too close for comfort. 'Seem to me, they gonna have to strip it, then blow it. They ain' gonna drag that baby out, no way. The trees, they don wanna let go. They like it the way it is.'

'Are we going to have to climb down?' said Hardin. He gazed around at the expanse of greenery, mile upon mile of it to the horizon, all points of the compass.

'Uh-uh. There a clearing beyond that li'l bitty titty of a hill. I seen better LZs, but it okay. I can set down, you guys can beat it.' He glanced at Hardin. 'You lookin' pissed, babe.'

Hardin shook his head. 'It's the back-up I'm worried about. There was supposed to be a whole bag of EnVee heading towards this area, but it hasn't showed.'

Marco chuckled.

'You wanna cheer, man. Bagga EnVee gonna make life tough down there. You can do without it.'

'I'd be happier if they were there,' said Hardin. He was watching a fat little Loach dipping down towards the jungle-top, scurrying over the sea of green. 'It'd actually make things a lot easier.'

As he said that the Loach disappeared in a flash of fire that made him wince, blink his eyes shut. When he opened them there were just bits of the tiny scout crashing into the trees.

'Shee-*it!*' yelled Marco. '*Now* who put the fuckin' hoodoo on!'

As Hardin stared, mesmerised, at where the remains of the Loach had tumbled into the Big Green, the tail-boom of a nearby Huey disintegrated in a smear of angry red. The chopper canted over, its main rotors shearing into top-growth. The whole machine was flung away upside down, and men, clinging to the ladder that had been dropped into the trees, shot into the air as though hurled from a sling. The Huey seemed to bounce against the trees, then it broke up in a red-cored explosion, the rotors whirling off at an angle. Hardin could see puffs of smoke coming from the jungle, muzzle-flashes winking against the green carpet. The various choppers were diving away from the immediate area in a state of utter confusion. Now Hardin could actually see missiles erupting out of the jungle, shooting up into the air, heat-seekers sniffing for engine-exhaust. On the horizon, to the east, the F-4s were wheeling round, hurtling in towards the fire-zone. Rockets spurted from them, lanced into the jungle, geysered flame, earth, tree-chunks high into the air.

'There your fuckin' back-up, man,' snapped Marco. 'I'm gettin' the hell out. Charlie north an east of the wreck an I headin' west!'

'No, wait!' Hardin grabbed his shoulder. 'Drop us in the trees, other side of the wreck.'

Marco turned in his bucket-seat, gaped at him. 'You fuckin' crazy? There gonna be all kindsa shit flyin' down there – not to mention I be a fuckin' sittin'-target!'

'Do it, Frank. There's about sixty grunts down there, on perimeter defence. With the EnVee throwing shit, I need some more men – gonna steal me a squad from the guys in the forest.'

Outside all hell had broken loose. The F-4s were rocketing the jungle to the north of the downed wreck and missiles were tearing up the trees. Smoke was beginning to drift thickly across the scene like a curtain. Another Loach blew apart, boiling into flames. Small white puffs of smoke were now appearing amidst the greenery like instant mushrooms. Up here, Hardin could hear nothing, but he could imagine the sound-pandemonium that would be going on below: the thud and krump of mortars; the crackle of rifle-fire; the tearing hiss of rockets through the air, the ear-shattering explosions as they impacted.

And the closer they were to the jungle-roof, the easier it would be for a heat-seeker to blow them all over the trees.

Hardin shrugged. It had to be done. He pointed to a spot where foliage was clustered thickly amongst the branches of medium-height trees.

'There. We can jump into that. We'll be twenty seconds, top – but I need to do it, if it takes fifty.'

'Won't take fifty fuckin' *micro*-seconds before we fire-ballin' into the fuckin' trees,' said Marco sourly.

He told his door-gunners to lay down as much suppressive as they could.

'Jus' remember, we got our guys down there too. Hit the trees the north of the wreck.' He turned to Hardin. 'Well, they got there, man. Victor Charles. You happy now?'

Hardin grinned. 'Yeah. It means they didn't link up with the guy I'm after. Way I see it, if they'd linked up, they'd've split fast, heading north. Bye-bye bag. But unless the little fuckers are just attacking from sheer orneriness, the runner is still running and I'm gonna catch him.'

'I jus' hope you know where you at,' said Marco.

Hardin unclipped his cans, made a circle with his finger and thumb, turned back into the main cabin area. He beckoned to Comeraro, glancing at his squad as he did so.

No fucking doubt about it, he thought, an odd squad. One L-T, two sergeants, a medic, a wireman, and a psychopath who got off on slicing guys' jugulars with piano-wire. It wasn't actually the tightest formation he'd ever headed, but, he thought, you could look at it another way. Comeraro was Special Forces and therefore very, very good. The two Sarges were old hands; they *were* tight. Doc Pepper got along; all he had to do was look after his supplies. Vogt could handle a radio, and otherwise was neither better nor, thank Christ, worse than fifty thousand other grunts in Nam. Garrett was a high class killer; he could use just about any weapon he was given, and to fierce, destructive effect. He, if anyone, was worth two or three other guys put together.

But he still needed another half-dozen men, to really beef things up the way he figured he might be needing it with Charlie on the rampage.

He said to Comeraro, 'We're gonna take a dive into the forest.'

Comeraro raised an eyebrow. 'Into that crap, sir?'

Hardin said, 'Yeah, I know. It's gonna be hairy. Olsen!'

Olsen came across. By now the chopper was curling in towards the jungle, as sneakily as only Marco could do it. The port-gunner was laying down his lines coolly and professionally, short tracer-bursts that lashed down into the top-growth, shredding it, flaying it apart and anything underneath it.

'We're going out on the hover, Olsen.'

'Yessir.' Olsen executed a neat double-take. 'You mean jump into the trees, Colonel?'

'Yeah, and fast.'

'Affirmative on that, sir. Be better, I gotta say, sir, if we could forget about the high stuff and maybe find us a low patch.'

'That's what Captain Marco's looking for. Just get 'em together, Sarge.'

Olsen whipped up a salute, began shoving Garrett and Vogt towards the open door.

They could now hear the sound of firing, explosions, above the racket of the rotors. Hardin clung on to a strut, eased himself behind the port-gunner's back. They were dropping fast. The tree-tops seemed to be hurtling up towards them. Leaves and twigs were whipped into the air by the rotor-downdraught.

The foliage below was thick; in places it seemed almost to be impenetrable even at this lower level – a dense and knotted mat of greenery. From Hardin's point of view it was ideal.

He jabbed his right fist down and to the left, away from the action around the wreck. He felt the chopper judder and shake, then she was hovering, no more than a foot above the trees.

Hardin judged his spot, holding on to the side of the door, then stepped out on the crouch on to a thick, flattish bough. He stooped, grabbed at a branch, plunged into the greenery, his boots finding an unseen but firm foothold beneath him. He was now clinging to the top of a tree, counting off the seconds in his mind. With his right hand he pulled at a machete at his belt, began shearing through the small stuff to create a space. The downblast from the rotors was tremendous, something physical that almost rammed him lower, and as he chopped and hacked away at twigs and thin top-branches so they were whirled into the air away from him.

He gestured with the machete. Olsen dropped down, almost lost his balance then regained it. He began smashing his way downwards into the foliage, then disappeared from sight completely. Vogt, with his own ruck and the radio, stood shaking in the doorway. Behind him Garrett was screaming at him. Vogt tentatively crouched down, put a foot out on to one of the boughs, then seemed to leap forward, as though finally having made up his mind to end it all then and there. Hardin cursed, knowing that Garrett had shoved the kid. With a wild yell Vogt disappeared after Olsen, his hands clawing at branches.

Below, Olsen heard the racket, braced himself with one arm round a sturdy bole and grabbed at one of Vogt's flailing arms as the kid came tumbling past. He heaved, felt Vogt clutching frantically at him, then yanked him bodily over on to the branch he was standing on.

'That fucker!' gasped Vogt. 'I'll kill the sucker . . .'

'Never mind!' snapped Olsen. 'Stay here. Help the rest down.'

He glanced upwards, saw Garrett shinning expertly downwards. Garrett grinned at Vogt, who scowled back.

'Hey!' said Garrett loudly.

'Shut it!' snarled Olsen. 'Garrett, you're a heapa dung. Don't fuck me about or you're gonna be in a worlda hurt. Follow me down. There could be a reception committee.'

He began scrambling lower, until he'd reached well below the top-foliage level. At his feet there were now the tops of monstrously tall ground-ferns, shimmying slightly. Olsen reckoned there was about another twenty feet to drop, maybe a little more. Garrett landed beside him.

'It's still better than the slammer, huh? There's a degree of fuckin' elbow-room out here.'

'Yeah,' said Olsen sourly, 'an' 7.62 rounds up your ass.'

Shock-waves of rocket-fire impaction from the F-4s above

were reaching them even here, though blunted by the intervening foliage. Explosions thundered, both grenade and mortar. Both men could hear the high-pitched and distinctive chatter of AK-fire as a leitmotif against the steady roar of the more muscular hardware.

'Look for gooks,' snapped Olsen. 'The little yellow men probably surrounded the wreck before they began throwin' the crap around. They could be anywhere.'

He began climbing down even further, now with his unslung M16 in one hand. It was easier down here; the hand- and foot-holds were firmer and the fact that he was nearer the ground was a psychological boost. The less you had to drop, the less it mattered.

He peered down through the leaf-screen – and froze. Charlie *was* below, although on the move. Two EnVee regulars sprinted past through the bushes carrying a 75mm recoilless rifle.

'Jesus,' muttered Olsen. He flapped a hand up at Garrett to tell him to hold on, shut up, don't do a goddamn thing. His hand was suddenly caught in a firm grip and he almost fell. He jerked round, about ready to take a swing at Garrett, when he saw that Hardin was above him. It suddenly dawned on him that he was no longer hearing the clatter of the Huey's rotors above. Hardin dropped down on to his branch.

'We're all set.'

'Gooks below.' Olsen pointed, left and right. 'Comin' from, goin' to. They got an M20.'

'Shit, we better kick 'em in the ass fast,' said Hardin. 'That won't do the guys by the wreck a hell of a lot of good.'

'Affirm that, sir.'

Crouching beside the burly sergeant Hardin muttered, 'I'll take Fuller, Garrett, Pepper, Vogt, hit 'em from behind. You and the L-T guard our rear but keep moving in our direction. We're heading for the wreck.'

'Yessir.'

Hardin slid down past him, dropped to the forest floor. Vaguely he was aware of voices to his right, an excited jabber. He crouched down at the foot of the tree and rapidly but expertly took in the scenery. He could hear nothing from the direction in which Olsen had gestured, could see nothing either. Hugging the tree, he shifted his gaze to the right, saw bushes with huge red flowers that drooped sadly; dense, tangled undergrowth. Charlie was either in the bushes or beyond them. He beckoned urgently to Olsen.

First down the tree was Garrett, who plunged into the undergrowth in front. Vogt scrambled down and Hardin grabbed him, shoved him round the tree. Pepper and Fuller dropped down, followed by Olsen and Comeraro. The L-T and the sergeant vanished left, rifles at the ready.

Hardin muttered, 'We're heading for the wreck and there's Charlie in between, maybe a couple, maybe more. Hit 'em hard and fast, and keep on the move. There's an M20 out there somewhere, so even if you hit nothing else, hit that.'

He moved through the undergrowth, headed into the bushes. He eased branches aside, kept moving, all the time alert for sudden confrontation.

Beyond the bush with the big red flowers two EnVees were setting up the recoilless rifle, and Hardin froze where he was. They were lining it at a wall of vegetation beyond which, Hardin guessed, lay the wrecked chopper. To the left of the M20 was a mortar with its three-man team. One of the men flipped out the bipod, dropped the ugly weapon into the ground so that its barrel pointed, too, at the forest wall.

Hardin could hear that a fierce battle was raging beyond that wall. He could imagine the Americans, abandoned by the choppers, grouped around and in the wrecked Huey. In many ways it was a solid position, but it was also terribly vulnerable. He now remembered that thick curtain of creepers and midgrowth behind the wreck, and it was clear that no one had thought to throw a defensive line on the other side of it – *this* side of it.

Hardin realised that the F-4s were rocketing well away from the wreck. They had to, or risk blowing their own men away. There was thus a circle around the downed chopper, a no-fire zone which the EnVees had penetrated. They were safe from the air-barrage, and if there were enough of them they could overwhelm those on the ground with comparative ease.

Hardin knew that at some time, Command were either going to have to drop more men in – a fuck of a lot more men – or do their utmost to pull up those left down here. But it was a no-win situation. Such was the nature of the terrain at this spot, that both manoeuvres were virtually impossible. Men rappelling out of choppers were going to be dead long before they reached the ground; likewise men scrambling up ladders thrown down into the trees. And the choppers too were going to be easy meat for those EnVee inside the magic circle away from the rocket-fire from above.

Just about all ways and every way, the grunts down here were in trouble. Big trouble. Still, Hardin thought, he could at least take some of the weight off. He glanced round, spotted Fuller inching his way into the centre of a mass of shrubbery overhung with creepers so thick you could probably do a Johnny Weismuller on them. He pointed to the M20 team then gestured at the mortar-men. Fuller signalled a brief acknowledgement.

Hardin looked over his shoulder, beckoned to Vogt who was a couple of yards behind him. Vogt slid into the bushes, M16 out.

Hardin dropped to his knees, his AK-47 in his right hand. He slunk forward, close to the ground, nearer to the EnVees. He was in the act of gently pushing the barrel of the assault rifle forward into an optimum firing position when he paused suddenly, frowned. He stared at the rotting leaves on the jungle floor, saw splashes of red, not fresh but not old either. He moved his head to gaze beneath his body. The splashes were there too. He put his finger down, touched one. Then another. Gummy.

He was looking at a blood-trail.

He felt a tingle of excitement ripple through him, the nerve-quiver of the hunter. He was looking at a blood-trail that was at most twenty-four hours' old – which meant that when he'd blazed away at the bushes yesterday he'd hit the runner. Not badly, maybe, but enough to make the fucker bleed, enough to make him leave his calling-card all over the jungle-floor.

Hardin nodded briefly to himself, then pulled his mind back to the present problem. To his right he could just see Vogt, looking at him. He jabbed his hand forward at the EnVees then settled down, squeezed a short burst at the M20 team. A moment later Vogt joined in, and seconds after that firing erupted from his left.

The EnVees didn't stand a chance. Hardin caught both the M20 men with his burst, stitching them up across their backs and sending them sideways where they were picked up by Leroy Vogt, a long chattering burst that tumbled them back again, crying out, across their weapon.

Two of the mortar-team fell to the floor, jerking, riddled with rounds from Fuller and the unseen Garrett. The third man turned and did the starkly unexpected. He dived straight for where Hardin was lying, screaming with fury and crazy blood-lust. Hardin let him have it in the chest. Rounds hammered at the man, punching bloody holes across his heart and left shoulder. He somersaulted backwards like a circus clown whose act has gone terribly wrong.

More firing broke out, this time far to the left. Hardin crouched where he was, trying to pierce the screen of shrubbery beyond Fuller's position. Then a pith-helmeted little guy burst out of it, running hard. Hardin saw Fuller firing, and the man was slung across the clearing, his helmet flying from him as rounds burst his head apart like a blood orange.

Comeraro's voice, low but penetrating, broke the sudden silence.

'It's tight behind and to your left.'

Hardin's eyes raked the vegetation on his right but he saw nothing out of place or threatening. He got to his feet, waved his men on. They grouped round the Envee weapons with Garrett and Vogt on guard one end of the clearing, Olsen and Fuller the other.

Comeraro said, 'There was a small team heading this way. We got behind 'em, took 'em out.'

Hardin nodded.

'Okay, we go through the screen. But casual. I don't wanna get carved by the good guys.'

He led off into the matted vegetation, pushing his way through in a stoop, holding an arm over his face to protect himself against thick thorn branches. It smelt dank here; the ground was a slick carpet of rotting leaves. He spotted another blood-splash, much bigger, then suddenly it was dark above him, the bulk of the chopper cutting off the light. He paused, pushed leaves aside, peered through greenery. There was a grunt staring at him, open-mouthed, M16 barrel aimed at his face.

'Don't pull the trigger,' said Hardin, almost pleasantly, as though he was saying 'Hi, pal', knowing that a sudden screamed order was far more likely to panic the guy into doing just that.

'Jesus, what the fuck . . .' The man almost blushed. 'Uh . . . sir. Where'd you spring from?'

Hardin grinned, beckoned his men forward. They scrambled through the creepers and foliage and out into the clearing made by the Huey. Men had dug themselves in around the chopper and Hardin saw at least two M60s stabbing fire into the forest; one was actually emplaced in the wreck itself and controlled a high field of fire across the bushes to the north. A mortar was thumping to the east somewhere, a continuous *Krump-krump-krump*, and there was a steady rattle of M16 fire punctuated by grenade explosions and laced with the higher-pitched song of the Kalashnikov. Hazy smoke drifted through the trees, turning them into ghostly shapes. There was an intense and steely stink of battle.

An L-T hurried up. He looked harassed. 'Where the hell did you – Oh. Sir. Where did you appear from?'

Hardin gestured behind him. 'You want some guys the other side of that vegetation, Lieutenant. We hit Charlie sneaking up on you from the rear. Who's in charge here?'

The L-T looked even more harassed.

'Christ knows. They hit us before we could really group up solid. Some of the guys here I've never seen before in my goddamn life. It's a fucked-up mess, sir.'

Hardin noticed a group of grunts heading towards the chopper, a Captain with a thick moustache in front. The Captain stared at Hardin.

'Who's the Captain?'

'Christ, sir, I dunno. He ain't mine's all I know. Mine got his head blown off about ten minutes ago. It's a real fuck-up, sir . . .'

A heavier burst of firing suddenly broke out and two grunts were spun into the bushes. Someone yelled, '*They're in the fuckin' trees!*' Men dived for cover. The M60 in the chopper began blazing away at a high angle, lashing the forest roof with tracer. Shrieking figures were dropping from unseen positions, crashing down through the mid-foliage and hitting the ground with ugly thuds. Hardin pushed his men back towards the chopper, unwilling to get them involved in a situation that looked likely to interfere with his own business.

The EnVee were now pouring MG-fire at the chopper. Rounds hammered at the steel carcase with a deafening tintinnabulation, ricochets whined and hissed through the air. The Captain with the moustache rolled into cover beside Hardin.

'Shit! Too much lead in the air,' he gasped. 'It's Colonel Hardin, isn't it? Seen you around.'

Hardin didn't recognise the man but acknowledged his own identity. 'You looking for someone, sir? Maybe I can help. Captain Renucci. Tom Renucci, sir.'

Hardin said, 'This your company, Captain?'

Renucci frowned, then laughed. 'Hell, it's kinda complicated, sir. Thing is . . .'

There was a loud hissing scream of air disturbance. The L-T howled '*Incoming!*' Hardin buried his face in the dirt and leaf-mould, jammed himself into the ground as far as he could get. There was a cracking burst of sound and he felt himself shoved sideways into Renucci. They picked themselves up, and Hardin scrabbled for his fallen AK.

'Renucci, I want six good men. Get your CP wireman to raise Command and tell 'em. Any crapchat, tell 'em I got an A-1 priority from General Halderling.'

Renucci nodded. 'Yeah. Right, sir. Do that.' He stared around, then said, 'Matter of fact, sir, I can get you five easy, plus me. This situation's heading for the tube, and frankly, I'm caught down here. My company's in the choppers up aloft somewhere, almost to a man.'

There was another drawn-out scream of sound and Renucci groaned 'Oh shit!' and flung himself at the ground again with Hardin. The earth heaved, there was a flash, a pounding crash. Hardin jumped to his feet and yelled at Renucci, 'Okay, get 'em!' He galloped for the L-T, grabbed him by the shoulder.

'There's gonna be no time for Command to pull you guys out and they can't call in arty because these fuckers've penetrated too close. You'll get pounded too. Get your men together – anyone that's around. Break out to the south. There'll be less of an EnVee concentration there. Flare for choppers when you get through.' He gripped the man's arm, staring down at the young white face smeared with mud and blood. 'But do it fast, or Charlie's gonna be celebrating tonight!'

He turned away, bawled for Comeraro. 'Back the way we came. I've found a blood-trail. With luck the EnVee are gonna be too busy here to bother us.'

The blood-trail was not difficult to follow. Every so often there were large scarlet splotches on leaves. Deep scarlet.

'Whoever you're after,' said Renucci, 'he's in a bad way. This stuff's from deep inside.'

The Captain had pulled five men with him: a Sergeant, Creed, and four grunts; three whites, Laguna, Rand, Snell, and one black, Hallings. Creed, to Hardin, was of a type: brutal, surly, as tough as a nail-head.

'Jesus,' said Renucci, 'it was such an all-fired mess back there. We were dropped in to supply support, but like I said, most of my guys didn't even make it to the ground. *Jesus!*' He glanced at Hardin questioningly. 'This guy we're trailing. The blood doesn't look fresh to me. Not today-fresh anyhow.'

Hardin shook his head.

They had travelled for over three hours. The fire-fight back of them had long since dwindled to a faint mutter, then to nothing much at all. The odd long-distance thump. Hardin hoped the L-T had made it out of the circle; the EnVees had been very muscular.

He hoped this was because the man they were following had not linked up with them, and the EnVees back at the wreck were closing in tight because they assumed their advance-squad had failed in its objective to get the bag.

In his mind, he gave a phantom snort. If there was a bag! If he hadn't gotten the entire sequence utterly wrong!

And then he thought: No! That hand had to be carrying *something*! He had a strong feeling about this, was positive he wasn't on a fool's errand. The wounded EnVee was still carrying whatever it was that had been chained to the civilian's wrist. Nor had he dropped it and stumbled on without it. Hardin had two lines of men out on each side, searching as they went.

And still the drops of blood blazed the trail.

The guy had been hurt more than he'd originally thought. It was possible he was delirious, which could be why he had not curved round to the north. He ought, of course, to have gone straight back the way he'd come, doubled round and met the EnVee back-up as they advanced. But, again of course, he couldn't. Not with the choppers that had pulled up Hardin and Marco buzzing around, and the arrival of more choppers, more men. He'd probably holed up someplace for a while, hoping the fucking Yankees'd split. But no such luck. There were a whole raft of Americans in between him and salvation.

Hardin could follow through the man's thinking. Get as far away as possible from the Americans, *then* curve round and back. But, like Renucci said, he was bleeding bad; there was indeed every likelihood that he was starting to see things that weren't there by now. All he would know was that he had to keep moving, keep dragging himself forward. Hardin had been in the same mental and physical state himself before now.

He grinned suddenly. It really wasn't going to be that difficult to tag the guy.

Ahead, out of sight, Comeraro was on point, with Garrett as slackman. Just behind him, Vogt was humping the radio-ruck and breathing hard.

He said to Renucci, 'It's a no-account mission. We figure one of the EnVees grabbed something from the chopper, beat it into the jungle. I just needed some more muscle in case we ran into another buncha Cong.'

'Shit,' said Renucci, nodding. 'I guess there was plenty intelligence material in that bird. Charlie'd dig getting his hands on all that.'

Hardin pondered exactly how much to tell Renucci. On the one hand, he always liked to keep things tight with strangers, but on the other there wasn't much to tell anyway. Hardin himself didn't even know what was in the bag.

He said, 'Yeah, but we think it was more than just intelligence. The guy could've gone for the log, code-books, that shit. He didn't. There was something else on that chopper, and he's got it.'

'Whatever it was,' said Renucci.

'Check.'

They kept moving. The land began to rise. The forest now was opening out to the extent that no longer were they ploughing through dense tracts of near-impenetrable jungle, but walking between tall trees that were yards apart. It was like walking through an endless cathedral, the roof of which, the top-growth of the trees, could hardly be seen at all. The sun shone through in pillars of blinding light. They were now on a trail that wound between tall ferns and brightly-flowered bushes, red and white and a blazing yellow.

Suddenly, over the brow of a low hill, the ground fell away on the left of the trail in a deep, wide gorge. Below, a river flowed slowly. On the far side of the gorge the land was lower, the jungle thicker. Hardin saw the lush green and yellow of quinine trees, tall and graceful sugar palms, banana trees. The blood was still around, but now they were having to search for it. He called a halt.

He used Renucci's squad for sentries, plus Garrett; two men each, north, east and west. South didn't matter. That was the edge of the gorge.

Comeraro stared at a topo map while Olsen busied himself with a couple of C-rat cans which doubled as stoves. He filled two large canteen cups with water, set these up. Then he collected two more stoves, placed heat tabs under them and simmered containers of beef slices with potatoes and gravy, and franks. Under the water cups he placed small broken-off chunks of C-4 explosive which he lit. The chunks were slow burners for several seconds, then – *whoomf!* There was a flare of intense, white-hot flame, dazzling to the eyes. The water boiled instantly. Olsen made coffee, checked the meat.

Comeraro sipped coffee and said, 'We have a small plantation any moment. Rubber.'

Hardin said, 'Local?'

'Uh-uh. French.'

'Shit.'

'Trouble?' asked Comeraro, frowning.

'Difficult to say how to treat with some of these old-timers. They got harassed by the Minh back in the fifties because they used their workers like slaves. But the weird thing is, they seem to rub along with the Cong. They pay out protection of course, but you get the impression they don't mind that so much. You actually get the impression they do more than pay out protection.' Hardin thought for a moment. 'If it's a rubber plantation, the guy probably won't be too goddamn friendly anyway.'

'Why?'

Hardin smiled. Sardonic. 'Goes back to when we wiped the French rubber plantations couple of years back.'

'Yeah, but that was because they were streaming with Charlie,' objected Comeraro. 'The Air Force had to do it, for Chrissakes. The fuckers were gathering on the French plantations, using them as sanctuaries, because they figured we wouldn't touch 'em.'

'So it was said.'

Comeraro glanced at him warily. 'Okay, I'll buy it.'

'Well,' said Hardin. 'The weird thing was, only the Michelin plantations got creamed. Nobody else's. That was weird.' He lit a cigarette. 'Didn't do our own tyre boys any harm, though.' He blew smoke into the air thoughtfully. 'I heard profits were astronomical that year. Astro-fuckin'-nomical.'

Comeraro gazed at the map without taking any of its features in. He didn't know what to make of Hardin. There were times when the guy didn't seem to be rooting for his own side at all, and yet what he said was often true, and often made sense. Comeraro himself had ambivalent feelings towards the war and the conduct of the war and the American presence in Vietnam, but then he supposed this was a natural state of mind for anyone tugged into a conflict that, strictly speaking, had nothing at all to do with him and was in any case half a world away from his own country. Of course, they were basically here to cream Reds, but the trouble was the Reds were fanatical: they *wanted* to win, *all* of them wanted it. The Americans, Comeraro thought gloomily, by and large had no such strong feelings, and now that Nixon was pulling out guys by the thousand it did seem that, whatever Command liked to say to the Press, back in Washington they felt the same, were giving up the whole business as a bad job, a global write-off.

Comeraro turned to Fuller, who was spooning chicken fricassee out of his can.

'What d'you think, Top?'

'Whad I think about what, sir?'

'You think Command would order an air-strike against French rubber plantations just to cream the competition?'

Fuller laughed harshly. He finished his stew, lit a cigarette. Like the old stager he was he kept the cigarette cupped in his hand as he smoked it.

'Sure, Lieutenant. Smart move, ta piss on the French so's our boys get the gravy. Ain't no fuckin' ethics in this business, lemme tall ya, sir.' He stared sourly at the glowing end of his cigarette. 'Ain't no fuckin' ethics left any more.'

'You sound pissed, Sarge,' said Hardin, amused.

Fuller shot him a dark look. 'Well, I'll tell ya, sir. I been thinkin'. This war's a fucked-up deal. Ain't nothin' tight about it. I get to thinkin' about Command, the guys at the top, and I'm thinkin' maybe they're not so fuckin' squared away theirselves.' He spat tobacco shreds out of his mouth. 'I been in this man's army a long time, sir, an I seen changes. But nothin' like the changes I seen in this bitched-up war. There's kids out here, they're smokin' dew, they're shootin' up on the crappin' white stuff. I'll tell ya, they don't give a *shit*! An it's not only them. *No one* gives a shit!' He looked almost desperate.

Hardin knew how the man felt. Sometimes it seemed as though the tightest fighting force in the entire world was cracking at the seams; fragmenting, falling apart. A lot of guys like Joe Fuller, lifers, men who knew almost nothing of life outside of the army except the whorehouse on R-and-R, were feeling the draught, were utterly confused by the greyness that had clouded their relatively simple black-and-white world.

Hardin pulled in his perimeters and then moved off, heading down now out of the high forest and back towards the steamy jungle. He put Fuller on point. It would wind him back up again.

As they stepped along the trail Hardin saw that his other Sergeant, Olsen, was looking as stripped-sour as Fuller. Clearly, this was not a good day for Papa Sierras.

'Loosen up, Olsen.'

'Shit, sir, I gotta say these new guys need some goddamn attention,' Olsen grumbled. 'With all respect, I don't believe that Captain Renucci runs a very goddamn tight ship, sir. I went around the perimeters, an they was fuckin' laughin' an smokin' – Jesus! I hadda square 'em away, sir. I'll tell ya how bad it was.' He shot Hardin a stunned look. 'Even *Garrett* was pissed! The guy was with him kept goin' ta fuckin' sleep!' He growled, 'That Creed, he don't know his fuckin' business, I gotta say it.'

Hardin glanced at Sergeant Creed, who was moving along to his right, M16 on the trail. He was short and squat, with narrow eyes set deep in a bullet skull. He'd struck Hardin already as a man he wouldn't care to trust at his rear, not in a heavy situation. Sergeant Creed looked the type to shoot you in the back and skip, if things fell apart. But all that was probably just on the surface. If it meant anything at all Olsen himself ought to be considered as the least trustworthy of all of his men. Olsen had, after all, fragged his own Lieutenant in a gesture of rage and frustration that went way further than Joe Fuller's verbal bitching or Creed's morose and surly attitude. Yet Hardin trusted Olsen without reservation. It was all a matter of degree, he supposed.

He was suddenly aware that in front there was some kind of stoppage. Alert, ducking low, he moved forward, Olsen behind him. Round a bend in the trail ahead, Rand, Hallings and Laguna were grouped. They were laughing. Laguna, a tall, olive-complexioned man, had his hand hidden from Hardin's view by the bulk of the black grunt, Hallings. He seemed to be pulling at something. A second later Hardin knew what it was. Not something, someone. Not it, either. This was a girl.

Laguna had her by the hair and Hallings was stopping her crying out by clutching her mouth. She was small, young – Hardin figured not yet in her teens, but you could never tell for sure out here. Her eyes were wide with terror. Laguna was now gleefully tugging at her wrap-around.

Hardin froze. He snarled, 'Let her go!'

Creed jumped past him.

'Hey! Fuckin' dink chick!' His voice was hoarse. 'What I could do with some pussy right now, even dink pussy.'

'Fuck off, Ben,' grinned Laguna. 'Waitcha turn.'

'Nah. I'm the Sarge in this squad, buddy. I get first lick.' Creed guffawed. 'As ya were – *she* gets first lick!'

'Too small for you, Ben. She got an ant's ass for a slit. Too tight, man.'

'I kin make it bigger. Whatsa matter with you guys? She'll take the fuckin' pork when I ram it in!' He grabbed at the girl's breasts.

Hardin went forward fast. He clamped a hand on Creed's shoulder, wrenched him away. The squat man staggered, fell backwards into the grass. Then with a grunt of fury he almost catapulted himself back on to his feet again, his face scarlet, his eyes popping. He had his M16 in his hands, pointing at Hardin's stomach, and for a second Hardin thought he was going to use it there and then, open up with a burst straight at him, unstitch his guts. Then Captain Renucci stormed past.

Renucci's right hand went back then forward, like a piston. His balled fist exploded into Creed's face and Creed was jolted backwards like a poleaxed steer.

'You stupid fucker!' hissed Renucci. 'Don't you know where you are! Don't you know *who* you fucking are!'

Creed dragged himself to his feet. He glared murderously around. It was clear he was going through incredible mind-contortions to control himself, to stop himself blowing them all away. He was breathing hard, harshly; blood was seeping out of his nose. He wiped the blood away with the sleeve of his fatigures.

'Yeah . . .' he said thickly. 'Yeah . . . I know . . . *sir*.' He ground out the last word as though it was poisonous.

Renucci turned to Hardin. He too was now breathing quickly, as though he'd just finished a 100-metre dash. He made a flapping gesture with his right hand.

'Of course, sir,' he said hoarsely, 'I'll see to it . . .'

Hardin snapped '*Shut it!*' in a voice that would have stripped paint. He swung back to Creed. 'I oughta fucking kill you, mister,' he whispered, jabbing his forefinger at the man as though he was going to drill through into his brain. He turned to the other three and saw that they were gazing at him with barely concealed resentment. He put one hand on the girl's shoulder, softly squeezing it.

Laguna said, 'Shit, sir. She's a fuckin' gook. Could be VC. Ain't no one gonna be worryin' if we have us a little fun . . .'

'You dumb shit!' snarled Hardin. 'There's only about a hundred fucking blow-pipes aimed at us right now!'

Laguna's mouth dropped open; his face seemed to crumple. His eyes began to flick round, taking in the bushes at the side of the trail.

He whispered, 'Ya kiddin . . .'

Leroy Vogt, watching from behind, felt his stomach turn over. He forgot about the radio he was humping, suddenly felt very vulnerable. He saw Hardin hold the girl to him, soothing her, then the Colonel put up his right hand, made an odd curling gesture with it, fingers splayed. He began to talk loudly in a language Vogt didn't understand.

Hardin was facing the jungle and suddenly Vogt could see a vague figure, half-hidden by bushes. Utterly motionless. Vogt winced his eyes and now saw the man more clearly. He was dark-skinned, naked except for a loin-cloth and beads, which hung in necklaces and bracelets down his chest, over his arms. Parts of his face were chalk-white and his body was painted with circles and ovals and ripple designs, red and white and black. Now Vogt could see another figure. And another. His eyes widened. There seemed to be a score of them, standing like statues. He glanced up and his stomach executed a double-flip this time. They were in the trees too, overlooking the trail, squatting on branches and staring impassively down. Christ, they were *everywhere!*

Hardin suddenly stopped talking. He pushed the girl gently towards the bushes. Without a backward glance, the girl plunged into the bushes and they could hear her running, crashing through dead twigs and leaves. The sound died. Vogt stared at the jungle again and this time there was no one there. No one at all. He didn't bother to look up into the trees.

He saw Hardin turn on Creed again, grab him by the throat. He'd never seen the man so coldly, icily angry before.

Hardin said, low-voiced, 'You scumbag sonuvabitch sackashit. You got about as much brain as a dead rat. When we get back, mister, I'm gonna see you're crucified for ever. If it wasn't that I need you, I'd bury you now.' He swung round, glared at the other three. 'And that goes for you shitbirds.'

He turned to Renucci. 'Get these assholes outta my sight, Captain. Square 'em away, or I swear to God I'll burn for the bastards.'

Renucci's face was white. He started to say something, then thought better of it and turned on Creed.

'*Move!*' he snarled.

Garrett hove into sight. He grinned sharply at Vogt.

'The shit we get in this man's army. Even that Renucci's a prick.'

Hardin marched across, his face tight. 'What the hell are you doing here, Garrett? You're slack to Fuller. Why the fuck aren't you up front?'

Vogt watched Garrett, could see that the burly man was wondering how close to the edge he could go with Hardin in his present mood. But this act of contemplation only took about two seconds. Vogt could see Garrett deciding to play it safe, or as safe as he ever played it. This was clearly no time to piss around too much. He wiped the grin from his face.

'Sir, we found us some more blood, sir,' he snapped out. 'Sir, I left Snell as slack.' He shut his mouth.

'Okay okay. Get back there.'

'Sir!'

Garrett whipped up a snappy salute, double-timed it off up the trail.

Comeraro said, 'These Montagnards, sir – we in deep shit?'

Hardin slowly shook his head. 'Shit, but not deep shit. Not yet. But it was close. I used a sign I know, told 'em I was gonna kill those sonsabitches. It pacified 'em. They can be touchy if the mood suits 'em. If we'd had any ARVIN with us, or a Kit Carson, there'd've been a massacre. They hate the Vietnamese.'

Garrett re-appeared. He stepped up to Hardin, grinned again.

'Oh yeah, I forgot.' He jerked his thumb back over his shoulder. 'We got us a centre of population down there. Fuller says to tell ya it looks tight.'

Hardin stared at him for some moments and then said, 'Garrett, if it wasn't for the fact that you kill good, I'd nail your nuts to the floor, use your head for a kick-ball.'

'Sir!' rapped Garrett, grinning fast, like a shark. 'Appreciate that!'

It was about as much of a compliment as he was ever going to get from Hardin.

IX

'You put me in a difficult position, Colonel,' said the tall, bronzed man. He was in his fifties, Hardin guessed, and in superb physical condition. He wore whites which were white, freshly laundered, and he had his shirt-sleeves rolled up, exposing dark brown arms with a covering of black, curling hair. His name was Jean Diderot and like most men of French origin who had drifted to South East Asia in the old days of colonial rule, he had stayed; probably, thought Hardin, he hadn't seen France in over three decades. Most expatriates, having once tasted the laid-back life-style of the Orient, never went back.

Hardin said, 'I can understand that.'

He lounged back in the cane easy chair, his eyes taking in the wide, airy room, the souvenirs of France – almost collectors' pieces now – cluttering up the shelves, the comfortable chairs. It was a long room with two tall windows on one side, and one at each end; a fireplace was set in the only blank wall. A glass door led out on to a patio overlooking the garden, which stretched down towards the river. There was a profusion of blooms, of gorgeously-hued flowers. If he inclined his head slightly, he could see a landing-stage to the right. A small boat could just be glimpsed chugging upriver.

Diderot said, 'You understand?'

'Sure. I know the score. You have to keep in with Charlie to a certain extent, or he's going to destroy your plantation.'

Diderot stared at him, a cigarette hanging from the corner of his mouth. There was a lively intelligence in his eyes, the hint of a smile at the corners of his broad, full-lipped mouth. With the cigarette, he looked very French indeed.

'That is very forthright of you, Colonel.'

Hardin leaned forward. 'Look, sir. All I want to know is if a wounded man has arrived here in the past few hours. At this bungalow.'

'None of my workers, to my knowledge,' said Diderot carefully, 'have hurt themselves.' His English was almost accentless.

'This isn't one of your workers, and you couldn't mistake the guy. He's bleeding bad with at least one round in him, maybe more. Almost certainly more. He's lost a lot of blood. And he's somewhere round here.'

Diderot stubbed his cigarette, lit another. He was clearly a chain-smoker. Even though the windows were open and the room well-aired, there was a pungent stink of French cigarettes. It was a reek which had built up over many years.

'One can imagine then, Colonel, that this wounded man whom you are seeking is a guerilla. When you first came in you asked me my attitude towards the Viet Cong and their northern collaborators. I repeat what I said then: you put me in an uncomfortable position.' He stood up, wandered across to one of the windows and stared out. 'As you implied – and it is no secret – one has to be diplomatic in a situation like this. It can be dangerous if one nails one's colours firmly to one particular mast. I am happy to work with the Americans; it distresses me to see this beautiful country ravaged by war and violent confrontation.' He was still speaking to the window. 'Nevertheless, out here it is a long way from the towns, from the centres of population – from the American presence. Your Command has made it perfectly clear that it is not in the business of guarding foreign non-combatants or their property and possessions.

My plantation is by no means large, but it is the only plantation I have.' He turned, flashed Hardin a smile of singular charm. 'Under the circumstances, one must do the best one can. One must make one's own arrangements . . . deal with each individual situation as it arises.'

'So that if a wounded VC or EnVee regular collapsed on your front mat,' said Hardin in a neutral tone, 'you would naturally hide him and get word back to the Cong that you have him and could they collect?'

The smile vanished from Diderot's facc.

'That is a little too forthright, Colonel. And it would not be accurate.' He paused. 'Not . . . in every case. It would depend on the circumstances.' The smile appeared again. Diderot lifted his arms in a Gallic shrug. 'In any case, all this is academic. I am merely putting forward one point of view. To my knowledge there is no such man as you are looking for in my house.'

'Your house,' said Hardin flatly.

'Or in my outhouses, garden, the territory under my immediate control.'

'What about your workers?'

Diderot shrugged again. 'I cannot, of course, speak for them. It would not be difficult for a wounded man to be concealed in one of the long-houses, but I hardly think it likely. I employ Montagnards.' A sardonic smile flickered across his face. 'Doubtless, Colonel, you are aware that there is no love lost between the Montagnards and the Vietnamese. If a wounded guerilla crawled into the hamlet, he would probably end up with his throat cut.'

'Unless you had some kind of working arrangement . . .'

'Really, Colonel, I'll begin to think you don't believe me soon.'

There was a hint of anger in Diderot's voice and Hardin was gratified. So far, the guy had been altogether too cool, too smooth.

He said, 'I've been following a blood-trail all day and it ends here. To be accurate, it ends up in the woods behind your compound. My men have searched the woods. No more blood-trail. You don't have to be a genius to be able to figure out the wounded man could have ended up down here.'

'But yes,' said Diderot, 'there is a possibility. He could have done. All I am saying, Colonel, is that to my knowledge he did not.' He puffed at his cigarette. 'What has he done, this man?'

'Security, sir.'

Diderot laughed. 'Forgive me, Colonel, but that word covers many things, a multitude of, ah . . . sins. He must be very important, for you to pursue him with such zeal. You simply want this man? Nothing else?'

'I want that man,' said Hardin flatly.

Diderot walked slowly across the room. There was a roll-top desk, its pigeon-holes overflowing with papers and dockets, against the wall up from the ornate fireplace. The Frenchman stared down at the desk, picked up an ivory paper-knife, tapped the point on the blotter-pad that was centralised on the writing-top.

Hardin said, 'I'd like to search.'

Diderot's head came up. His gaze was frosty. 'And if I refuse?'

'I'll search anyway.'

'You Americans do not help your own cause, Colonel,' snapped Diderot. 'This is not your country yet, not the 53rd State. You have caused enough misery here already. I shall complain to your authorities.'

'You're perfectly at liberty to do just that, sir.'

'In the strongest possible terms.'

'Frankly, you can do it how the hell you like.'

Diderot stared at him coldly for a moment, then he breathed out slowly. He tossed the cigarette he was holding into the fireplace and fumbled in his shirt pocket for the packet. He lit another cigarette, laughed suddenly.

'Let us forget what I said, Colonel. Search, of course. I will not make trouble for you. I understand your position, Colonel, believe me. All I would ask is that you try to understand mine.' He made an open-handed gesture, as though to take in the house, garden, forest and the entire terrain unto the ends of the earth. 'We can at least be civilised about this.'

'Sure,' said Hardin softly.

He followed Diderot out into a passage. A Vietnamese houseboy in white coat and dark pants emerged from a room at the far end of the corridor, from which came the unmistakable crackle of a powerful radio on open channel.

'You don't use Montagnard houseboys,' Hardin said.

Diderot laughed shortly. 'The Montagnards are not suitable for domestic work, Colonel. They dislike work of any kind, except as a means of gratifying their love of alcohol. As plantation workers they are, at best, adequate. But they know better than to interfere with my personal servants.'

Hardin gazed into the radio-room. Most out-of-the-way settlements had a radio; it was a prime necessity. One end of the small room was cluttered with electrical equipment. There were tubes and bulbs, two open canvas holdalls with valves inside, a briefcase leaning against some rolls of copper wire, cardboard cartons of spare fitments. The radio itself had a highly sophisticated console.

'I noticed you've got a chopper-pad outside,' said Hardin.

'It is useful for one's friends. The journey up-river can be exhausting, even hazardous. You will, if you are still in the vicinity, hear a helicopter arriving tonight. Some old friends. Coming to stay.'

Hardin grinned, saluted casually.

'Yeah, we'll still be in the vicinity.'

Olsen was priming a Claymore. He inserted the blasting-cap in the hole at the top of the mine, flicked open the metal struts on which it would stand, pushed the mine down so that the legs sank into the earth. He shifted the mine very slightly, aiming its concave face outwards from the base-camp position, towards the jungle. He started unwinding the wire, moving backwards through the grass, muttering, 'Come on, slopeheads, you take a face fulla this, huh?'

Garrett, behind him, covering his rear with an M16, chuckled.

'You reckon the dinks're round here?'

'Sergeant!' said Olsen testily, steadily unwinding the wire on its metal reel. 'Goddamnit, Garrett, cut out that insubordinate bullcrap. How many goddamn times do I have to tell you, you say "Sergeant" when you speak to me. This may be a fuck-irregular unit, but you're still a pissing grunt and I'm still a pissing Sergeant!'

Garrett grinned with his teeth. They were white in the moonlight, but they did not show for very long. Garrett's smile rarely lasted more than a second or so.

'Well, I thought you'd been busted, ya know? I thought they banged ya back down to grunt status again, you shreddin' ya Loot up an all.'

Olsen shot him a dark look. 'Maybe, but the Colonel, he says I'm a Sergeant and that's good enough for me, dumbfuck.'

'I been busted up an down,' said Garrett reminiscently. 'I been a grunt, Corporal, back to grunt. Up and down. I been busted all over.'

'Yeah? Well I get any more bullshit from you, Garrett, and I'm gonna be busting you all over the China fucking Seas. Myself. Personally.'

They arrived back at the position Comeraro had chosen. It was beside the river, on a knoll clear down three sides. There were bushes on the knoll, prime cover. It was a defensible position.

Olsen led the wire into the hootch area. This, like any other hastily erected hootch area in the whole of Nam, was basically crudely-dug foxholes covered with ponchos. Olsen reflected sourly that no one was going to be using the foxholes for sleeping much this night; with only nine men it was going to be difficult to mount a guard-roster, especially as five of those men weren't at all damn squared away and he was going to have to use his own men to cover for them. He checked the rest of the Claymore lines, testing the firing devices, flicking the safeties back and forth to make certain they were not going to jam at an inopportune moment. In a conflict that depended to a very large extent on mechanisms of one kind or another, the greatest fear of all was that the machines would fuck up just when you needed them, just when the Indians were jumping over the stockade.

He stared around the hootch area. Men were cleaning

weapons, smoking, brewing coffee. He saw Hardin talking to Comeraro and Captain Renucci, and then he frowned, puzzled. He gazed around again, checking his men off in his mind. Creed. Where was that fucking Creed? The dumb fucker was missing.

'Olsen!'

Hardin was beckoning. Olsen strode across.

Hardin looked extremely pissed. He said, 'You found nothing at all in the ville?'

'Nossir. Nary a damn thing. Just a Monty ville is all. They didn't look like they was hiding anything either, sir, I gotta say. You know them Montys, sir, they ain't so damn sneaky as the Veets. Veets can look ya in the eye and ya don't know what the fuck they're thinking. The big blank face. But the Montys – well, they ain't so, like I said, sneaky.'

'That bastard's round here somewhere,' said Hardin tightly. 'He didn't just vanish into thin air.'

'With all respect, sir,' said Olsen, 'that trail was dryin' up. There were like gaps between the drops. He coulda veered off after that last blood-mark, gone off at an angle, away from the trail. We just searched in the straight line down towards the Frenchy compound, sir.' He said glumly, 'Could be anywhere sir, I gotta say that.'

To himself, Hardin acknowledged the truth of this. Although they'd searched the more open wooded slopes above the river, they had only mounted a minimal trawl of the forest nearby. The guy could be anywhere in there. He could be watching them now, laughing his fucking boots off.

Except – whatever he was doing he wasn't actually doing that. He'd lost too much blood to be able to laugh at anything.

And wherever he was, he sure as hell wasn't in Diderot's bungalow, either, or his outbuildings, or anywhere in the Frenchman's compound. That was certain. Hardin had gone through that house with a fine-tooth comb. He'd looked through closets tall and squat, he'd opened up large, ornately-decorated native chests; he'd even, for Christ's sake, peered down into water-tanks, used a long-handled broom to probe their depths. Towards the end of his search he could hear Diderot's subdued snickers of laughter as the Frenchman escorted him round. But that hadn't caused him to relax his search.

Hardin couldn't make his mind up about Diderot. He didn't like the guy, and there was something weird cooking at his bungalow, something Diderot didn't want anyone else to know about. But it didn't have to be connected with the wounded EnVee. It could be the guy was smuggling; could be he was a staging-post on the Laos-Saigon dope trail; could be he was shifting arms to the Cong; could be he was in the Goddamn white-slave traffic! Anything! Or it could simply be that his shifty attitude was merely a symptom of a general dislike of Americans. Those Frenchmen who'd remained in Vietnam tended for the most part to detest those whom they saw as the new colonialists. There was no reason for Diderot to be an exception to this.

In fact, when you got right down to it, there was actually no reason at all to link Diderot with the wounded North Vietnamese, who was probably dead by now anyway, lying in the undergrowth still clutching that goddamn bag. Or case. Or pig's valise. Whatever the fuck it was he'd sliced off from the civilian in the chopper.

Hardin spat irritably into the grass.

He said, 'I'm going on the prowl.'

Olsen wondered whether to tell Hardin about Creed, who was still, as a glance behind him confirmed, missing, then shrugged his shoulders. Time enough for that later. The guy could be simply taking a leak somewhere.

The forest was very near to the bottom of the knoll. Here Garrett and the black, Hallings, were set up. Hardin went past them, slipped into the trees. He had it in mind to circle the Montagnard hamlet and slide round the back of Diderot's bungalow, check out the action there, if any. It would do no harm.

The moon was not full. Even so, there was enough light to see – the forest canopy, the top-growth of the trees, was not as densely packed here as in the jungle of a few miles back. If he kept to the forest, he would skirt the Montagnard ville and there would be no one to see him, the Montys being a convivial race who tended to celebrate something or other just about every night of the year.

The moonlight, shining down through the trees, lent a strange and eerie quality to the scene. Unlike sunlight it sharpened objects – trees, bushes, patches of fern, the ground itself, carpeted thickly with rotting leaves, grass hussocks, dead wood. Here, in the more open forest, there were few sounds, just the odd rustle and crackle of tiny creatures foraging on the forest floor. A bat swooped. A light wind soughed through the branches of trees, sending leaves scuttering along the ground.

It was the wind that caused Hardin to glance to his right and miss his step, as he was threading his way through a shrubbery-like tangle of chest-high bushes.

He caught a flutter of movement to his side and stared at a leaf caught by the wind over the bushes and spiralling upwards before losing momentum and spinning sideways towards him through the air. Involuntarily, he ducked, stepped backwards into the bush, felt his boots sink into the earth. It felt like a hole of some kind; could be some animal's earthwork or burrow. Anything. He parted the bushes, let the moonlight chase away the shadows.

And saw that someone had been digging.

Whoever it was had tried to disguise the fact by scattering dead leaves across the patch. But the effect was wrong, and in any case Hardin could see broken earth, under-soil on top of the rotting matter.

He checked his position carefully, stared round at the surrounding trees, noted positions of clumps of fern. Then he moved fast, back the way he'd come, making no sound at all. He reached Garrett's position.

'Bring an ET. Hallings, give me yours.'

Garrett, for once, didn't argue or ask questions. He untied his own entrenching tool from his ruck and followed Hardin into the forest.

'What we got?'

'I don't know. Fresh digging. Could be what we're looking for.'

'Shit,' grumbled Garrett, 'ya see life in the army. Fuckin'

grave-digger now.'

Hardin followed his own trail back into the bushes and pointed downwards.

'Yeah,' he agreed. 'Somethin' under there okay. Not too deep, by the looksa it.'

It wasn't. They dug, though hampered by the bushes until Garrett got mad and dragged one branch back, snapping it. The sound, even in the night-silence, was not loud. Hardin shifted earth carefully, building up a mound to one side.

'Looks like ya win a Kewpie,' observed Garrett, staring down at what lay in the shallow depression at their feet. 'That's one dead dink.'

It was the EnVee all right. Hardin could even recognise his face, although the expression on it was no longer one of tense suspicion, wariness, hostility. His mouth gaped open but there was earth inside; loose soil trickled down his cheeks. His eyes gazed blankly upwards. He was in a curled position, so placed that Hardin could see exactly where he'd hit him. One round had thumped into his back and emerged through the stomach wall. The North Vietnamese had tied a scarf round himself to staunch the blood; the cloth was crusted blackly. It had not been at all effective. For nearly two days his life had been oozing slowly out on the forest floor.

Hardin knelt down, felt the man's wrist. It was cold, waxy. He tried to move it but *rigor* had already set in. It would not be long, in this climate, before the body would begin to rot.

'Hey!'

Garrett stooped, shifted earth with his ET. Hardin gazed at what the spade revealed.

A hand.

A hand sliced off well above the wrist. It looked like some fat and obscene insect from a horror movie, and for an instant Hardin thought it might suddenly start moving, scrabbling round dementedly in the earth. It was greyish in the moonlight, black around the hacked stump. There was a secure wristlet around the wrist, a chain attached to it.

Garrett put the point of his ET to the end of the chain and lifted it.

'Cut,' he grunted. 'Clean as cheese. Wire-cutters. Ain't no Monty done that.'

As Garrett said that, it suddenly flashed through Hardin's mind that he'd been looking at all this from the wrong angle. What if the guy had been making for here all the time – *heading for Diderot's compound*?

Maybe, when he realised he couldn't link up with the rest of his buddies, he deliberately drove himself, wounded and probably half-crazy, eastwards because he knew there was sanctuary here, a safe haven. And because he knew that what was in the bag was important to Diderot as well as the EnVee. Christ, maybe it had been Diderot who had somehow – yeah, the radio! – alerted the EnVee to the chopper wreck and the importance of reaching it before anyone else.

This could all be wrong too, but one thing was for sure. Like Garrett had implied, it could only have been Diderot who had clipped off the bag from the chain.

'Shit,' Hardin muttered. 'That sonuvabitch! He probably had the goddamn bag there even while I was searching the place! But I wasn't looking for a bag, I was looking for a man. No wonder the bastard was laughing!' He glared at Garrett, enraged. 'Goddamnit! I'm gonna tear that place apart, and Diderot with it!'

That was when the scream rang out.

It was not loud but in the night-silence it carried, sharp and keen, and cut off abruptly at its peak. Hardin jerked his head up, gauging the direction. He grabbed for his AK.

He snapped: 'Stay here!' Then he was sprinting through the bushes, keeping to grass as much as possible, still not making much sound at all, his eyes alert for creepers that might entangle him, logs that might trip him up. He came to a halt, listening, peering around. He heard a moaning sound, a man's tones, deep-throated. The sound puzzled him; he could not identify it precisely, but it served as a sound-beacon, drawing him to the spot from which it emanated. He moved forward more slowly now, parting bushes stealthily. The sound was louder, almost abandoned;

the man was making hardly any attempt to control himself. And as he thought that Hardin suddenly understood exactly what he was hearing, and what the sound meant.

He jumped into the bushes, dragging branches aside. In front of him was Sergeant Creed, his fatigues pants round his ankles, his heaving buttocks an ugly, leprous white in the moonlight. He was on top of a girl. Not the same one as before, the girl on the trail, but another one. It hardly mattered who or how. Creed had his hands clutched around her throat as he grunted and moaned and thrust.

Hardin suddenly realised he was still holding the entrenching tool. With a snarl he dropped his AK and swung the spade, smacking it in a sideways swipe at the back of Creed's head. There was a dull, ringing sound and the man gasped then slumped sideways, off the girl. She made no sound, no movement. Furiously Hardin dropped the spade, his AK, and reached down, grabbing at the back of Creed's collar and yanking at him, heaving him bodily to one side. The stunned man crashed into a bush. Still the girl made no vocal response, no movement.

Hardin bent down, gazed at her face in the moonlight. Her eyes were open but they were like pebbles, as blank and unseeing as those of the runner. Her throat still bore the marks of Creed's thick, spatulate fingers, deep indentations into the soft young skin. Hardin felt for her pulse, but there was nothing, not even a faint flutter. Nothing at all.

A cold rage surged up inside him, a near-berserk fury that threatened to overwhelm him totally. All kinds of violent emotions flooded through him, not all of them entirely altruistic. He hated Creed then not only because the man had raped and murdered the girl and clearly had not one spark of humanity in him. That was appalling enough. But the mindless animal had also, and this had to be faced, now seriously jeopardised the success of the mission, which had looked like it might be completed without a hell of a lot of hassle, and thrown the lives of all of Hardin's men into terrible peril.

Earlier, on the trail, the Montagnards had been on the verge of killing all the Americans; he had had to talk fast to stop them, had had to offer a drastic revenge as a sop to their outrage. The fact that he never had any intention of killing Creed was beside the point. He had had it in mind to throw the fucker into the brig as soon as they reached Do Thon, pile so many charges down on his head that he wouldn't see daylight for about a decade. But the Montagnards were not to know that, and had been satisfied with what he'd promised. And now this had happened. It was a fucking disaster.

Sure, the Montagnards regarded the Americans as a kindly white race who, like the French of former times, would look after them, protect them from the greedy and detested Vietnamese. When the Montagnard Special Forces' mercenaries had risen in revolt a half-dozen years before, they had massacred the Vietnamese, but had not touched their American officers. But they were a volatile and bloodthirsty race, and after an outrage like this their fury would not be appeased by any more vague promises of death to the principal culprit. Only blood would assuage them now.

Hardin stared down at the dead girl. He was sickened by the sight of that defenceless, ravaged body, the piteous expression on that child's face. He turned towards Creed, his own face a mask of loathing and fury.

Creed was stumbling to his feet, tugging at his pants, clipping them up. He gazed at Hardin with a mixture of unease and defiance on his face.

Hardin whispered slowly, 'God damn you to hell, Creed . . .'

Creed took a step forward, his hand rising in a defensive gesture.

'Hey now, wait up, mister. Ya got no fucking cause to . . .'

'Cause!' snarled Hardin. 'You sonuvabitch, there's every fucking cause right behind me!'

'Now come on, buddy.' Creed nervously wiped a hand over his chin. 'Less forget it, huh? Fuckin' dink bitch. What's the odds? Who cares? I mean, who fuckin' cares, buddy?' His voice was rising.

'Say your prayers.'

'Jesus, mister! Ya can't just ice me for *that*!' Creed's voice was now high-pitched; his breathing was ragged.

'Sure I can. This is a court-martial in the field, Colonel to Sergeant, and I've just found you guilty, guilty as hell. You're a dead man.'

Alarm flickered across Creed's face, and something else, some other emotion Hardin couldn't identify and in any case was too enraged to bother to try.

'Wait,' said Creed hoarsely. 'Forget that crap. Ya don't know what the fuck ya talkin' about, buddy, ya got it way-out wrong. Look, I can deal ya in. . . .'

His eyes were shifting to left and right wildly. Suddenly he lunged forward, stooping, and grabbed for Hardin's fallen AK, scooped it up. He began to breathe more slowly, more easily, an expression of ugly triumph surging across his features.

'Yer a sucker, pal,' he said. He started to laugh. 'Yer a real fucker-sucker.'

Hardin put his right hand down to his belt and unclipped his holster-flap. He drew his .45 smoothly up and out of the soft leather holder.

Creed stepped back, his face working. He could not believe what he was seeing.

He said, 'Ya stupid fuck,' and squeezed the AK's trigger. Nothing happened.

Hardin said softly 'Safety.'

'*Shit!*'

Creed's scream was stiff with blind panic; his fingers scrabbled at the weapon's stock. Hardin shot him once in the stomach. At such close range the bullet punched Creed backwards and his arms flapped uselessly in the air, the assault rifle dropping to the forest floor from his suddenly nerveless fingers. He crashed down in the bushes, his body twisted, his hands now clutched at his guts. Blood was welling past his fingers, black and thick in the moonlight, looking almost like hot chocolate. For a split second shock flooded through his system, numbing the pain – then the pain triumphed, lanced through him like an incandescent knife-blade.

'Jesus,' he whimpered. 'It . . . hurts . . .'

'I'll put you outta your misery,' said Hardin icily. 'In an hour or so. Maybe . . .'

Creed stared up at him. His face was grey and clammy with sweat; it looked like he had a heavy dew on his skin.

He said, 'Ya stupid . . . fuck. Ya don't . . .'

Hardin shot him again, this time in the chest, to the left of the heart. The round tore through bone and cartilage, its ferocious impact sending Creed tumbling backwards, deeper into the undergrowth. The man's hands, as the bullet struck him, flew upwards and blood from his fingers sprayed thickly into the air. His mouth gaped open; he was trying to speak but nothing came out except wet and ragged gargling sounds from the back of his throat.

Suddenly he articulated 'Got it all . . . wrong . . .' He said something else, something that sounded like 'haws', and then blood gushed up out of his mouth like an oil-strike.

Hardin stared down, now sickened not so much at Creed but at himself. He said coldly, 'Horseshit yourself, damn you,' and put a third bullet into Creed's heart. The squat man lurched, one hand clutching at grass spasmodically, and croaked. Then he was still.

From behind Hardin a voice said, 'Jesus Christ!' and he whipped round, ducking, the automatic now held two-fisted.

Garrett yelped '*Don't shoot!*'

Hardin relaxed. He plugged the .45 back into its holster, stared at Garrett threateningly.

Garrett said, in a voice that, for him, was almost nervous, 'Ya sure messed him around.'

'I said to stay where you were.'

'Jesus,' complained the big man. 'I heard the first shot, came running. Fuck it, I thought that was a right cool thing ta do. Ya won't get me bustin' my guts ta help ya out next . . .' His voice tailed off; he shrugged, dead-pan. Then he stared at the girl glumly. 'That Creed, he's put our nuts in the vice, for sure. The Montys're gonna get mad at this.' He looked up at Hardin, who was stone-faced in the moonlight. 'Whadda we do?'

Hardin had already made up his mind. The Montagnards would not have heard the shots; the village was too far away, and in any case round about now they'd be laying into the booze strong. He had a responsibility to his men which had priority over everything, even the mission. He stooped and pulled the girl's wraparound across her body, then said, 'Dig.'

The two men used their entrenching tools to scoop out a shallow grave, then they lifted the girl into the hollow. Hardin gently arranged her arms across her breasts, straightened her legs. They shifted the earth back, and carried armfuls of leaves and dead vegetation to the grave, piling them over in a long mound. Although this was a compassionate gesture to a certain extent, it was also a very necessary one. The Montagnards would look for the missing girl, might even find the grave. But it would take time, Hardin hoped, and by the time they did discover the body he and his men would be well away from the area. He pushed branches back into place, then nodded at Creed.

'We'll dump that bastard in with the other. Grab a leg.'

It took them five minutes to drag the heavy body back through the forest to where the EnVee lay in his opened grave. By that time they were sweating.

'See what he's got in his pockets,' said Hardin. 'I'll check out Charlie.'

Garrett said, 'He don't have nothin'.'

Hardin stared at him. Garrett shrugged.

'I looked.'

'Garrett,' said Hardin warningly.

'There was nothin'! I swear ta God! You can search me, for fuck's sake!'

Hardin thought it was typical of Garrett, scavenger that he was, to go through the pockets of a stiff. He made a quick search of the big man, who protested throughout, but found nothing.

'Okay, now Creed.'

While Garrett squatted down beside the dead American, Hardin began to dig some more, widening and deepening the hole that had been made by whoever had found the

North Vietnamese first. After a while he was satisfied that he could cram both bodies in and turned to Garrett, who was looking puzzled.

'He don't have nothin' either. No dogs, no IDs, nothin'.' Garrett peered up at Hardin. 'Kinda weird.'

Hardin shrugged. It could be weird, but there could be a simple explanation. Renucci could have his men's dog-tags, for one reason or another. It often happened out in the field that a CO would be asked to hold his men's personal documents, letters, whatever.

'The hell with it. I'll check with Captain Renucci. Let's get these bastards under.'

They heaved Creed's bloodied corpse on top of the EnVee and heaped the earth back into the grave, scuffed more leaves over it. As they laboured over this Hardin was aware of a faint clamour in the distance, a steady '*Thappa-thappa-thappa*' that grew louder and louder until it was directly overhead, roaring above them through the night sky. The sound decreased in volume, dwindled to a distant mutter.

Garrett mopped his brow.

'Hey, is that it? We bein' lifted?'

Hardin remembered what Diderot had said. That must be his buddies arriving for their month in the country.

'The Frenchy.'

'Well, that sounded to me like onea ours. A fuckin' Huey. That didn't sound to me like no fuckin' private job.'

'So he's got friends in the goddamn military,' snapped Hardin. 'One of these days, Garrett, someone's gonna open up your skull, turn the volume down. I might just do it myself.'

Garrett shrugged. 'Okay, okay.'

The trouble was, Garrett was right. The doubt he'd expressed had already blossomed in Hardin's own mind. Then he remembered that in any case he'd originally set out to take a low-level recon of Diderot's compound.

He said sourly, 'Just don't say anything, Garrett, right? Not one fucking word. Just pick up your piece and be my slack, and we'll check out the Frenchy.'

Garrett's smile travelled across his craggy face so fast it looked more like a snarl.

The bungalow looked dark, as though everyone had gone to bed, but Hardin could see chinks of light through the blinds at the front. He and Garrett were crouching in the bushes that lay to the side of the long lawn that fell away from the house down to the river. To one side, higher and to the left of the house, stood a Huey with Air Cav markings, on the flat concrete bed Hardin had noted earlier. There seemed to be no one guarding the chopper as far as he could see.

Looking at the silent helicopter Hardin thought about the Huey that had been shot down in the jungle originally, and also the Huey that had shot him and Marco down. This business was getting out of hand. Nothing made sense. And yet it was perfectly possible still that the Air Cav chopper had nothing to do with either events, that those who'd flown up in it were, in fact, US military who happened to be friends of Diderot on R-and-R. Powerful friends, sure, to be able to annex an Air Cav helicopter as private transport, but stranger and far more outrageous things were happening all the time in this crazy war. It was even possible that Diderot *was* on the level, had not cut the chain that held the bag, did not even know of the EnVee's existence.

He nudged Garrett and muttered, 'Round the back.'

They made their way silently and inconspicuously through the lush garden, half-circling the bungalow. There was a back-verandah at the rear, three doors. All of the windows were dark.

Hardin was trying to orientate himself. One of those doors opened into the passage with the radio-room in it, and as he'd just been pondering on whether or not Diderot really was on the level he'd suddenly had a visual flash of that room and what it contained, which had in turn triggered off a memory of a dictum that Halderling had hammered into him at an early age – in intelligence work the best cover is often no cover at all. That could apply here, if his memory was not at fault. He made his mind up.

'Right hand door,' he whispered to Garrett. 'Could be locked.'

'No sweat,' said the big man. 'Leave it to me. No noise, sweet and clean.'

Hardin's eyes took in the bungalow. No one at the windows that he could see. No one watching from the garden. They shadow-hopped to the edge of the verandah, slid along to the steps and up. The floor was wooden boards; they kept to the edge, holding the rail, until they were opposite the door. Garrett tried the handle, but it was locked. He felt in his pocket, bent down beside the keyhole.

Hardin flattened himself up against the wall, his back to the wood. He was perfectly positioned to control the whole of the rear of the garden visually and his eyes flicked from shadow-patch to shadow-patch for any sign of movement. But there was nothing. There was no sound either, no sign of life from the bungalow itself – until Garrett suddenly grunted to himself, a mutter of triumph. The door was open.

'Watch my back,' murmured Hardin. 'Don't do anything unless you hear shooting.'

'There gonna be any?'

'Not if I can help it.'

He stepped inside, into the corridor. Ahead, at the far end, was a door, the door to the comfortable room in which Diderot had not given him a drink or offered him a cigarette. Hardin grinned a mirthless grin. Bastard'd pay for that, with any luck. He could now hear the mutter of conversation and he stepped forward, keeping to the side of the passage in case of loose boards which would creak even under the thick matting laid over them.

There was a door on his left and it was partly open. He peered in. Although no light was on he did not need it. Moonlight filled the radio-room with its sharp, picked-clean brilliance. Hardin moved across the room, past the big transceivers, to where the clutter of spare equipment lay under the window. He checked what was there, then grinned. It had not been moved.

The briefcase that lay across the copper-wire rolls.

He stared at it, almost unwilling to go forward and pick it

up. After all, it could be any old goddamn bag. He had only glanced at it briefly before, simply taken note of the fact that it was there, and the fact, subconsciously registered, that it seemed maybe a little out of place amidst all that electrical junk.

He thought: The hell with this.

He leaned forward, picked it up by the handle. It was fat and heavy; there was more than merely paper in it. There was a short length of steel chain attached to the handle, cut off neatly. There were stains, too, now he came to look at it more closely, dark blotches on one side as though it had been clutched close to one whose blood was oozing slowly, unstoppably, out of him.

He checked the flap. It was still locked and without a key it was going to be a bitch to open. It was going to have to be blown off, in fact. That was one damn fine lock on it: combination. The bag was weighty, and Hardin knew exactly how it was constructed: thin steel plates beneath the soft black leather.

He turned, went out of the room and down the passage fast. Garrett was crouching beside the doorway, M16 cradled in his arms.

'Can you lock it again?'

'Even less sweat.'

Hardin waited while the big man fiddled at the keyhole. He wondered what to do, and then suddenly realised that he very much wanted to see who was closeted with Diderot. Sure, the wisest move, having at last gotten his hands on the case, was to split fast. But Diderot's military buddies intrigued him, and, he knew, they would also intrigue Lew Halderling, who was never averse to gleaning any kind of information – however small, however large, however dull, however outright bizarre – about anyone.

Garrett whispered, 'All set.'

Hardin handed him the case.

'Get this back to Lieutenant Comeraro. Tell him hold it. Also tell him, I want Olsen, Fuller and you back here in twenty. If I don't come out in another ten come in and get me. But it could be cool, don't make a big deal about it.'

Hardin grinned sardonically. 'I mean don't come in spraying lead unless someone's spraying it at you.'

Garrett nodded. He held the case to his chest with one hand, his unslung M16 with the other. He showed his teeth in the moonlight.

'Okay. See ya in thirty.'

They went down the steps of the verandah, and Garrett vanished into the shadows. Hardin watched him go. He had no fear that Garrett would beat it; after all, where would he head for? It was a day's hard trek through the jungle just to get to the chopper wreck, which would in any case be overrun by EnVees by now, and another day and a half, optimum-march, back to Do Thon. As for the river, he'd have to swim it, unless he stole a boat and that was not really feasible, all things considered. In any case, there was no reason for Garrett to make a run for it; every reason for him to tough it out with Hardin. The reward, once Halderling got everyone's shit together, would be worth the wait: no execution, freedom, money, even a goddamn ribbon or two!

Hardin moved round to the front of the bungalow, and unslung his AK-47. There were some flowering shrubs at the edge of the lawn, in the shadows of trees. He parted one and placed the assault-rifle and his two spare mags on the ground inside the bushy growth. Then he walked part-way across the lawn in full view of the shuttered windows and strode up the path towards the door. He mounted the verandah, banged on the door.

There was a brief interval of nothing then the unmistakable sound of army boots crossing the hallway inside. The door opened. A man in off-duty fatigues and Captain's badges stared at him in surprise. Hardin didn't say anything. The Captain frowned, puzzled.

'Were you already here, sir?'

Hardin said, 'Yeah. I was already here.'

The Captain, now looking even more puzzled, ushered him in. Hardin followed him across the hall and into the room he had been in earlier that day.

There were a number of men there, some military, some civilian. Or at least, men dressed in civilian clothes. All had drinks; most were smoking. There was a buzz of conversation which slowly died as Hardin advanced into the room. Diderot was talking to a tall man with a thick moustache. They were beside the roll-top desk, and Diderot had some papers in his hand which he was showing to the tall man. Hardin didn't recognise anyone of the military, although he noted at least one full Colonel and a couple of Majors, one of whom was wearing Intelligence flashes. Diderot glanced up and stopped talking abruptly, his face not quite registering shock.

'Why, Colonel. So you are still here.'

Hardin nodded. 'That's right. Thought I'd drop by. Socially.'

The tall man said, in French, 'Who is he?'

Diderot said, also in French, 'No, no. Wait.'

He shoved the papers at the tall man and came across to Hardin.

'My dear Colonel, will you accept a drink? Scotch, gin, rum, even some bourbon, although it is not to my own taste. But,' he gestured vaguely at the gathering, 'my friends, you know. A little party.'

'I'll take a scotch.'

'Single malt, or blended?'

'Single malt'll be fine. More than fine.' He laughed, and thought: For a guy's who's only got one small rubber plantation, this dude's living high.

He wondered if this was some kind of bizarre gay gathering. There were no women present, and all these guys looked macho to a degree. Was that what was bothering Diderot? Did they all strip down and beat each other with chains after dinner?

Behind him, Diderot said, 'I take it you will have it straight, Colonel? No water and no ice?'

But he said it in French.

Hardin took his cigarettes out of his jacket pocket, offered the pack to those nearest him. No one accepted; conversation was creaking back into life again.

Diderot said again, in French, 'Water or ice, Colonel? Or nothing?'

Hardin lit a cigarette, gazed around, beaming fatuously at the gathering. Conversation became general. Diderot appeared at his elbow holding a glass.

'I assumed you'd take it straight, Colonel,' he said in English, smiling. 'You don't look the type, if I may say so, to adulterate fine liquor.'

'Yeah. Straight it is. Thanks.'

Behind him the tall man with the moustache said, 'Who the hell is he? He's not one of ours. What in the name of God is going on?'

Diderot snapped, 'They are chasing the Vietnamese. It's a mess. But don't worry, I've got the bag and they won't find the man. He's under the earth.'

The tall man said, 'You don't think he's one of *them*, do you? My God, have we been set up?'

'Calm down! He's genuine. We've got the blasted bag back. That could have been a disaster. Now, thanks to our friends, everything's back to normal again. Don't you see?' He laughed harshly. 'It's a sign! They shoot down our transport and we *still* get the merchandise!'

Hardin sipped his malt. It was smooth and dark, smoky; it slipped down his throat like cream. He hadn't tasted such a fine whisky since he'd been in Hong Kong a couple of years back. He wondered what else the tall man and Diderot were going to spill.

The Major in Intelligence came across, a broad-shouldered man but stout. He smiled affably.

'You're on some kind of mission, I understand, sir?'

Hardin said, 'Not really. Or I wouldn't be here. It's a two-bit thing. I may abort, and head back to civilisation tomorrow.'

The tall man said, 'There's a leak somewhere, Jean. Someone told them of our flights, all the details. Someone close. You don't think it's that snooty English bastard?'

'Hardly. He knows nothing of that side of the business. He simply provides contacts and takes his cut. And keep your voice down. Even if this pig doesn't speak French, the Englishman does.'

'Well, when the hell are we going to get down to business?

This is an emergency!'

'Don't worry. I'll get rid of him.'

Hardin was saying 'Yes' and 'Oh?' and 'Sure' to the Major in Intelligence while his eyes were drifting round the room. At the far end from him he saw a middle-aged civilian with greying hair, a thin nose, an expression of elegant distaste on his narrow, patrician features. Presumably the Englishman. The man shot his cuffs irritably, yawned.

As he did that a new voice suddenly bellowed in French, '*What the bloody hell is he doing here? Have you gone bloody mad, Jean?*'

At the sound of that fierce, rasping voice, Hardin felt as though someone had thrust a red-hot poker into his central nervous system. He actually felt the hairs at the back of his neck bristle, and a jolt of sheer, naked panic lanced through him. That took no more than a micro-second of time, and then he was moving into a blur of action.

Even on entering the room he had taken note automatically of furniture positions, windows, doors. Now he slammed into the Major and sent him reeling backwards into two or three men behind. He jumped forward, bounded towards the glass door that opened out on to the garden, his right hand reaching for his automatic even as he careered across the room, smashing a path through the crowd of shouting drinkers.

'*Stop him!*' howled the voice. '*Stop that bastard!*'

Hardin hurled himself at the glass door and gasped with pain as it withstood his charge. With sickening clarity he realised that the fucking door opened inwards, not outwards. And the glass was reinforced. He was flung back on the rebound and someone banged at his hand which by now had dragged his gun out. The automatic spun away from him.

He dived for it, and then something hit him in the back and jolted him off-balance. A hand caught at him, swung him round.

'You swine!' hissed the man who had once begun calmly to extract his back teeth in the stinking cellar in that pretty villa in the suburbs of Algiers. Henri Guerini. The Corsican.

The man they called La Bête.

Hardin threw a punch at him. It was a good one, a solid right to the jaw. The Corsican laughed. His left fist came up and out, with all the force and speed of a steam-hammer. It thudded into Hardin's stomach and the impact actually lifted him off his feet. He jack-knifed, collapsed to the floor, vomiting the single malt all over the carpet.

Guerini's boot descended and Hardin screamed shrilly as a blaze of agony erupted up from his groin, shooting through every nerve-fibre in his body.

Through a haze of nausea and pain he heard the Corsican say, 'Pick him up – *pick him up!* I want to do this slowly . . .'

X

Hardin gagged but nothing happened, nothing came up. There was nothing left in his stomach but pain.

He lay on the floor, curled round in an agonised crescent-moon shape. Every nerve-end throbbed, every bone in his body seemed to ache. Bloody saliva drooled from his mouth; he saw the carpet near his face through bleary, dazed eyes that could not register details.

And yet a part of his brain was still alert.

At first he'd fought. He'd fought hard and viciously. There were at least three men who were now damaged seriously, one of them – from two stiff fingers, jabbed like steel rods at the face – had even lost an eye. But one man against maybe a dozen, maybe more, could not hold out for very long.

At last he'd buckled to the floor, pounded down by brutal blows to the head and body. Then he'd been dragged up again, held firmly by the arms – and La Bête had started in on him. Savage kicks to the groin, haymakers to the stomach and chest, brain-dislodging blows to the side of the head.

And all the time, while pain flooded and surged through his body, while he gagged and threw up until he could vomit no more, while his head seemed to ring with a thousand bells whose sound seemed to transform itself with each jolting punch or kick into wild flares of agony that coursed up and down his nerve-ends, he still managed to retain a vestige of intelligent thought in his brain. Something held back and covered over automatically, something defended in the furthest caverns of his mind: a spark of intelligence that had to be kept alive at all costs.

Now he lay on the floor trying desperately not to drift into the oblivion of unconsciousness. It would be easy to let go, so easy. Let go and fade into the comfortable, soothing darkness.

Too easy.

He marshalled what strength of will he still possessed and fought the urge.

A long time ago – it seemed like goddamn millennia, lying here on the floor surrounded by enemies – he'd learned the trick of taking terrible body-punishment. You took so much, and you let them think you were taking it all. There was a way of rolling with the punches, letting the kicks only get so far but no farther. As long as you took some, and it could be seen that you were taking it – *punishment must be seen to be done!*, he thought, and as he thought it he knew he was beginning to crawl back – there were ways you could fake the rest. Now, dazed and blurry-eyed, he forced himself to relax, to let new strength seep into his muscles; he forced himself to think, and listen, and plan.

Above him Diderot was saying angrily, 'How the hell was I to know he was some damned enemy of yours! Am I expected to recognise every man in the past twenty years who's crossed you? Ridiculous!'

'Marais and Bellemain recognised the swine. Tried to knock him off, but he was too fast. He was always fast, like a blasted snake. He moved fast when he did this.' The Corsican tore at his shirt, tugged it out of his pants and exposed his brown, scarred stomach. He jabbed a finger at one old, long-healed wound, a gash of white running down towards his groin. 'There! By God he moved fast then, when those dirty OAS swine blew the Villa Dar Es Saada and he grabbed a knife and stuck me. The bastard nearly finished me with this one there and then. I swore I'd use his entrails as a rope to string him up if I ever got my hands on him again, and by God I'll do that and more before I'm through. He'll be eating his own prick before I've finished with the bastard.'

Diderot said sharply, 'This is no time for your private feuds. He has men out there. What the hell happens when they start getting restless?'

'We have men too, loyal to us.' That was the tall man with the moustache. 'What is the strength of his force?'

'How the hell should I know? D'you think I went out there and counted heads? The first thing I knew was when he walked in earlier and started asking questions about the EnVee. It seems they were chasing him, presumably for the bag. Although the impression I got was he was simply after the man.'

'How can you be so certain?' the tall man snapped. 'I think he's one of the enemy. We have brothers in the US forces, they have too. Italians, Sicilian trash. That's how they're able to shoot down our couriers. If we can manoeuvre our men to do special jobs for us without their Command knowing a damned thing about it, so can they.'

'But they can't do that without knowledge in the first place, concrete information! Goddamnit!' That was the Intelligence Major; Hardin recognised his voice. The French accent was almost flawless. The oath at the end was spat out in English, though, and he went on in that language, bitterly. 'Someone's blowing our routes to the enemy!'

'That's what I said.' That was the tall man again. 'I said that to Jean. It's the only answer. It has to be someone working with us at the top. It could be one of us *here!*'

'In the name of God!' Diderot. 'Whoever it is, it can't be this pig, can it! Talk sense! And we don't even know he was after the bloody bag at all! Maybe he *was* just after the man, without knowing what the man had.'

'Crap!' The Corsican. 'Don't tell me a force of Americans, and one headed by this swine, chases a man through the forest just to capture him. One man! My God!'

'Maybe he has back-up . . .'

That was the Intelligence Major. He said it slowly and

there was a sudden silence, broken by hurried footsteps leaving the room, the slam of a door. Then there was the scrape of a match, an intake of breath, a loud exhalation.

'If he has back-up, and it's muscular, and it's heading in our direction,' the Major said, 'I'm getting out. No argument. As far as I'm concerned you can deal me straight outta this one. I'll slide information to you, cook the books, do all I can to shift the stuff along nice and easy. I'll shake hands with as many of the goddamn gooks as you like, so long as things are sweet. But if the shit's hitting the fan I'm running for cover damn fast. I don't mind taking risks. I'm a brother. But they've gotta be, for Christ's sake, calculated risks – and this deal's starting to run wild. The goddamn brake-fluid's leaking.'

'Such loyalty,' sneered the Corsican.

'I don't have to prove my loyalty to you, mister!' snarled the Major. 'Could be the situation would've been cleaner if you hadn't come in like a fucking bull just now.'

'Little friend,' said the Corsican in harsh Marseilles French, 'you are beginning to annoy me.'

'Might I point out,' said a voice, new to Hardin, English, a cultured but acerbic drawl, 'that our information is that the opposition have put aside three hundred million dollars to destroy us.'

'And what the hell's that gotta do with this?' snapped the Major.

'Merely that they need not have bothered. They need not spend a cent. We can do the job ourselves, for nothing. Might I also point out that we don't know anything about this man! We don't know whether he knows our business or not, whether he has, as you put it, back-up, whether it's simply bad luck that he's here at all.'

'So let's find out,' said another American voice.

Hardin felt hands gripping him, pulling him up. He forced himself to become a dead weight; not difficult, under the circumstances. He groaned with pain, muttered incoherently. He was dragged to his feet, held upright. He gazed blearily at the American Colonel.

He was a Marine, 1st Div. Tall, sandy hair in a close

crew-cut, long bony chin. He was in his fifties. He was smoking a pipe and he stared at Hardin impassively, but Hardin could see unease in his light brown eyes.

'You'd better make it easy on yourself. Did anyone send you here? If so, who?'

'I don't know what's going on,' said Hardin thickly. 'I don't know what the fuck you're talking about.'

The Major stared at him thoughtfully. His brow was creased up into vertical lines of puzzled suspicion.

'You can do better than that,' said the Colonel.

'There's no way I can do better, mister,' mumbled Hardin. 'There was a chopper crash in the jungle. The EnVee attacked. We beat 'em off. I got sent out to chase the survivors. We tracked one guy. What the hell else is there?'

'You tell me,' said the Colonel.

'For Christ's sake! There's nothing to tell!'

Hardin put everything he had into that, every nuance of weariness and misery that he could summon up. The Colonel gazed at him reflectively, slowly puffing at the pipe. He suddenly turned to the others.

'You know, I think we fucked up. I got a gut feeling this bastard's on the level.'

'This one? On the level?' The Corsican spat at the floor.

The Major suddenly snapped his fingers. 'Hardin. Wait a minute. He's with Halderling. I remember now.'

The Colonel shrugged. 'So what? He works for Halderling. So Halderling runs an undercover hit-group. Still doesn't mean dog-shit.'

All at once the Corsican gave a grunt of fury, leaned forward and smashed a vicious backhander across Hardin's face. Hardin gasped, staggered backwards. His mind was a buzzing kaleidoscope of pain.

'Let me have the pig,' snarled Guerini. 'Even if he's got nothing to talk about, I'll make him talk. I'll make the bastard *sing!*'

The door behind them crashed open and the group of men swung round almost as one. In the doorway stood Diderot. His face was pasty-white with rage; his right hand, which clutched at the door, was trembling.

'The bag,' he managed to get out, 'the blasted bag! It's gone!'

Hardin closed his eyes wearily and wondered where the hell Olsen, Fuller and Garrett had got to. The US cavalry seemed to be taking its own sweet fucking time in arriving.

Garrett was staring down at the contents of the bag, now revealed in the moonlight to his stunned gaze. In fact he was almost in a state of shock, although not so much that he could not whisper incredulously, 'Fat *city!*'

After leaving Hardin he'd threaded his way back through the trees, circled the Montagnard settlement – which seemed, now, oddly quiet – then headed round into the thicker jungle back towards Comeraro's fire-base.

He could not have said exactly when he'd formulated the thought that maybe a glance through the contents of the bag he was carrying might not be such a bad idea; if he'd thought about it at all he would probably have said that it came by degrees, slid into his mind slowly and sinuously and insidiously, until he suddenly jammed the case down on the ground, levelled his M16 on single shot, and blew the lock away.

It occurred to him that Hardin was going to be pissed, and then it occurred to him that Hardin need never know. The contents of the bag were probably top secret, or why all the fuss? But the odds were that all he'd find would be paper: documents, maps, all that garbage. Nothing you could make a buck on. Well sure, you could probably make a hell of a lot of bucks, but you had to have the contacts. Garrett did not have the contacts. Not now. As for Hardin being pissed about him blowing the lock off, he could say Comeraro did it, and he could tell Comeraro Hardin did it. Simple. They were neither of them going to be arguing a fucking post mortem about it.

He wrenched the clasp of the lock off, unflapped the bag, pulled it open. Even in the moonlight what was inside was instantly recognisable.

There were ten clear glassine bags filled with a white powder.

It wasn't sugar and it wasn't flour and it wasn't refined salt and it wasn't, for Chrissake, any other commodity in the entire Goddamn world but heroin.

There were ten kilos of heroin hydrochloride in the bag.

Ten fuckin' keys of horse!

And it was white, too. It was snow white. It was No. 4 heroin, so pure that if you hit intravenously you died, you goddamn *died!*

'Holy shit,' muttered Garrett.

When this junk was cut and cut and cut again – with powdered milk, quinine, lactose, mannite, talcum powder, starch, what the hell – the value of each individual key would be heading up towards one million dollars.

Which meant that right here in front of him was horse to the value of maybe ten million bucks!

Garrett gazed at the sight in awe.

He groaned 'Jesus H. *Christ!*' as though he was in acute pain.

He banged the bag shut, glanced nervously over his shoulder. He was literally appalled. He did not know what the hell to do. He had a fortune here in his hands and he was in the middle of the fucking jungle in the middle of fucking Vietnam half a world away from the fucking World and he did not know what the *crap* to do.

He squatted down in the grass and tried to figure out a plan of action.

He could not go back to Comeraro. He could not go back to Hardin. He could not hijack that chopper at the Frenchy's compound because he could not fly and there were going to be too many problems trying to find someone who could fly. He could not take to the river because he did not even know where it led to and he might capsize or get captured by gooks. He could not set off into the jungle because that was the stupidest thing ever a lone man could do with no food, no water, no equipment, and he might be bitten by snakes or eaten by tigers. Or captured by gooks.

Garrett said, low-voiced, 'Gimme a solution, God, an spare my life so I can use all this dough, an I swear, I fuckin' swear, I will be a motherfucker of a right guy from now on.'

There was no sign that God had heard. Or if he heard, he made no reply. Garrett, sighing, racking his brain for some way out of this sheerly hellish situation, reached for the bag and stood up.

And froze in horror.

The cavalry were not going to arrive. And now Hardin knew what was in the bag he also knew why the cavalry were not going to arrive.

It was obvious. Garrett must've opened the bag. It was the only solution. He'd opened Pandora's Box and the fairies and evil spirits had flown out and Garrett wouldn't ever be seen again. The irony of it was that the greedy fucker would almost certainly try and strike out alone into the jungle, heading east without even a ruck, and if he made ten miles without being killed by Charlie or savaged by the wild-life he'd be lucky. And Garrett had never struck him as a man on whom Lady Luck smiled too often.

Hardin wiped an arm across his face and slumped back wearily against the wall of the cellar. It was not actually a cellar, but with the Corsican within striking distance it sure felt like one; it felt exactly like one. For Hardin, it brought back a deal of memories.

Actually, it was Diderot's liquor store, slightly below the ground-floor of the bungalow. Because it was situated on a small hill, the bungalow was not constructed on piles but set into the ground. Outside the door was a wide, well-lit passage and although there were plenty of possibilities, weaponswise, in the room – scores of bottles of wine and spirits – the door opened inwards flat against a wall and there was a commanding fire-line from the wide doorway. Tom Swift might've been able to coldcock a guy standing in the doorway with a bottle but the guy would have to be pretty dumb. These fuckers upstairs were by no means dumb.

Hardin had been left his cigarettes and a book of two matches, both of which were damp. He fished out a cigarette and began scraping away with one of the card matches. After some moments it spluttered into life and he was just able to catch a sparking flame before it died. He sucked smoke greedily.

He now had a rough picture of what was going on and what he didn't know he could fill in without too much brain-pain. It was really very simple, when you got the hang of it, and it explained everything, every weird, seemingly inexplicable angle.

The French were running heroin from Laos to Saigon, and thence to Marseilles.

Simple. Well, maybe not quite that simple, given what had been happening recently, but simple enough. The French were mostly Corsicans, of course, the *Union Corse*. They'd had a stranglehold on South East Asia for decades; it was their prime source of the drug. Opium from the Golden Triangle transmuted into pure heroin from the morphine base in the laboratories of Laos, then shipped to Marseilles for further refinement and then sent to the States, where it would be cut down in the narcotics mills of Brooklyn or Queens or Manhattan's East Side and shifted out on to the street in bags containing probably one-in-ten (one part heroin to nine parts crap) or in the case of the pure No. 4, 'croak-dope', one-in-fifteen, or maybe more depending on the sheer genuine zap of the original.

The South East Asia goldmine was a gigantic enterprise, and thus a prize of stupendous proportions, and it now appeared that the Italians – or, more accurately, the Sicilians, the *Unione Siciliana*, getting right down to it, the goddamn Mafia – had decided that they wanted a piece of the action. Not just a piece, come to think of it; they wanted the whole fershlugginer pot. And if, as Hardin had heard while slumped on the floor, the Mafia were willing to lay out three hundred million dollars simply to eliminate the Corsicans, they weren't kidding around.

And although three hundred million bucks was no big deal in the wider context of the entire drugs industry, it was more than enough to bribe politicians, the fuzz, Narcs, and especially members of the US armed forces over here in Nam, many of whom were of Italian extraction anyhow and would not need that much bribing. It would all be in The Family. Exactly how the Mafia liked it.

And of course they'd already started. Hardin could follow the chain of events almost from the beginning, and doing just that was a relief from contemplating the bruised and aching shell that was his own body.

The chopper from Laos had been a regular runner for the Corsicans, a black flight no one in Command, or lower, would know about. Easy enough to set up a regular cross-border courier flight. The Corsicans had money too, and plenty of it to spend on guys who would man the choppers or be only too happy to look the other way.

Somehow the Sicilians, in their take-over drive, had gotten wind of this and spent some of their money, fixed for their own choppers to shoot the Corsican transport down, a first nail in the coffin. Panic for the Corsicans! But they had another angle. The Corsicans were French, and the French in this country – certainly those who had plantations out in bandit territory – were closer to Charlie than they were to the Americans. Maybe there was an EnVee element in this anyhow – both the Cong and the North Vietnamese needed bread bad; they could subsidise arms- and materiél-buying by helping out along the line.

So the Corsicans told the EnVee to make the pick-up from the wreck. Which they did. And that brought Hardin back to the here and now and his own position in the deck.

He was a wild card; to put it another way, a kick in the Corsicans' butt from fate. It was sheer irony that one of the Corsicans happened to be that bastard Guerini; sheer irony, too, that he had been tugged into this business by being knocked out of the sky by the Mafia-linked flyboys nosing around the wreck when he and Marco were only out for a goddamn spin! Irony was funny the way it worked. Hardin reflected that unless he could think of something to get him out of this fast, it was going to be killingly funny.

He pulled at the cigarette again, started flexing his arms, his legs. It would be a hell of a time before his aches disappeared – and maybe he'd be dead before they did – but he wasn't feeling too battered right now. His stomach hurt like hell, but only if he remembered to think about it. He promptly forgot about his stomach.

From what he'd heard, after Diderot came back into the room, there were ten kilos of pure in that case that once had been chained to an unknown man's hand. That was a lot of pure.

At first he'd thought they were going to ice him right there, but in fact, although they pushed him around some, the steam had gone out of them. Diderot genuinely believed it could not have been Hardin who'd taken the bag. He based this on the fact that all the doors to the rear of the bungalow were still locked, and the locks themselves were shit-hot, specially-fitted, supposedly burglar-proof. Hardin reflected that he must remember to congratulate Garrett on his lock-picking skills – after he'd finished kicking his ass all over Nam.

Even Guerini's tide of murderous rage had ebbed away from Hardin as target to the unknown who, it seemed, had been blowing all their secure stuff to the Sicilians. Furious arguments had broken out. If the bag was missing and the doors were still locked, the bag had to be still in the bungalow. The traitor had to be actually in the room.

Hardin had his own ideas about that. He was remembering who Will Steeger had bumped into at the Continental Hotel's street café. There was a Frenchman: that was Diderot. There was a gorilla: Guerini, La Bête. There was an aristocratic type: that was the Englishman, name unknown.

And there was Luke Dowling.

Luke the Spook.

It was an open secret that the CIA, using their straw-airline, Air America, was running heroin across South East Asia. That was an indisputable fact. Sure, it was supposedly part of their own master-plan of economic warfare – the more Vietnamese you got hooked, the less they're gonna turn to the Cong; the more Cong you got hooked, the less they're gonna fight: *smart!* – but someone was making money somewhere. The spooks weren't doing this for free.

And what if someone out at Langley had been playing with his abacus and had suddenly been struck by the stunning economic truth that one group of guys running heroin would get better profits, more jack, than two groups of guys, working independently.

Hardin had no doubt at all that the CIA, or at least an element of the CIA, had teamed up in an unholy alliance with the Sicilian Mafia to smash the French-Corsican control of the South East Asian heroin market. It would be entirely in keeping with all he knew about the Company, and everything that he himself had experienced at its hands, and as someone who, as a member of Halderling's SSG, had often worked along parallel lines with that power-hungry organisation. Hardin knew for a stone-cold fact that the CIA had links with the Mafia that went way beyond the Bay of Pigs, right back to the forties.

Dowling had been infiltrated into the French set-up. He'd worked in Vientiane, in Laos, and he knew the heroin trade. The Corsicans would have been delighted to welcome him into the fold: his own network of contacts would be a rich prize. They probably loved him like a brother.

And all the time, Hardin thought, the fucker was selling them down the river.

The cellar door suddenly opened. With a sinking heart Hardin saw his entire squad being hustled through the doorway towards him.

'Christ,' said Comeraro in an aggrieved voice, 'I mean, what the hell was I supposed to do? There's this guy, he's a full fucking Colonel, and he's got more brass with him, and he marches past our pickets and says we have to haul ass over to the bungalow. So I think the hell with this and I'm about to refer him to Captain Renucci when I discover that Captain Renucci isn't goddamn there, and this Colonel is very clearly getting very uptight and saying this is an emergency, shift your butts. So we head this way fast and get jumped on as soon as we enter the door. There's an assortment of evil-looking grunts with M16s covering our front and the brass at the back covering our rear.' He shrugged helplessly. 'And that's it.' He stared at Hardin. 'They worked you over, sir. What in Christ's name is this all about?'

Hardin shook his head and said, 'Later. So they don't know about Renucci?'

'Nope. He's out there somewhere. I dunno where.'

Hardin thought: Renucci could be *my* wild card, except for one thing – *why* wasn't he there when the Corsican contingent arrived? He suddenly had an odd feeling about Captain Renucci. 'When did he split?'

'Couldn't have been more'n a few seconds before these guys reached the top of the knoll. We could see 'em from there, as they came past the guys I'd posted at the bottom. Hallings, here,' he jerked a thumb at the black, 'was just about to get his ass chewed by me because he'd moseyed up from his position bitching that you'd taken Garrett and that was a time ago, and then I saw that Colonel and his group heading towards us. Renucci must've gone to take a leak, maybe.'

And maybe not, thought Hardin.

Olsen said, 'Beggin' your pardon, Colonel, but I gotta say that that Creed split, too. He ain't come back.'

'Forget about Creed.'

'Oh. Okay. Right, sir.' Olsen, a wise and experienced Papa Sierra, recognised a certain tone in Hardin's voice. 'But I haveta say these other guys ain't too squared away. They need, frankly, to be thrown back to boot camp an' screamed at a lot. That's actually what I think, Colonel.'

Hardin said, 'You know something, Sarge? I agree with you – hundred-and-one per cent.' He turned to Snell. 'Gimme your name, number.'

Snell stared at him. He said, 'Uh, sure. Snell. James Snell. Uh . . . Five Oh Six, uh . . . Three, uh . . . Five . . . sir.'

Olsen glared at the man. He opened his mouth, but Hardin waved him down. He jabbed a finger at Hallings.

'Now you.'

The black grinned nervously.

'Ri' – uh, Phil Hallings, sir. Six Oh Five Three, uh . . . Four.'

'Now you.' Hardin pointed at Rand.

'Rand, William,' snapped the man. He stared disgustedly at the other two. 'Seven Six Nine Three Four One.'

'Congratulations,' said Hardin dryly. 'You got the right number of digits. But even Garrett could beat you in delivery. Let's hear it from you, Lieutenant.'

Comeraro looked at him blankly for a moment, then stamped to attention. 'Comeraro! Arthur! One L-T! Oh Nine Eight Oh Six Four! Sir!

Hardin nodded. He turned to Laguna and smiled at him. It was the smile of a wolf. He now knew why Creed had no dog-tags. Laguna licked his lips, his eyes wary.

'Let's cut out the crap, Laguna – if that is your name. You're not in the army. None of you are. You're working for the Mafia. To be precise, you're working for the Sicilians.' He smiled again. 'Okay?'

Laguna stared at him. 'You're crazy.'

'No – "You're crazy, *sir*",' said Hardin gently. 'That's how you address an officer when you're in the armed forces of the United States. Now, can I hear that again?'

'Look, mister . . .' said Laguna dangerously.

Hardin hit him. His left fist thudded into the olive-skinned man's stomach and he jack-knifed. Hardin sent a driving right into the man's face, slamming him backwards. Laguna hit the wall, slid down it, blood flooding from his nose.

Hallings jumped for Hardin but Fuller was in between. Fuller's left arm swung out stiffly, smacking into his throat. The black shot sideways with a strangled yell.

Hardin massaged the knuckles of his right hand thoughtfully. He said, 'Laguna, your balls are on the table and I got me a hatchet. You're in shit neck-deep. Those guys upstairs are very pissed. They're *murderously* pissed. There's some talk of maybe ten keys of scag gone astray and they're ready to massacre everyone in sight, but especially they're ready to massacre anyone who might have some connection with a certain Sicilian organisation who are trying to elbow them out of a very profitable business. All I have to do is give 'em the nod and they're gonna strip the flesh off you just for starters. Then they're really gonna get mad. Get me?'

Laguna stumbled to his feet, wiping the blood from his nose with his sleeve. His face was grey.

'Look, I don't know nothin' about any Mafia,' he said shakily.

'That's a double negative,' said Hardin. 'It actually means you *do* know *something* about any Mafia.' He said to Comeraro conversationally, 'Did you notice that? Classic case of the Freudian slip. His subconscious was giving the game away.'

Laguna gazed at Hardin, his eyes wide. There was a wild expression on his face. He swallowed a couple of times.

'Renucci brought us in. With a whole buncha other guys. We were given these jungle outfits, see, all the gear, the pieces, ammo. There was a bag in this helicopter wreck. We had to get it. We had to waste anyone trieda stop us. Military, anyone. They said no one'd bother us anyways when we were flown in because there were like a thousand other guys down there. But we hadda get that bag, whatever.'

As he spoke, Hardin remembered the harassed L-T at the scene of the wreck: '*Some of these guys I've never seen before in my life!*' He remembered too what Creed had tried to say just before he'd died. 'Horse' not 'horseshit'. He'd been trying to deal Hardin in, to save himself. Too bad about Creed. He wasn't going to be getting any of the profits. Where he'd gone, he wouldn't be getting anything!

Laguna said, 'Then when we got down there, into the jungle, we came under attack and that's when things went down the sluice. Most of the men were left upstairs, in the helicopter. Then you arrived and Renucci, he recognised you. He's actually in the army, works behind a desk in Saigon. He said there was only one reason a dude like you'd be down there and that was to get the bag. He said he knew your rep, knew you worked for some special group. He said it was too much of a coincidence. So we tagged along. And that's it.'

'Yeah,' murmured Hardin. 'That is surely it.'

Renucci must've recognised some of the military here too, he thought. Could be he figured they might ask awkward questions: like, what's a Remington Raider doing up in the jungle with a combat unit? They could start getting suspicious. Although it was more likely that he knew them for what they were, knew of their affiliation with the *Union Corse*. He probably suspected a trap of some kind.

But all this was academic. He suddenly turned on Rand. 'You're a deserter.'

'I ain't sayin' nothin',' growled the man.

'It doesn't matter,' shrugged Hardin. 'The way things are, you'll soon be a dead deserter.' He said to Comeraro, 'Where did they put your weapons?'

'Just slung 'em down in the hallway. They took everything.'

'With all respect, sir.' Olsen stepped forward. He was grinning broadly, but there was a touch of something else on his face: a hint of craftiness.

'They actually didn't take everything, sir.' He pushed a hand deep into his pants' side-pocket. 'Got a hole in this one, sir, an' it goes right down to the lining, and frankly this just might pull our nuts out, I gotta say, or at least damage those bastards around a little.'

He held out his hand. Hardin stared at what lay in it.

He said admiringly, 'Goddamnit, Olsen, I'm gonna put you up for a Silver Star if we get outta this.'

They'd brought him back to Diderot's living-room, the Major in Intelligence and a surly-looking grunt. He wondered just how many grunts had come up with the chopper. It couldn't be that many. Comeraro had counted seven when he'd been disarmed. Hardin hoped there were no more than that although, the way things were heading, it might not matter how many spare grunts the Corsican faction had brought with them as honour-guard as far as he personally was concerned, because it looked very much like they were going to knock him off right here and now, no argument.

'I want him,' La Bête was saying. 'I want that bastard for myself.'

Diderot snapped, 'I told you, forget about your private feuds! This business is too damned important for us to be bothered with side-issues!'

'It's no side-issue . . .'

Diderot smashed his fist down on the desk. 'By God, this

time you'll do as *I* say!' He swung round on Hardin. 'No more prevarication. Where is the bag?'

'I've already told you, I don't know what the hell you're talking about. We were chasing a gook. We lost him. We got here. That's it.' Hardin suddenly noticed there was a lighter on the desk. Diderot's furious assault had cleared papers off it. It was what he desperately needed. He'd been thinking that maybe he could mug it up a little, ask for a last cigarette – but that now seemed, the mood these guys were in, out of the question.

'Look, Colonel, we don't believe you.' The Major crossed the room, stood just out of arm's reach. 'You're the only guy who could have taken the bag. You picked the lock, relocked the door. It's obvious.'

'Last time I was here,' said Hardin, 'you were hot for someone in this very room, someone on your own side. Someone very close to the top echelons of your own organisation, as far as I can gather, is blowing your secrets. So why shouldn't he have grabbed this bag?'

'I'll get it out of him,' growled Guerini. 'I'll *cut* it out of the pig!'

'That's not the answer!' snapped Diderot.

But the huge Corsican took no notice. He lunged forward, grabbed for Hardin's throat. Hardin jerked to one side but the Corsican kicked out and Hardin, pain spearing up his leg, staggered. La Bête caught him, gripped his wrists together behind him with one huge hand and pulled him close, his right hand hooking up to Hardin's neck.

'Talk,' he snarled. 'Talk or I'll pull your throat apart with my bare fingers. You know I can do it, swine. You've watched me in the cellar, strung up like a piece of meat. I should've finished you off long ago.'

The strength of the man was frightening, even to Hardin. He tried to shift his position, tried to twist himself away from Guerini so that he could get in a knee to the groin. But he could barely move, and Guerini, wary of just such a manoeuvre, had so positioned himself that he was almost sideways on to Hardin. He was smiling, his face only inches away.

'Either that or I'll twist your head in a circle, my friend. Three hundred and sixty degrees.'

He inched his fingers upwards slightly, pushed at Hardin's jaw. Hardin felt the right side of his neck begin to burn with pain. The fingers were digging into him, feeling for his pressure-point. He began to black out.

Then, through the dull roaring in his ears, he heard the sound of breaking glass. Instantly, the pressure was relieved as Guerini thrust him aside with an animal-like growl of frustrated fury. Hardin reeled back against the wall beside the desk. Almost automatically his left hand scrabbled at the papers, closed around the lighter, scooped it up. He winced and focused on the room as more glass shattered.

It was the windows. From outside the blinds were being torn aside by brown hands. It was like a horror movie he had once seen – crazy people in cells, and the only parts of them you could see clearly were their hands clutching out blindly from barred hatchways. Other objects were being thrust into the room through the broken glass – M16 barrels. The group of men in the room stood as though paralysed. A few had started to reach for their own guns at the first crash, but as more and more rifles, not only M16s but AKs and even older weapons, were shoved through the window it seemed like suicide to move.

There was a heavy blow on the locked French-window door; something thudded at the reinforced glass. Then an assault rifle stammered briefly and the wood and metal around the lock erupted into the room. The door was kicked open. A Montagnard holding an Armalite appeared in the doorway.

He wore a loin-cloth, although incongruously the upper half of his body was cloaked in an olive-drab jungle fatigues jacket. A medallion on a thong bounced on his chest as he suddenly jumped fast into the room, gesturing with the rifle, followed by six more men, similarly garbed. All wore paint-marks on their faces, mud and vegetable dyes; one wore a grunt's helmet.

The total effect – the outright weirdness of their clothes – was almost laughable. But no one laughed. No one who looked into the naked, savage fury on their faces even so much as twitched.

Certainly the Englishman did not move. He stared at the men as though they were apparitions, hideous phantoms come to drag them all down to some unspeakable Hell. England seemed a million miles away. In fact he felt as though he'd been transported to another planet. His stomach was churning, his hands were shaking, trembling almost uncontrollably. He was looking for nothing now except salvation. The money, the drug deals, the power and the contacts gained via close association with the Corsicans were all useless, as insubstantial as shadows. His career, his own personal power, his lofty aspirations, the glittering prizes that had been heaped upon him in his own country were just so much dust.

He saw Diderot shouting at one of the men in French – What were they doing? Had they gone mad? He had never treated them badly! What in God's name did they want? – but the man simply stared back as though the Frenchman had not said a word.

Then he stepped to one side and another man – another bloody cannibal, thought the Englishman, shuddering – entered the room. The man was slightly taller than the rest, certainly plumper, and with more markings on his face and body. He held a machete in one hand. The Englishman felt as though nothing was going to stop him from being sick.

The man whom Diderot had shouted at said in French, 'Lao very angry. Only blood will appease.'

Diderot said shrilly, 'For God's sake, what the hell is this? What d'you want? Just tell me!'

The man said, 'There is a girl. Daughter of Lao . . .'

He got no further because there was a sudden movement at the back of the room and the Englishman saw the American Colonel – the one they called Hardin, the one against whom that animal Guerini seemed to have some kind of grudge – move forward, begin to speak in a high-pitched chattering voice quite unlike his normal tones. The man listened to what Hardin was saying impassively, his head on one side. Then he seemed to be asking questions, and Hardin made an odd motion with his right hand – a movement that all at once transformed itself into a gesture directed towards the Corsican.

There was a sigh from two or three of the savages – long and drawn-out. Then three of them pointed their guns at Guerini, jabbering at him menacingly. The Corsican gazed at them uncomprehendingly.

Hardin said, in English, 'They seem to want you, Guerini.'

The Corsican tensed, then swung round, glaring at the rest of the room.

'What? What is this?'

'You,' said Hardin. 'They want you to go with them.'

At a shout from the man who had spoken before, more Montagnards advanced through the door, armed like the others with rifles. They circled the Corsican, who stared at them in utter disbelief. Then they began to make jabbing motions with their guns. Guerini let out a bull-like roar of fury.

'What the hell is this? You swine, Hardin! What've you done?!'

'You,' said Hardin softly. There was a chilling smile on his face.

Guerini grabbed at one of the rifle-barrels, lugged it towards him as his left arm slammed round at dark brown faces. He caught at one of the men, tried to pitch into the rest but a second man jumped behind him, began clubbing at the back of his head with the butt of an Armalite. With a terrible roar of fury and pain the maddened Corsican lashed out with fists and feet. Another Montagnard rammed the butt of his rifle into Guerini's face and blood sprayed into the air from a gash over one eye. Guerini's flailing movements became feebler and feebler; it was like watching a film slowing down. He staggered forward, groaning, blood pouring over his eyes and down his face, then fell to the floor with a crash that the Englishman could feel even where he was standing. The Englishman had one hand over his mouth; he was trying to stop himself from throwing up.

But he still watched, mesmerised by the horror of the scene, as the Montagnards dragged the twitching, bloody hulk out through the French windows. It took three of them to do it.

The man who had spoken from the first said, 'You stay. No move.'

The Major whispered, 'For Christ's sake, what did he do?'

'He didn't do anything,' said Hardin.

He used the lighter to set fire to one of his cigarettes. He was wondering what had happened to Comeraro and the rest. They should have been out by now, and then the kid had to do what was necessary – but they were taking their goddamn time. He hoped to Christ there wasn't another vicious fuck-up, a reprise of the Garrett disaster.

He watched the Englishman. The dude looked to be in a bad way, trembling, shaking, sweating. He looked like he was going to do something very foolish any second. He wondered who the guy was. He looked like a fat cat who'd had it his own way for years, decades; a guy who really didn't know reality from fucking Christmas.

The Englishman suddenly stepped forward, one hand half-raised. He stuttered, 'Look, you .... you don't understand . . . who I am . . .'

He took two steps and the Montagnard swivelled round and fired. In the tense silence of the room the sound was nerve-shattering. Bright scarlet blotches appeared across the Englishman's white shirt, his mouth seemed to spring open and he was flung backwards, blood spouting up from his throat. He landed in a slumped heap in one corner.

The Montagnard backed away through the open French windows, the gun now pointing at the rest of the men in the room. Hardin flicked at the lighter and passed the flame over the object he held in his left hand. The Montagnard faded into the night and Diderot turned on Hardin, his face white and drawn.

'What the hell did you say? What was . . . what . . .?'

Hardin did not look down at his hands because that would have directed the attention of the others to what he was doing. The lighter-flame seared his skin. He didn't flinch. He grinned at Diderot.

'There was some trouble over a girl. She was raped, murdered. I thought I'd hidden her away, but it seems like the Montagnards were keen to find her.'

'Jesus,' the Colonel whispered. 'You fucker! You told those goddamn savages . . .'

'They wanted the guy who did it. I said it was Guerini. I mean, hell, I remembered he liked 'em young. I guess it was poetic justice.'

Diderot said, 'Kill him. Kill him now.'

Hardin said, 'Catch.'

The object in his hand was now alight. He tossed it at Diderot and it curved through the air, high, between them. Diderot stepped back, put his hands up defensively. The chunk of C-4 Olsen had discovered in his pants' lining exploded blindingly in a sizzling, incandescent flare about two inches from the Frenchman's face.

Hardin didn't stop to check the result. He didn't need to. The intense flame would have instant-fried Diderot's face, brains, the back of his head and anyone who happened to be close behind him. Hardin simply hurled himself at the open French windows.

This time he made it. He went out into the night in a high, lancing dive and landed on the patio outside, rolling perfectly and precisely and shooting off on to the grass of the lawn. Behind him he could hear screaming. It was of no interest to him at all. The only important thing to him now was his AK-47 and it took him a half of a split-second to find it where he'd dumped it earlier.

He grabbed it, scooped up the spare mags and turned to send a burst into the front of the bungalow.

But he didn't.

Clouds drifted from the face of the moon and its light revealed figures running up the lawn towards him from the river.

EnVees.

Scores of EnVees.

XI

Hardin knew who they were, knew who they had to be. They were the guys who'd attacked at the chopper wreck. They'd either cleared up the Americans there, or bypassed them and kept on moving this way. Whatever, they were linked to Diderot and the Corsicans, and this bungalow, for them, would be a sanctuary. They would not be expecting a hard time.

Which was a prime reason to give them exactly that. A plenty hard time.

He crouched down on one knee and sent a long burst of automatic fire spraying across their front runners.

It was like shooting at a carny side-show. Every one a winner. He knocked them down like pins and sent another burst hammering into the second line. Sheer shock was on his side.

Then he dived for cover as the shock factor was washed away and AK-47s chattered viciously and rounds howled above him, stripping leaves off trees, flaying twigs and branches.

He crawled fast and low through a dense mass of ornamental shrubbery. Now he wanted the lights out and a healthy darkness cloaking his movements. The thought uppermost in his mind was: Where was Comeraro? That group must still be in the cellar. The one match he had left them could not have fired, in which case they had nothing with which to light the other piece of C-4 plastic explosive to blow out the door. In which case . . .

Hardin cursed. In which case he had to go back into the bungalow to get them out. He'd have to make for the rear and hope to Christ the EnVees weren't round there as well. He turned and sent an aimless burst of fire ripping through the vegetation, just to keep them on the hop. He wanted them mad, and concentrating on the front of the bungalow. He wanted them to flay the house with fire-power. He wanted chaos because that was the only situation that was going to help him. Once the unnerved Americans started firing back he and his men would be relatively safe.

The irony would be that the Corsican element would be shooting it out with their own side, EnVees who had obviously entered into a business pact with Diderot on the heroin railway. If Diderot were still alive he would be able to shout out passwords, make signs, turn the EnVees' fire on to Hardin. But Hardin knew that the C-4 blast had killed the Frenchman instantly. No one could survive that intense blast of searing fire at such close quarters.

All the Americans would see were North Vietnamese troops advancing towards them and firing. In their jittery, demoralised state they'd jump to the only conclusion possible. They were under attack. Hardin doubted that anyone there other than Diderot himself had any close links with the enemy. In any case, after losing men as they had done just now, the EnVees would be in no mood to halt their advance. They'd be as murderous as a nest of disturbed wasps.

As he emerged from the shrubbery he heard M16 fire, and grinned fiercely to himself. Let the fuckers fight it out among themselves; it gave him the time he so desperately needed.

He shadow-hopped across more grass, keeping to trees and tall shrubs, heading round the side of the building. And now he realised that there was a simple way out of this, if only he could extract his men from the cellar.

The chopper.

There was only one problem. The Huey could be seen from the upper lawn, an easy target for the Vietnamese once they reached that position.

He pushed his way through another small jungle of shrubbery, sprinted across moonlit grass, dived into a tangle of bushes then emerged from the greenery and pulled up short in stunned amazement.

The chopper's rotors were lazily creaking into life.

The Huey's nose was facing him and in the moonlight he could see the pilot clearly.

'*Renucci!*' he bellowed.

He threw up his AK and squeezed the trigger.

Nothing. His last burst had emptied the mag.

He ripped the mag out, groped for a spare, then threw himself back into the bushes as Renucci leaned from the cockpit and blazed automatic fire at him. Rounds tore through the branches above him and the spare mag spun out of his fingers as he rolled, squeezing himself into the damp earth. He scrabbled for the mag, cursing as he heard the chopper's turbine whine into life, the clatter of the rotors as they whirled faster and faster. He heard something else too, and raised himself as he at last found the mag, sliding out of the bushes on his stomach.

The chopper rose into the air with a bellow of engine-sound, but Hardin was staring at a man sprinting in towards it from his left, screaming dementedly. It was Garrett.

The stocky man had his M16 and he raised it, fired, kept on firing. He emptied the entire mag at the rising bird, lashing it with rounds, and all the time he was screaming. Hardin could see him in the moonlight quite clearly, although his words were lost in the roar of the chopper.

Garrett's withering blast of rounds smashed plexiglas, hammered the rotors to scrap, and tore at Renucci, punching him over in his seat. The chopper rose still higher then lurched drunkenly, keeled over sideways. It seemed to hang in the air above the bungalow for seconds upon seconds, and then it fell. It plunged into the roof and there was a terrible rending sound as its dead weight crashed through the roof, buckling timbers, tearing masonry apart. She blew. There was a blazing spout of flame that shot high into the sky and then an ear-shattering explosion that ripped the chopper apart and sent the front of the bungalow erupting outwards over the advancing North Vietnamese.

Wincing, Hardin staggered to his feet and stumbled towards Garrett, who had been bowled over by the explosion's shock-wave. Garrett glared up at him, his face a devil's mask in the leaping flames of the burning bungalow. His voice was a thin, high scream.

'That fucker! That motherfuckin' cocksucker!'

Hardin whacked a hand across the demented man's face, spinning him sideways. For a second he thought Garrett was going to blow him away with the M16. Then he stopped yelling and his face seemed to pucker up like crumpled cardboard. It almost looked like the big man was going to cry.

He whispered, 'A fuckin' fortune . . .' gazing up at Hardin with eyes that were full of pain.

Even in this desperate situation – with a horde of kill-crazy yellow men after them – Hardin started to laugh. Garrett *had* opened the bag, and then Renucci had presumably bumped into him and grabbed it.

'He came at me outta the trees,' babbled Garrett. 'Clubbed me down with his piece. That fucker! May he rot in fuckin' *hell!*'

It solved a number of problems, not least what to do with all that goddamn scag with guys like Garrett in the near vicinity. He glanced at Renucci's funeral pyre. It was maybe the most expensive inferno of the whole damn war.

'Come on, Garrett, get the goddamn lead out. We got Charlie up our ass.'

He pushed the spare mag up into the AK and grabbed the big man's collar, shoving him towards the rear of the blaze. As he did so he heard some firing, this time from M16s. That was bad. It sounded like some of the Corsican contingent had got out before the chopper had death-dived.

Then he saw Joe Fuller running across the rear lawn followed by Vogt, then Comeraro. Comeraro skidded to a halt when he saw Hardin.

'Shit, I thought you were in there.' He jerked a thumb at the flames.

'So did I.'

'There's a raft of yellow men on our tail.'

'Likewise.'

They bolted across the short stretch of grass and dived into the friendly darkness under the trees. Comeraro was breathing hard.

'Your match fizzled out. We spent hell's own time finding another. One of Renucci's men had a half a one in his pocket. We nearly shit ourselves getting the fucker to light.'

'Lose anyone?'

'Uh-uh. But before we got out the house we had to mix it with some of the grunts that Colonel had with him.'

'Did Vogt use the radio?'

'Rodge. That was what took us so long. We had to hold the radio room while he was getting through to Do Thon. Came out of the window, and then that goddamn chopper fell out the sky. Jesus!'

Hardin said, 'Get Olsen and Fuller to round up. We'll head for the Montagnard ville.'

'We need ammo,' said Comeraro. 'We grabbed some guns from the house but we don't have enough. There's all our materiél at the hill, up-river. Long as the gooks' heavy stuff is in their rear and not up front, we could maybe hold that position.'

'Check.'

They filed out in line and moved fast through the trees, not bothering to hide the sounds of their retreat. Hardin figured that the EnVees would spend time at the bungalow before throwing out feeler-squads, then moving *en masse* after them. It gave them more time, not a hell of a lot. The Montagnards would give them more.

He broke out of the trees and found himself above the ville. Then he stopped, transfixed by the sight that met his eyes, the scene illuminated by the brush-fires in the central plaza.

Comeraro joined him.

'Jesus,' the younger man muttered, aghast. 'Jesus Christ. What do we do now?'

Hardin breathed out.

'Forget the village,' he said harshly.

La Bête was in a world of pain. Logical thought had almost ceased inside his brain. All he had now were nightmarish impressions; all he could hear was the rumble of chanting from the Montagnards which beat at his ears, rising and falling like waves upon a rock.

He stumbled on, round and round the thick wooden stake to which he was attached by ropes tied to his wrists. Shapes danced at him, arms swung, pain flared excruciatingly from his naked shoulders, buttocks, arms and back at each light cut of each precisely swung machete, hacking into him, but not so much that he would tumble to the ground for good. Vaguely, he knew that he must keep on his feet. It was almost to please them, these wraiths who rose up from the firelight and fell away again, leaving him with more and more agony, letting out more and more of his blood.

His head slumped forward on to his chest as he tottered onwards in his fixed orbit. He saw his body below him, but it did not seem to be his at all. He saw the cuts and the blood seeping out of him, saw his groin where there was nothing at all except for what seemed to be an open mouth drooling scarlet thickly over his thighs.

He staggered on, steel slicing into him, and he began to laugh. He could not stop himself, although the sound was strange and rasping because of course they had taken his tongue from him before they had taken anything else.

But the weirdest, most bizarre image had occurred to him and it would not go away. The picture of a cockroach, its antennae flickering busily.

Vrai', c'était absurde! Très fou!

La Bête blundered onwards, round and round and round . . .

'They're comin'! I can see the little bastards! Sweet fuckin' Jesus, there's some fuckin' crowd down there!'

Sergeant Fuller stared from under his poncho which was draped over the top of the foxhole. He nestled in closer to his

M16, feeling good. Fuller had spare mags now and his own piece. That always made him feel king of the mountain even in a bad situation like this where there was a strong possibility that no one was going to make it out alive.

He muttered to Snell, who was squashed up next to him, 'Them choppers, they ain't gonna make that hundred klicks in time, son, you betcha ass. We're all gonna fuckin' die here.' He gave an evil, throaty chuckle.

Snell, in a stricken voice, said, 'I don't even gotta be here!'

'Tough titty, turdbird. Ya wanna get out there with a white snot-rag, tell 'em they made a mistake?'

Higher up the hill Hardin in his foxhole watched the North Vietnamese troops advancing along the river bank towards them. They were well spread out, and they were half-circling the knoll. Another few minutes and they'd be within his range.

Comeraro said, 'Maybe they'll bypass us. They got no firm reason to think we're anywhere but running like hell through the forest.'

Hardin shook his head in the darkness.

'This hill's too good. They'd check it out anyway. What they'll do is toss grenades and see what happens, but I want them closer. It depends how smart their honcho is. If he thinks we're hiding up here on a quick decision he'll come in and look us over. If he thinks we've already had time to dig in, make it a defensible position, he'll stay back and mortar us.'

'Let's hope he's not smart,' said Comeraro. 'Couple of mortars'd turn us into hamburger damn fast.'

'Let's hope he's not smart,' agreed Hardin, 'but let's pray that Olsen's as good a Papa Sierra as I'm always saying he is.'

The enemy moved through bushes out on to riverside scrub. They seemed to be heading away from the knoll at a lazy angle. Comeraro grunted with suppressed excitement.

'Grenade launchers.'

'Yeah, he's not so smart. Only one thing can shaft us now, and that's Renucci's men panicking and jumping out of their foxholes.' He suddenly snapped, 'Here they come!'

Grenades curved high through the air, exploded on the hill. The men in the foxholes crouched down, clawing themselves deeper into the earth, became suddenly burrowing worms that prayed and cursed. The explosions were short and sharp, cracks of sound that did not linger. Another salvo burst on the hill. Earth was flung into the air in clods, torn out by the blasts.

Hardin peered out again and a lethal smile crossed his features.

'They're easing round. They're gonna take a look-see. They don't think there's anyone here but they wanna make sure.'

The North Vietnamese began to move slowly up the lower slopes of the little hill.

'C'mon, c'mon,' breathed Hardin. 'I want that second wave.'

More men filtered up on to the rising ground. Hardin gripped the claquer firing device in his right hand, and squeezed.

A Claymore mine, facing outwards to the second line of men, crackblasted, shattering the silence. On cue, other Claymores burst into deadly life, spraying out hundreds of steel shards into the advancing wave of men with a devastating accuracy, and a horrifying result. Now the night was awash with sound: the screams of men who had suddenly lost stomachs, arms, legs; more cracking explosions. Those who were at some distance from the detonations were staggering about like blind men, shrieking and wailing. Those who were close enough to receive the full appalling impact of the blasts were literally minced, shredded by the lethal spray of steel splinters hurled at such savage velocity.

Hardin shoved aside his poncho and rose up out of the foxhole like an avenging angel. He swung his AK-47 round and sent a stream of fire down at the North Vietnamese front line, those who had passed beyond Olsen's hidden Claymores. He fired high so that his fire-lines burned air above the heads of his own men lower down the slope. The string of men, spread out in a semicircle round the hill and half way up it, were caught at knee-level and chest-level. They had no chance. They were scythed down like corn in a field, and those that were not hit began to run.

Hardin howled, *'Grenades!'*

Already he'd dropped his gun, and was hurling splinter-grenades, lobbing them high and far so that they struck the ground ahead of the fleeing EnVees – and as they reached the bottom of the hill, so the grenades burst, red-cored eruptions of flame and vicious sound that hurled them back the way they'd come, back up the hill. More M16 fire stabbed at them, any survivors who were still able to crawl or stagger or squirm along in the mud. The hill was a litter of bodies and bits of bodies; the air was a reek of smoke and TNT.

Hardin sank back down into the foxhole. 'I guess that blew our cover,' he said.

Now fire from the rear lashed the hill, machine-guns and assault rifles. More grenades burst, ripping at the earth and scrub, gouging chunks out of boulders. Hardin's men shuddered in their foxholes, deafened and shaken by the grenade blasts and the unceasing, brain-tearing clamour of automatic fire.

In one of the lower foxholes, Snell couldn't stand it any more. It was like nothing he'd ever experienced in his life. He was a small-time gorilla whose previous experience of violence, in the employ of Renucci and men like Renucci, had been solely in meteing it out, usually to guys who owed more money than they were ever going to be able to pay back or guys who had simply annoyed someone else and needed a lesson. It was a matter of cracked arms, or cracked legs, or cracked heads. Nice and easy. But this – Snell couldn't believe it: the horrifying and continuous thunder-storm of sound, the heaves and lurches in the ground as grenades pounded and crashed. And there seemed to be no end to it. It seemed to be going on for ever. His head was throbbing, pounding with pain. He thought he was going mad.

Suddenly, with a shrill mindless wail, he clawed himself out of the stinking, muddy hole and began running. He didn't know where to, but it had to be anywhere that was far from this nightmare of hellish sound and violence.

But he got no further than a half dozen paces before

tracer blazed into him and flung him to the ground. There were a thousand hammers beating at his flesh, a thousand spear-points stabbing into him. Fire-lines swerved and homed in on him. Rounds lashed through him and ripped him apart, burst bones, tore ligaments, smashed blood vessels, pulverising his body so that what was left bore no resemblance to a human being at all. So that what was left was a lumpy, shredded mass of bloody gristle, still bouncing and juddering and quivering as fire-lines caught at it and tossed it around on the hillside like a ghastly, scarlet football.

And still the EnVees kept up the ferocious, punishing onslaught of fire.

Comeraro bellowed, 'What the fuck are they doing?!'

'Laying down suppressive. They're gonna come in again.'

'Christ, I know that, sir! But all they need to do is bring up their mortars! They could *level* this goddamn hill!'

Hardin grinned in the flame-torn darkness. 'Is that what you want? Jesus, Lieutenant – you got a death-wish on you or something? I'll take this any day rather than mortars!'

'But their honcho really must be crazy! Why expend men needlessly?'

'They want the bag.'

'But we don't – Oh Christ!'

'Right!'

Hardin had figured it out almost as soon as the incredible barrage had started. The EnVee honcho knew about the heroin. That was now clear. His line of reasoning was that anyone who'd escaped from the scene of the pulverised bungalow must still have the heroin. It was a reasonable assumption, and he would do anything to capture that supreme prize. If he brought in his mortars he could almost certainly destroy the knoll and everyone on it – and just about every thing. Including ten fragile glassine bags of horse worth millions of dollars.

So he couldn't bring up his mortars. He had to storm the position and take it, and with all that loot as a possible reward he wouldn't mind how many of his men he used up.

'Jesus!' snarled Comeraro. 'That means we're dead already.

They've got more ammo than us, more men. They're just gonna keep on coming, keep on coming.'

'You got it, Lieutenant.'

'Maybe we could beat it to the river?'

'They'd hit us before we could even touch the water.'

'The choppers!'

'Oh sure! But how long are they gonna take? They could be here in thirty seconds. Could be thirty minutes. If they arrive in thirty minutes, forget it.'

All at once he caught an easing in the sound bombardment. He knew instantly what it meant. Half of those firing had stopped firing, because they were now running. They were running madly for the hill under the fire-lines of those at the rear.

Hardin heaved the poncho aside, poked his AK out and blazed downwards in a long sweeping burst. The moon had gone; apart from the stabbing fire-flies of muzzle-flashes from below, it was now almost pitch black.

'Give us an illum! Towards them!'

Comeraro fired an illumination round and seconds later it burst high in the air over the EnVee position. The light was spectacularly bright, as bright as daylight, but at the same time possessed of all the sharp and strange qualities of moonlight, a ghastly, picked-clean radiance that threw everything into razor-sharp relief.

It showed a wave of North Vietnamese washing over the lower slopes of the hill, lapping fiercely higher and higher even as Hardin watched.

'Down to the lower level,' he snapped. 'You take the east side, I'll take the south. Keep firing illums.'

He slid down in the churned up earth to Olsen's position, firing as he went. EnVees stumbled, spun away, fell back as the rest of his men opened up. There was only one good thing about this, he thought, and that was that the honcho was pouring men in and they were easy to kill. Christ, they were easy to kill.

He jumped down into Olsen's slit-trench and began squeezing off bursts at the advancing troops. More holes appeared in the EnVee ranks and more men filled those holes. Darkness cloaked the scene for some seconds and then another illumination round burst high in the night sky, stark and cold. Hardin and Olsen heaved grenades down the hill, firing blindly into and beyond the flame-eruptions. More grenades roared; automatic fire was a seamless blare of sound. And still the North Vietnamese advanced.

'Do we move back up top, sir?' yelled Olsen.

'Not unless we have to. Use your bayonet if it gets to close quarters. We can only retreat to the goddamn river.'

Light died again and then burst spectacularly over the scene. The slope of the hill seemed littered with bodies; in places they were in tangled piles. Hardin stared at the slope. He almost couldn't believe they'd killed so many, and only just in time too – there were stiffs sprawled out only yards away.

He jammed another banana clip up into the AK, leant the gun on the earthwork ridge of the trench, sent sprays of rounds hammering down the hill, every so often glancing to his left and behind, just in case Comeraro's group had been over-run and the enemy started to pour over the top of the hill towards them. A few yards away he glimpsed Vogt and Garrett firing desperately at the stumbling troops who did not seem to give a shit about dying at all. Darkness descended. Light blazed.

More bodies, more sprawled figures; even more than before, and closer than before.

'*Jesus!*' Hardin ripped out to Olsen. '*The fuckers! They've been sliding up in the dark!*'

EnVees suddenly rose up in scattered bunches, only paces away from them down the slope – dead bodies suddenly erupting into shocking, horrifying life. For every two seconds of non-illum darkness men had been rushing up the slope, slumping to the ground in feigned death, dashing nearer, sprawling in the mud.

'*They're on us!*'

Olsen poured fire at the nearest men but there were too many of them and they were too desperate. They rolled up and on to the trench-top and Hardin swung his AK wildly through the air in a wide, hacking sweep, the bayonet slashing blood out of men as they lunged at him. He was firing as he swung and rounds blew men back, exploded their faces, jack-hammered their chests and stomachs. The AK was knocked out of his grasp and he fell towards Olsen and his eyes caught at something fixed to Olsen's ruck lying in the bottom of the trench. He reached for it and grabbed it even as hands tore at him, fists punched and pounded him.

He grasped the handle of the object and wrenched himself away from those clutching hands, those shrieking men, and swung out. Olsen was a hell of a Papa Sierra, just like he'd always said. He'd come up with the C-4 plas just when it was needed, he'd set the Claymores right and tight – and he'd kept his machete honed down to a razor-sharp perfection.

Hardin lashed out with the machete and took a man's head right off – the blade sliced through the neck, through bone and cartilage and veins and fat, as though it was just so much thin air and the head bounded high in a great scarlet spout. He was drenched with blood and he was mad. He whirled the machete round and struck and struck again at those flailing arms and lunging bodies until he'd cleared the trench as though he was cutting his way through the jungle. Men fell away from him redly, collapsed in their own blood, spun off the trench-top leaving chunks of themselves behind.

Olsen had regained his fire-superiority and was now pumping death at more EnVees who were stumbling up the slope, cutting them down and slamming them away.

Hardin yelled, 'Make for the top!'

Both men scrambled up the torn slope as the light died on them again. Comeraro was at the top, grouped with his men, and Garrett and Vogt stumbled up behind from the side foxhole.

Comeraro said breathlessly, 'Panicsville! I got but one frigging illum round left. That's it. No more.'

'Shit. Don't use it yet. Wait till the bastards are on top of us. We need to see who we're killing.'

Hardin spread his men round the hill in a half-arc, pointing outwards to all directions but the west. To the west was the steep slope of the knoll that fell down to the river.

He said, 'If it looks like they're gonna take us, slide down to the river and beat it any way you can. Fuck the choppers – doesn't look like they're gonna make it, so as a last resort we don't need to stay bunched up together for a pick-up. Head down-river for the gorge we passed yesterday. Just any way you can. Just – *Down!*'

Tracer lit the darkness starkly in a pyrotechnical display from two sides. Long flaring lines that curved down towards them – a harsh, spluttering death-staccato that tore the silence to shreds.

'*Holy shit!*' screamed Vogt. '*They're comin' up from the river!*'

Hardin whirled, leapt to the western edge of the knoll, the steep, almost unclimbable slope that fell away to the river below, and saw, in the tracer-torn blackness, faces so near he could almost touch them. Vogt poured rounds down at them and Hardin jabbed at heads with his bayonet, but this was a truly muscular wave of men who had sneaked round to the side and determinedly dragged themselves, snake-like, up that steepness, their movements hidden by the fire-concentration on the other side of the hill.

And now those other sides too were a scrambling mass of North Vietnamese who scented bloody victory over just ten men who were running out of rounds, and running out of hope.

A shrieking man leapt at Hardin, stabbing with his bayonet, and Hardin danced aside like a matador and gutted him with his own bayonet, kicking the man off the point back into the others who were jumbled behind. He had no more mags. He pulled his .45 out and point-blank blew the head of the next man into a grisly pulp.

'*Fire!*'

He fired, and fired again. At this range you couldn't miss. It was impossible not to deal out bloody death to man after man as they rose around him in the muzzle-flash-lit darkness.

'*Fire!*'

He wondered who the hell was bawling out the most obvious order in the whole damn world when scores of

EnVees were pouring over the top of the hill and the only damn thing you *could* do was . . .

'*FIRE!*'

All at once it hit him how strange that voice sounded, how boomingly hollow, how goddamn *loud*, and he glanced upwards and was for a moment transfixed by the sight of a shifting kaleidoscope of flickering, winking lights high in the sky to the east. He thought: Jesus. Choppers. Using their psy-ops loudspeakers.

And now, even above the deafening clamour of battle he could hear the roaring racket of rotors, the pounding cacophony of hard rock music.

He yelled 'Illumination!' – and Comeraro, clubbing the barrel of the pistol at men who tore at him, tried to smash him down, fired high.

The round sizzled skywards; night exploded into eerie day. An armada of gunships hurtled high towards them, loudspeakers blaring:

'*I am the god of hell-fire*
And I bring you –
FIRE!'

Rockets blazed into the area around the hill, volcanoing earth and rocks and bushes; blasting, searing, destroying. Hardin screamed at his men, hurled himself into a foxhole, gasped as someone else landed atop him, winced as cannon-fire from above sliced and scythed down EnVees on the brow of the knoll. He huddled in the earth, let the ear-splitting sound-mix of cannons and MGs and death-screams and rotors and that blaring, devilish music wash right over him.

Hardin stared down at a moon-landscape of death and destruction – smoking craters and jumbled bodies and torn earth and discarded weapons sharply picked out by the blaze of searchlights from the hovering gunships.

His men were grouped with him on the top of the hill; some sitting, some standing, some muttering dazedly to themselves, some smoking, some simply staring, like Hardin, at the fearful carnage spread out below.

Lew Halderling is going to be pleased, thought Hardin. I have a tale to tell him which is going to flip him out – a tale of junk and junk-men, power-plays and corruption, millions of bucks burning to nothing in a funeral pyre. It wouldn't have ended there, of course. What was maybe nine or ten million dollars in an empire of evil that had spread itself across South East Asia? You couldn't stop it. The trade would go on, just as the war within a war – the fight to the death between two powerful clans gouging each other to bloody shreds for a billion dollar empire, hidden by the greater battle of two powerful ideologies wrestling for the hearts and minds and souls of an agony-racked people – would go on.

Maybe you could stop bits of it, bits of the smaller war, but it was like the Hydra-headed monster of ancient legend: cut off a limb and two more would sprout in its place.

An investigation would be mounted – Halderling would see to that; would gleefully set it up – an investigation into the rot of organised crime spreading its poison insidiously across the most powerful army the world had ever known – but it would bog down after a while in a morass of lies and cover-ups. Hardin knew the form: you could never tie all the loose ends up.

But at least you could maybe burn as many of the threads as you could find.

Garrett ambled across. '*Now* are those basstuds gonna give us ribbons an' stuff, honourable discharges, kick us back to the World?'

Hardin shrugged. 'Who knows?'

He lit a cigarette and watched as the gunships eased themselves out of hover, began slowly to descend towards them.

AFTERWORD

Over a 12-day period in 1970 – July 4th to July 16th – US Mafia capos held a summit meeting at the Hotel Sole in Palermo, Sicily. The main item on the agenda was South East Asia, and it was agreed that the area should be transformed into the main source of world heroin in place of Turkey and Marseilles, where too much pressure was being exerted by international anti-narcotics organisations. Amongst those present at the summit were Santo Trafficante, Jr, right-hand man to mob overlord Meyer Lansky, and a number of agents from the Central Intelligence Agency.

The main stumbling block to beefing up the Asian connection as far as the Sicilians were concerned was the Corsican element, which had controlled the Vietnam–Laos–Cambodia heroin trade for decades. $300M was voted from central Mafia funds to be invested in the bribery and corruption of the Corsicans' principal friends, allies and associates amongst governments in the area. $800M was set aside to maximise opium production in the Golden Triangle. It was unanimously agreed by all parties that the Corsicans had to be eliminated.

A month later – August, 1970 – a hastily convened Corsican counter-summit was held at the Continental Hotel in Saigon. War was declared on the Sicilians. Here too, oddly enough, CIA operatives were in evidence.

JHT